AN OBSESSION UNDER THREAT

seademons

First edition

Cover art by Jordana M. Andrade (@danailustra)
Page dividers by Freepik

ISBN 978-1-7357485-3-5

This book contains sexual encounters and adult content. It is intended for mature audiences only.

CONTENT WARNING: mentions of sexual and physical abuse, self-harm, drug abuse and alcohol abuse.

Table of Contents

Chapter 1

The abandoned gas station

We circled each other,
wary, abandoned, full of longing.

- Jeanette Winterson, *Why Be Happy When You Could Be Normal?*

His father's office was much bigger than originally thought. He didn't know why, but he'd always imagined it to be a small room in someone's basement where Henry typed numbers on a screen, and from time to time, his boss would show up to make sure he was doing his job.

This place was huge. The front door opened into a very impressive entrance hall, where the floors were made of marble and a massive chandelier hung from the ceiling. In the center of the room, a mahogany counter with two layers kept the secretary's things out of view, except they weren't here today. It was the weekend, after all.

Despite that, some people had still come in. They worked in the next room over, which was only accessed through the keycard in their lanyard. That room looked a lot more like the image of the accounting office Theodore had had in mind, except fancier and bigger. Desks were grouped up in four or six with partitions between them, carpets covered the floor and every window had blinds. It was daytime, but the blinds were drawn and the lights were on. Weird.

His father explained that this was the main office, HR was in the back and *his* office was somewhere else entirely. As they talked, a couple of employees greeted the two of them very shyly, without making much eye contact. Henry didn't introduce Theodore, but they could probably guess who he was.

The office was clearly real, with real people who had real jobs and even came in over the weekend. Did Henry actually work for Burman? The evidence

1

pointed to an overwhelming yes, but seeing this place, it was difficult to pin it as a front. It was easier to believe both theories were simultaneously correct, that this was a real accounting office and Burman was simply another client. Perhaps a big one that needed a little more of Henry's attention and care, but still. That was the only way Theodore could fit all the pieces of the puzzle together.

"Is this where I'm going to start?" His question was genuine, something he'd been wondering for a while. Alternatively, would he be assigned to Burman as well, or was that a bit of a secret? How many employees knew about it?

"Yes. Who's going to coach you will depend on what branch you happen to choose. We have bookkeeping right here on the left, tax accounting behind them and auditors on the right. You may also choose to specialize in HR."

"Um."

His pulse jumped. This was another conversation he'd been meaning to have for some time now. He'd thought the right time for it would be over dinner with his mother also present, but perhaps this was just as well. Rip it off like a Band-Aid. He breathed in, hands shaking. They disappeared into his pockets.

"Well, I was thinking, maybe—maybe law, actually?"

Henry's eyebrows raised, impressed. "Accounting lawyers make a lot of money. We will definitely benefit from having you with us."

Shit, that wasn't what he'd meant at all. Dammit.

"Let me show you to my office."

No, I meant I want to be a lawyer. I want to go to law school. Just say it. He licked his lips, hands gripping the lining of his pockets. Henry started across the entrance hall with him in tow, feet erratic and quick. Jesus Christ, just say it. The words came up his throat, but instead of coming out, they choked him. God, just *say it!* His lips opened and closed like a fish out of water. A shaky breath filled his lungs.

He couldn't do this. Swallowing the confrontation down, he let his shoulders droop. Another failure for his collection. His hand closed around an imaginary dagger, and in his mind, he stabbed himself in the neck.

It didn't matter.

On the right side of the building, another door locked by a keycard opened into two spacious offices and a flight of stairs. One of those belonged to his father. A long desk rested near the back wall with only a pen holder on it, a couch against the rightmost wall, and a round table on the opposite side of the room, by a whiteboard. It was very nice in here.

"Don't you have a computer?" he asked.

"Of course I do. It's at home."

Right, that made sense. At this point, he was in the pole position for Idiot of the Year; the only award he had a fair chance of winning.

"One day, I hope to see you take my place." There was a hint of emotion in Henry's voice, buried under solemnity. It almost touched him. "I hope to see you become greater than me, smarter and far more powerful. I want to leave you a legacy."

What if he didn't want it? The thought crossed his mind very heavily, followed by a keen sense of shame. How ungrateful did he have to be to refuse such a gift? Ryan would've killed for this. A lot of people would've killed for this, yet here he was, throwing it away like it was garbage. His father should be hitting him right now.

"Do you know what happens when people start losing control over their own lives?" This question sounded a bit harsher than any of the points Henry had made so far. "When they don't have a goal or a purpose?"

Theodore promptly thought of what Laith had told him last weekend, how feeling lost and worthless had pushed him to the bottom of the pit. "They get depressed?" That was his best guess.

"They turn to drugs. Every day is a void to be filled, so they get high and party, throwing their lives away, since they don't think they have one in the first place. Now, I'm sure you know where they end up."

His throat closed. "In the tunnels," he answered.

"Have you been there?"

That question flew at him so quickly that it gave him whiplash.

"No, dad." He almost choked. "Of course not."

Henry leaned against his own desk, arms crossed over his chest. "You're slipping, Theodore. You're letting your piece of shit friends drag you down, so they can see you waste your life too. You're a puppet in their game. Do you realize that?"

He grabbed his own hands, squeezing.

"I *need* you to see that," Henry continued. "That's where your new friend comes in."

Oh god, he hated this. Nothing good could come out of it.

"You'll meet him tonight."

The wait was harrowing. Back home, he was expected to act normally and see the rest of the day through as if he weren't counting the minutes until dusk. The only thing that helped was baking cookies with his mother, something that brought him back to the familiarity of living under her roof, their shared little hobby. She told him how much of each ingredient to put in the bowl and the order too, essentially baking it herself, only through his hands. That was the point, after all—to do it together. They made his favorite recipe, with lemon juice in the batter and lemon zest in the icing. He had a feeling she knew exactly what was going on.

"Do you know who dad's friend is?" He kept his voice low, eyes down on the dishes. "The one he's introducing me to."

"I haven't met him myself, if that's what you're asking."

"Do you know anything about him?"

"Of course. I know about every one of your father's associates."

The two of them spoke without looking at each other, voices barely above whispers as they did the dishes and put them away.

"Is he gonna hurt me?"

"That's entirely up to you."

That froze his heart and crushed it.

mmermemmen

Sleeping through the afternoon was impossible. Locked in his room, or the one his parents had curated for him, he tossed and turned, tired but too scared to fall asleep. Every time he closed his eyes, he saw a dark figure beating him up while his father watched and immediately gasped himself awake, heart beating wildly. Exhaustion warped that image with each new try—his father got closer and the figure took shape. Eventually, they merged together. It stripped him naked and spanked him in front of a crowd, darkness pooling at their feet, consuming them slowly. The auditorium flooded, but the figure didn't stop. His father didn't stop. It held his head underwater, face pushed into the black sludge. He swallowed it, choking, drowning until the world turned black.

mmermemmen

As the last minutes of sunlight filtered in through the front door, he waited. His pulse raced and his lungs barely worked, but he tried his best to keep calm. The glass panes behind him allowed the foyer to glow in hues of red and orange, shadows growing darker. The TV was on, he could hear it from here— his mother must be in the living room. In silence, he listened to the muffled voices, brain focused on trying to detangle them as a way to keep himself together. It worked well enough.

Once the sun fully set, his father came downstairs. He flicked some of the lights on and found Theodore by the front door, standing still, like a statue. That didn't seem to strike him any which way though, emotionless. With a jacket over his shoulders, he simply put on a mask and pulled the door open.

They traveled to the outskirts of town, an area Theodore had never explored on foot before, always passing through in someone's vehicle. At first, he couldn't exactly tell where they were, unfamiliar with the street corner where his father had parked. It was weird to be here with him, actually leaving the car to walk around. Why was his friend waiting *here*? This wasn't a place his father would ever go to.

As they walked, the unnamed subway entrance came up, always deserted. That one landmark allowed him to know exactly where they were. His mind went back to last weekend, Justin dropping everybody off before taking him home. Did Henry know about that? He'd figured everything out already; he must know about the others too. Justin must have told him.

They didn't approach the entrance. Instead, Henry kept on walking, rounding corners here and there, crossing deserted streets. Aside from the busy interstate, the rest of this whole area was eerily quiet, abandoned almost, with shut down businesses in every block and no one on the sidewalk. Dread crept up Theodore's chest, heart stuck in the back of his throat. This wasn't safe.

He stayed very close to his father the whole way, choking on pleas for him to let this entire thing go and just drive them back home. He'd be good, he promised!—except that card had already been played. This far into the game, his hand was empty.

The very end of one of these blocks welcomed them to an abandoned gas station. This place was clearly forgotten about; the pumps were broken, the convenience store was empty and an old chain fenced the corner, dismantled over the ground. A figure paced leisurely near the convenience store, all the way across, cigarette burning orange in the dark.

His breathing ceased, feet stumbling out of shock—this was it, the point of no return. That was the man who'd beat him into a pulp to make his father proud, to teach him a lesson, to make him behave. Would they strip him naked? Would they leave marks? His eyes watered as possibilities began to pile up in his mind. He fell behind for a moment, but remained on his father's trail anyway, following like a very small shadow. Would they make him bleed? His entire body trembled.

As the two of them walked, the figure slowly came to a halt. It was difficult to see, especially half-hidden behind his father, but the closer Theodore got, the clearer the figure's shape became. Tall and broad, this man was built like a brick; the pain he could inflict, the damage he could cause was unimaginable. The cigarette burned between his fingers, hanging limp by his side. Theodore wished he'd toke on it so his face would light up, but that thought soon became obsolete. Close enough to see the shape of his face, Theodore realized he knew him. The shock that struck him then grew roots twenty feet into the ground below. His lungs didn't even work.

Coming up to Laith, Henry motioned to him. "Son, this is the Great White Shark. He lives underground, but work has brought us together."

They both held the stare, speechless, eyes wide. Theodore didn't even know what to say. The only thought his brain was capable of producing was confirmation that Laith had spoken the truth when he'd unveiled Henry as the Crow earlier this year. That was it.

Would Laith beat the shit out of him?

"You see here, Shark, my son's been really interested in the tunnels lately. He's friends with a drug dealer and smokes dope. Next thing I know, he's underground snorting coke off a whore's back. So tell me, or rather, tell *him* a little bit about how things work down there. Tell him what you've been through."

Laith finally broke eye contact to pass Henry a brief glance. The way he held his shoulders, the way he carried himself was extremely tense, similar to how Theodore felt. "You know, it's a rough place." His voice made Theodore's heart jump, still shocked to see him here, caught in disbelief. "You get beat up and threatened at about every turn. The dogs—they're above the law. They'll kick the shit out of you if you're not careful."

The human dogs, right? The ones Hwan had mentioned weren't *actually* dogs. That must be yet another term for thug.

"Is that what happened to you?" Henry's voice was low, conversational on the surface, but something about it just felt menacing.

Laith stared at his boss. "Yeah. They got me good too."

"And you're what, six three, two hundred pounds?"

"Two fifty."

6

Henry nodded. "Do you think my son has any chance of making it down there?"

"He just doesn't belong there."

That comment cut into him like a razor blade. He already knew how Laith felt about that, but it still hurt to hear it. His heart choked him.

"Right." Henry glanced at Theodore next, eyes cold in the dark. "He doesn't."

"How come you guys work together?" That question left him on a whim, thoughtless. He barely even registered he'd said anything at all.

"We have an associate in common," his father briefly explained. "Now, son, the Great White will be checking up on you every now and then. It'll be random, whenever he has the time. He bashes skulls for a living, so he might not make it every night, but he'll find you if you're not home and he'll let me know where you were. He knows your friend Justin too—he'll tell me whether you've continued seeing him or not. Won't you, Shark?"

Surprise was written all across Laith's face. They must not have talked about this beforehand. Also, on an unrelated note, he bashed skulls for a living? Somehow, Theodore didn't believe that. "Yeah. Yeah, of course."

Henry turned back to Theodore. "Don't take this the wrong way; it's really all up to you. When you grow up, you'll understand this was for your own good." He touched Theodore's shoulder. "I love you, son."

This was the most dishonest his father had ever sounded, but those three words still doubled his heart in size. He couldn't remember the last time Henry had said them.

"I love you too, dad." That left him straight from the heart, a little piece of it in every word. He hadn't said them in such a long time. Still poisoned by sincerity, he added his honest thoughts on this arrangement, and as he spoke, his blood curdled with something toxic. "And thank you. I think this is exactly what I need."

His father was essentially handing him Laith on a silver platter, after all. The hand on his shoulder squeezed a bit, tugging an infinitesimal smile onto his face. "Shark, I expect you to report back to me tomorrow. Now, follow."

With that, Henry turned to leave. In the split-second of privacy that his back provided, Theodore glanced up at Laith only to see green eyes already down at him. As his heart bounced, a slew of questions passed through his mind, led primarily by *how*. How had any of this happened? It felt like a dream, or the very thin line that crossed into nightmare territory. He'd still get beat up, after all.

In silence, the two of them started after his father, veiled by a bizarre cloak that hid their true involvement. At the end of the day, his efforts to pull Laith close had been outperformed by his father's parenting. That said a lot in regards to what Henry thought of Laith, if he'd been the chosen one to run his son off the tunnels. In Henry's eyes, he was a staple of what the tunnels produced; a perfect example of the kinds of people that populated their dark corners. The message wasn't lost on Theodore, that he'd turn into somebody like Laith if he continued to explore drugs and get involved with the underground, but the reason it failed to have an impact was because his parents' morals didn't reflect on him. He didn't think the rats were inferior to him. If anything, Laith was above him in every conceivable way.

What would his father think if he knew they'd been sleeping together? The world would catch on fire. If Henry already thought of Laith as vermin and couldn't possibly imagine his son as anything other than straight, then learning of their involvement would shatter reality—*Henry's* reality, carefully crafted. Deep inside, he must know that interfering this much removed any possibility of organic growth, interpersonal or otherwise, but then, that was probably what he wanted. He'd always been obsessed with control. The real reason he didn't like Ryan had nothing to do with genes and family trees; it was because Ryan was the embodiment of all his failed attempts to control him too, to shape him into a perfect little box by sending him off to business school and giving him nice gifts, like an apartment downtown and a car for Christmas. Theodore, on the other hand, didn't know himself well enough to decline any of those things. For all he knew, he could fall in love with business school in the next two weeks and find that following in his father's footsteps was his true calling.

Henry ended up leading the two back to his car and telling them to get in. Theodore stopped in his tracks, eyebrows furrowed—were they going to a different location just to jump him? He got in suspiciously, taking the front seat to keep an eye on his father. It would also keep Laith from being able to hurt him at Henry's command.

It didn't take long for the turns that his father took and the streets he drove down to start looking familiar—they were going back to Theodore's apartment. So he *wouldn't* get hurt? His heart began to slow down, lungs breathing normally again. Of course his father wouldn't do that; it'd be fucked up, right? Yeah, it'd be fucked up. Henry had wanted to teach him a lesson, scare him a little bit, not get him hurt. He didn't even know why he'd believed otherwise; Henry had never so much as laid a finger on him.

The car pulled up to the curb. That allowed Henry to turn around and tell Laith what this place was—that he'd be coming here to check on Theodore. Then, he ordered him to leave, and obediently, Laith did. Theodore watched him through the side mirror, stepping onto the sidewalk, hands slipping into his pockets.

Suddenly, he needed to leave too. Every siren in his brain went off, screaming that it wasn't safe to be alone with his father. Who knew what could happen? He quickly thanked Henry for the ride and pushed the door open. Part of him expected the man to say something back, if not an anecdote then a simple *you're welcome,* but nothing came. Awkwardly, and a little disappointed, Theodore got out.

On the sidewalk, he glanced into the car only to find Henry staring back at him, perfectly impassive, unreadable. Theodore waited for a moment, holding the door with a hand, still under the impression that a comment would come. When it didn't, he waved goodbye and closed the door.

Chapter 2

Two of a kind

Now I'm going down
and set 57th Street on fire
to keep you warm.

- 1956 love letter from James Schuyler to John Button

As soon as his father's car disappeared around the first corner, he turned to glance at Laith. His arms moved out of frustration, palms up in the air. "What the fuck was that?"

Laith's shoulders raised in a prolonged shrug, eyes off in the distance. "Your dad's sick. He's been on a witch hunt down there, you know. He called me in to spy on Ryan, then persecuted the hell out of Justin 'cause he invited you to the farm, and now this, a fucking babysitting service. He's *on* you, bro." Laith swallowed, Adam's apple bobbing. "We're fucked."

Were they, though?

"How much does he know?"

"He knows you're friends with Justin and that you smoke weed, which, by the way, isn't even something you do. Like, actually do. I guess a couple times is just as bad to him, though."

Laith's comment brought the baggie to mind, the lighter he'd found in Cantaloupe, the paper he'd used to roll himself a joint and the very first one he'd gotten from Justin. Not to mention every class he'd watched while incredibly high this week. His father had a point—this was much worse than anybody knew—but he still didn't think it was *so* bad. It just wasn't as inconsequential as Laith made it out to be.

"So he doesn't really know anything," Theodore concluded.

"He knows you're not a saint."

"Which is nothing. I'm still redeemable; I still have a chance—that's what matters. I'm getting a car too. That's kind of the whole point."

"It's just a matter of time until he gets to me."

"How?" His shoulders raised, palm up. "*You're* his source of information. If you don't tell him anything, he won't know anything. Also, did you hear the part where I'm getting a car?"

Laith sighed, shoulders sagging. There was something incredibly defeatist about him tonight. "Congrats, dude. That's great."

"I'm thinking about running away."

Their eyes met.

"Straight-up?"

"Yeah. I don't know where I'm gonna go, but I know it won't be here. Maybe—maybe I'll drive down to California."

"Nah, that's too obvious. Nevada and Arizona are safer bets."

"You're probably right. I just—I don't think I can take this for much longer. It's..." His mind went back to the knife in his mother's kitchen, the violent glint on the blade, his grip on the handle. "It's been hard."

A light breeze swept the street, ruffling his hair a bit. The sky was entirely black at this hour, stars hidden behind thick clouds.

"It gets better, though. Things aren't gonna be this way forever."

"I have expectations put on me. I have an entire career plan laid out; a whole *life* planned out in front of me, except..." He shrugged. "I didn't get to decide any of it. I don't wanna work for my dad and I don't wanna marry my mom's neighbor. I don't even think I want kids! I just—I don't think I can tell them what I actually want."

"What's that?"

They held the stare. That question sent his heart flying into the roof of his mouth, hands squeezed into fists.

"I don't want what they want for me." That was the best he could do.

"Dude, you're gonna have to have that conversation at some point. Yeah, you could get your car and run away, but if you do that, you'll spend the rest of your life wondering what would've happened. You'll never get closure."

"I *know* what would happen."

"No, you don't. Parents can be very surprising, and judging how much your dad cares about you, things might take a different turn. Compromises are possible. You're young too; you might change your mind about everything tomorrow."

"I can't change who I'm attracted to."

"No, but you might end up liking the life your parents have planned out for you, even if for that you'll need to tweak a few things. You don't *need* to run away."

"Is that what you did?"

"I didn't have anything planned out that way, just the societal expectations that everyone has to live with." None of which Laith had probably fulfilled, considering everything Theodore knew about him.

"At least you have a job that you like."

"It's not one my parents approve of, though. Like I said, this stuff is a compromise; I don't have a job that they endorse, but I have a job. You might end up choosing a different career path, but you'll have a career. It's kind of like that."

"What do you do?" That question flew past his mouth. In truth, it'd been marinating in the back of his mind for so long that finally saying it felt like wrapping up a year-long project. "I mean, you work for Burman *and* for my dad and everyone down there kinda hates you. At least, that's the vibe I get. They call you a thug; my dad said you crush skulls for a living. What's going on?"

Laith scoffed out what was probably going to be a laugh that never actually formed. Partially hidden behind a mask, his face was a mystery; it was impossible to tell whether there was a smile there or not. "Man, I'm just a debt collector; it's really not that glamorous. I pick up Burman's money and give it back to her. Some days are just harder than others."

"The way you talk about it, you make it sound like every day is life or death."

"Sometimes it is. It depends if your dad's there."

"Isn't he always there?"

"Not always."

Voices echoed from across the front yard, familiar ones that ruined the perfect rhythm of his pulse. His watch read five minutes to nine—the girls must be coming down. Trying to keep his composure, he took Laith's arm and started for the corner. "The girls are here."

At this point, lying about that was simply fruitless; Laith had already figured him out. He didn't follow Theodore very willingly though, hesitant to duck out of sight. Two steps were taken, but overall, he lingered in front of the building. "Why don't you want me to meet your friends?" His question was very genuine, quiet in the silence that permeated the streets. It almost broke Theodore's heart, but on the verge of panicking, he couldn't exactly focus on it.

"You wouldn't get along," he spoke quickly, pulling Laith toward the corner. Two more steps were conquered. "You guys are way too different."

"You're judging them the way we judge you. The way you *hate* to be judged."

"The difference is that I know them."

Begrudgingly, Laith trudged down the sidewalk and rounded the corner. That put things in motion right on time. Focused on their concealment, without averting his eyes for a single moment, Theodore pushed him against the wall and held still.

The girls' voices grew closer, louder as they approached the gate— Theodore peeked around the corner to keep an eye on them. Conversing leisurely, they walked out and crossed the street, probably on the way to one of the house parties in that area, nearest the campus.

When they disappeared around the next block, a breath left Theodore's lungs, shoulders relaxing. It was only then that he noticed his palm pressed against Laith's chest and his entire body shoved in Laith's personal space. He promptly took a step back, all contact ceased. His heart jumped into his throat.

"They *want* to meet you," he commented, caught in his own embarrassment. If he kept talking, it'd redirect Laith's focus to the conversation. "They said I had to introduce them to the next person I met up with, but I obviously didn't do that. They're always asleep, anyway; it's not like I'd wake them up just for that."

"Who did you see this week?"

"Everyone but you."

In a move specifically tailored to send a message, he walked back to the front of the building without waiting for Laith or even looking back. The entire time, all he could think of was if Laith had followed or just left, but he refused to betray himself and break the façade. Instead, he slowed down and listened. Laith was very heavy-footed, so it was easy to hear his footsteps trailing behind, even if he was a few feet back. Breathing in deep, Theodore approached the gate, and from inside his cabin, the doorman buzzed the lock open.

"Are you coming up?" he spoke before turning to look at Laith.

As soon as their eyes met, Laith stopped walking, six feet away from him. "Who's everyone?"

"Why don't we have that conversation upstairs?" He walked into the front yard and held the gate open.

Green eyes squinted. They glanced across the yard first, then up the building itself, suspicious yet pensive. "Was it Justin?"

"I don't know."

They held the stare. Reluctantly, Laith walked over.

mmmmmmmmmmm

"We met up on Wednesday, I think. My sleeping schedule is all backwards, so it's hard to know for sure." He kept his voice quiet in the elevator, back resting against the mirror. "We hung out all night. It was nice."

"Are you talking about Justin?"

"Yeah."

"Couldn't have been Wednesday. That's when I saw him."

"Then it was Tuesday. He cancelled on me after. Now I know why."

Once the display changed to number six, the elevator elegantly halted and opened its doors. Laith walked out first.

"What were you guys doing? Talking to my dad?" Theodore asked, towing along.

"Yeah, actually."

"Is that when Justin told on me?"

"He said a lot less than he could have."

Inside the apartment, he flicked one of the lights on, above the dining table. His shoulders shrugged his coat off as the door clicked behind him, closed by Laith. That handful of actions together triggered a brief memory, his entrance in Hwan's apartment, except there was only one person with him now— the one who mattered. The one who should've been there the first time around, in the scenario he'd wanted from the very beginning. His chest grew warm.

With his coat on the hanger, he turned to see Laith leaning against the door, hands deep in his pockets. Every time their eyes met tonight, green ones had found him first. He could get used to it.

"You said I shouldn't run away but failed to mention how to go about telling them."

"My best advice is to only open that can of worms when you have someone to help you do it. A real, long-lasting relationship."

His head moved in a slow nod. A long-lasting relationship, huh. Someone he'd been seeing for a while, maybe? Who he trusted with his life, who'd already done this in the past? He took a step closer, eyes glued on Laith's face. "Except that's not what you did."

"I didn't get a chance to—my sister told them—which is why getting to the forefront of this is so important."

Oh, god. The weight of that knitted his eyebrows together, heart hanging precariously over the pit. That wasn't fair at all. "I'm sorry."

Laith shrugged. "I just don't think you should chicken out before knowing what you're working with. Sometimes, it's manageable and you don't have to lose your family. Sometimes, it isn't. At least find out before you leave."

The mere thought of coming out froze his body from the inside out, but somebody else doing it for him was a much worse alternative. Ryan immediately came to mind, even if chances of him outing his little brother were pretty much none, considering he didn't even speak to their parents anymore. Not to mention the same could be done to him right back.

"You could come to Cali with me." The invitation left him straight from the heart. "We'll visit Santa Monica and ride the Ferris wheel together. I bet it's as big as the one in Seattle."

The corners of Laith's lips curled into the smallest smile he'd ever seen, mask back in his pocket. "How are you gonna afford that?"

"Oh, tickets can't be that expensive. Ten dollars at most."

This time, Laith actually smiled, though it only lasted a second. "You know, people don't just run away like that anymore; they go into the tunnels. That's the whole reason they turned into what they are today."

"I don't belong there, remember?"

"No, but homeless kids do."

He scowled. "I won't be homeless; I'll have a car."

"That's not a home. Theo, the reality of running away is that you'll be starting from scratch. That means sleeping in your car and eating from convenience stores. You don't know what it's like to be poor."

"I'll get a job."

"And then what? You'll suddenly have a home and a fridge full of food? You won't even be making enough to rent a place. You'll have no furniture, no appliances and no utilities. I'm not saying you won't make it; I'm just saying it's much harder than you think. It's not just *running away.*" Laith quoted the air, eyebrows drawn together. "Leaving your old life behind without planning a successful future won't change things for the better. I know that because I left home too, but I did it on my own terms."

"How did you do it?"

"I made friends who led me to Burman. I got a job, then a place, *then* I left. We're lucky to have her."

He chewed on the inside of his cheek. "I'm glad that worked out for you, but the problem is that I won't be running from anything if I move underground. I'll still be living within my dad's reach. He could find me in seconds."

"He really doesn't have all that power. *Burman* is the one who calls the shots; he's just her accountant. His contract gives him access to some dangerous people, yeah, but at the end of the day, everything he does in *her* playground only ever happens because she lets it happen."

"Didn't he hurt you? Didn't he beat you up?"

"Yeah, and she watched it. I was an idiot; I deserved it. If she thinks his actions are justified, she'll give him the green light, but you didn't do anything. There's no reason for him to chase you down when all you want is to stay away."

"What if she thinks I deserve it?"

"What did you do to deserve it?"

They held the stare.

"She doesn't know me; she'll believe whatever he says. He'll give her some bullshit excuse for the green light."

"If you move down, she's going to know you. At one point or another, she'll get to you, and anyway, nothing's stopping you from going to her first."

Huh.

"Are you..." His eyes squinted jokingly, teasing. "Are you telling me to go down? The guy who has publicly stated that I don't belong there?"

Laith rolled his eyes. "I'm not *telling* you to do anything; I don't even think you should leave home. I'm just saying that if you do, driving all the way to California is a stupid way to move forward. In case you don't know, your dad can still find you there."

"I think you wanna be my neighbor."

His stupid antics succeeded in breaking the tension, pulling a scoffed out laugh from Laith's throat. "Yeah, right. And have your dad breathing down my neck? I think I'll pass."

16

"Isn't he doing that already? The only difference is that you'd get to see me anytime you wanted." His shoulder raised into a half-shrug.

"I can do that now. I already know your address."

"I'm assuming my apartment is too out of the way for you to actually visit, since you never have." He cocked his head aside, eyes big on purpose. The emotional appeal worked—Laith had to look away. "Isn't that it?" he asked.

"That's..." Laith shook his head.

"What?"

Their eyes met again.

"I'll be coming over a lot more often now, so it doesn't really matter, does it?"

"It does if you don't wanna be here. If you've never wanted to be here at all."

Laith scowled, but there was pain in the crease between his eyebrows, eyes soft with it. No rebuttal came, so Theodore continued.

"I don't wanna have you around if you don't wanna come over. I'm tired of chaining you to me just so I can see you, just so I can talk to you. It's not fair to you and it's not fair to me either. Running after someone who won't even turn around for me is exhausting. I..." His shoulders raised into a prolonged shrug. "I don't wanna do that."

Laith nodded, gaze dropping. "Yeah, that's not very fair, is it?"

"No, it isn't." His heart hammered, breath caught in his throat. This was a *very* risky move, but at this point, he really didn't have anything to lose. He'd never had anything in the first place; Laith had never been his to slip through his fingers. It was either this or absolutely nothing at all.

"I can try meeting you halfway." Laith's voice was quiet, shoulders moving up a bit. "I can't promise I'll be any good at it, but—well." His head tilted, causing a strand of hair to fall over his forehead. "I'll do what I gotta do."

A shit-eating grin almost burst through Theodore's face, but he managed to hold it back, smiling nicely instead, even if Laith still refused to look at him. "You can't quit me just as much as I can't quit you, huh?"

Finally, their eyes met.

"You're addicted to me too," Theodore continued, shaping his words around a big grin.

"Honestly?" Dark eyebrows raised, shoulders bouncing. "Yeah. Yeah. I don't know what you did, but I can't kick you for the life of me. All I did this week was think about you."

His eyes tripled in size, heart paralyzed in his chest, lungs flat-lining—what? He could barely believe his own ears. "Are you serious?" His voice floated from a disembodied entity, ears ringing loudly.

"Yeah, I—" Laith shook his head, eyes cast aside. "This is TMI, but I get this, like—this attachment to people and... I'm not gonna tell you it means anything it doesn't, but yeah, I—I wanna be around you. I'll meet you halfway; I'll do whatever I have to. It's stupid; you're the worst choice I could ever make and the moment the Crow finds out, he's gonna put a hit on me, but I just can't—I can't stand here and pretend I haven't thought about this all fucking week. So." Laith's hands left their pockets to fling up into the air, vague. "Yeah."

"You like me." A smile slowly cut through Theodore's face. "You *like* like me."

"Yeah." That word was almost a whisper, Laith's voice soft and low. "I like you a whole lot."

Theodore grinned so big that his cheeks hurt. Propelled by the beating of his heart, ten times its own size, he closed the distance between them with a hug. His arms squeezed Laith around the waist, face buried into the crook of his neck. When he breathed, tobacco and amber filled his lungs, chest warm with a feeling so precious and pure that it encapsulated this moment in a snow globe, kept forever. Laith moved in his hold, arms wrapping around him in return, much softer, much more delicate than any hug he'd ever received. It was different than the one from last week, on Justin's dance floor; this one harbored sentiment, a conscious choice. Nuzzling into his hair, Laith held him back.

Chapter 3

A date?

I won't forget how you looked at me then
I know I'm no sweet prince of love

- Glass Animals, *Pork Soda*

This was the first time Laith's presence didn't bring along the looming urgency to keep him entertained. They put on a movie and sat down to watch it—actually watch it. Laith hadn't seen it yet, so it was a new experience for them both. Unlike before, when doing this had only felt like the ticking of a clock until Laith got too bored to hang out with him any longer, this was actually fun. Not because the movie was interesting, but because Laith *wanted* to be here, watching it with him.

Throughout the runtime, he learned Laith was the kind of person who talked during movies. Whenever he noticed something, he pointed it out; little bits of the story that connected here and there, recurring items or characters that had appeared in a much earlier scene, details that he thought were important. Theodore had noticed them too, and if Laith happened to miss one, he was more than happy to point it out. It was nice to share an experience with someone who paid as much attention to things as he did.

Once the movie was done, they decided to make some dinner. To keep it simple, tonight's menu would be a couple of tuna sandwiches and cranberry juice. While Laith chopped up the tomatoes, onions and celery, Theodore assembled everything with a lot of mayo. That was when he noticed just how steady Laith's hands were, wielding the knife precisely, without hurting himself at all. It brought his sobriety into question, if he'd drunk anything before coming over. Thinking back to the gas station, plus the whole time they'd been together, Theodore couldn't remember a single sway or misstep. Holy shit, was Laith sober? Straight-up asking was out of the question—too vulgar and impolite—so he'd have to get creative.

"You know, we don't *have* to have cranberry juice; I could fix you a drink. I mean, I don't know if you pre-gamed or not, but we still have the gin and stuff from last time."

"Yeah, no; I'm on prescription, but thanks. Here." Laith slid the chopped pieces of celery from the cutting board into a bowl. "I'll get started on the lettuce."

Okay, so he *was* sober. Theodore didn't know what this prescription was or what it did, but the way Laith had put it hadn't given him the impression he'd taken it for recreational purposes. He probably wouldn't look and sound so sober if he had. It bore noticing too that the last time he'd talked about medication of any kind was on Justin's porch, when the hospital had come up; Theodore had no idea he was still on anything at all. He'd mentioned getting better, that he no longer felt how he used to, so what was this about? What was it for?

While he *could* ask, he decided not to; a question like that ran a very big risk of making things weird. The point he was trying to make was that, if Laith *was* sober, then everything he'd said earlier had been genuine, the whole thing about liking him back. His heart skipped a beat—had Laith meant the speech from last week too? He'd been very quick to dismiss it as drunken ramblings, but a lot of what had been said tracked with their conversation earlier, so maybe not *everything* had been forgettable. Maybe Laith really did like him much more than he'd been led to believe. Sherry's spiel had never really left his mind, and now, he was starting to believe that maybe she was right.

"You like me, right? You like me." That left him on its own, bypassing his brain straight for his mouth. It prompted Laith to pass him a glance.

"We've just been over this, Theo. I like you a lot."

"Okay, I just..."

What was it, then? He didn't even know what his soul was trying to get at, what gnawed on it, the source of such insecurity. In resigned distress, he set the butter knife down and turned to get the juice.

The utter normality that was two people sitting at a table over dinner crash-landed against his skull about halfway into the evening. He hadn't sat down to eat with the girls in so long that his first instinct was to compare this moment to dinner with his parents, except a better version of it, nicer, one he could find himself looking forward to, rather than contemplating to fake a cold in order to skip it.

The contents of their conversation were the same as they'd always been, with added comments on the movie from earlier, which should've been completely expected, but for some reason, it still felt rebellious, as if there were certain topics that shouldn't be discussed over dinner. This was a moment of politeness and respect, after all. In reality, he knew the only reason he felt this way was because dinner with his parents always came with a list of censored topics. Actually, any conversation with them came with that list attached. Discussing the movie's sex scenes and its homoerotic undertones was definitely not something he would've ever done with his parents, but with Laith, it felt natural, even if it tainted the sanctity of dinnertime. On second thought, Ryan's outbursts and all the fights that had broken out at the table were good enough reasons to make him believe dinner had never been sacred in the first place.

By now, it'd become a habit of his to do all the dishes directly after eating. It hadn't always been the case in his parents' home—his mother had been in charge of that for a while—but overtime, it'd been delegated to him, probably because he was the only one who'd cared to help her in any sense. Back when he still lived with her, they'd do it together, but last night, it was made clear that she'd no longer participate. It was fine; he didn't mind it.

Since he'd done it so often, it hadn't occurred to him that other people might do it too. Laith, for example. When Theodore very absently started on the dishes, he didn't expect Laith to grab a cloth and dry the plates, just like his mother used to do. The only difference was that Laith piled them up on the counter instead of putting them away, probably because he didn't know where they went. Still, it felt incredibly coordinated for something they'd never done together. Familiar in a strange way, like the time they'd gone grocery shopping.

"What do you do to pass the time?" That question left him as he shut off the water. "During the week, I mean, when you're not partying and stuff. I realized I need to get a hobby, or I'll just watch trashy romcoms all night. No one's ever awake, and the ones who are don't wanna hang out with me."

"You don't *need* people to party, dude. I do it during the week too. I go by myself." Laith shrugged, cloth wiping the last pot dry. "Depends if I feel like hooking up or not. If I don't, I usually stay in and research. The hauntings, I mean; Kant, Lewis and Armstrong."

"Oh my god." That exclamation erupted with memories of last night;

Ethel's dying silhouette in the dark. "I was at my mom's house last night, you know the one in Crestwood? She's always had this woman following her, Ethel. When she went to bed, Ethel would stand in the hallway and stare at her bedroom door all night. Except last night, she didn't. She came downstairs to where I was and died. She *died.* Like, wasn't she already dead?"

Dark eyebrows pinched together, curiosity written all over Laith's face. "Apparently not. Did she die in front of you?"

"Yeah, she slumped over and disappeared, but I touched her! I touched her while she was on the floor. She was the manifestation of my mom's fears and anxieties. That's what they are."

"So we create them. They come from inside us."

"How come my mom couldn't see her, though?"

"Why did she die?"

"Because my mom overcame those fears, I think—but why couldn't she see Ethel? She made her."

Laith pensively set the pot down. "Why are they dangerous to people who have nothing to do with them?"

"Maybe there *is* a connection. Ethel never hurt me, but I was afraid of her for a long time. I might be partly responsible for what my mom used to feel."

"Okay, but wouldn't that make *everyone* able to see each other's ghosts? If we're all resentful of one another, that should raise the number of hauntings."

Hm, that made sense.

"She told me a lot about my mom. Stuff I've always wanted to know, but knew she'd never tell me. She grew up in a trailer park too."

"Huh. Saved by a prince." Laith handed the cloth back to him. "My brother had a creature following him too—Abbas. It died along with him. I noticed the correlation, but could never reach any proper conclusions."

"Did you get to figure out what Abbas represented?"

"No, he scared the shit out of me. He used to hang from the ceiling and watch us sleep. All I could see was a vague outline in the dark with small, white eyes."

"How come they tell us their names but not what they are? With Ethel, it felt like I'd always known her, while not actually knowing her at all. She'd never said a word either—I just knew."

"Did she want to hurt your mom?"

"No, she liked her. She followed her everywhere."

"Abbas wanted to hurt Qasim really bad. He wanted to rip his arms off. He'd whisper it at night, all the ways he wanted to do it—with a knife, with a saw, with his own teeth. He'd chew his own cheeks for hours. I still remember what it sounded like."

"Was Abbas the only one?"

"The only one I knew. The other ones didn't have names; they just crawled around and hid in the dark, but Abbas hung right over me. He'd look through me like I wasn't there and whisper—*it's just a matter of time, it's just a matter of time.* He spoke through his cheeks, eating them."

"What did his voice sound like? I didn't even know they could speak."

"It sounded like three people talking at the same time, three of the same voice, kinda like a growl. He never told me his name either—I always just knew."

Huh.

"Well," Laith continued, clearing his throat. "At least your place isn't haunted."

"Yeah, I can be bored and alone without the dark terrorizing me."

Laith's teeth flashed as he tutted. "I told you, man; just go out by yourself. Don't give people so much power over your evenings."

"I don't know if I wanna do that, though. Being alone in a crowd is depressing."

"That's just the thing, dude—you're not alone; you're in a crowd."

"You can *feel* alone in a crowd; that's what I meant. When you look around and none of the faces you see are familiar. It's like reaching for someone who you think is your mom, but then realizing she's not your mom at all and you're still lost at the mall."

Laith gave him a look. "How come none of your friends wanna hang out with you?"

"They have normal sleeping schedules, so we're never awake at the same time. We're awake for class, but that's it."

"What about the others?"

"What others?"

"Tae-hwan and his friends."

"Oh, uh." His face caught on fire, mind briefly replaying the events of last Friday. "We're not very close."

Green eyes squinted. "Sure." Laith didn't sound convinced at all. "In that case, either make new friends, get to know the ones you already have, or learn how to live with yourself. Actually, that last one goes regardless."

"That's the problem, like, I only ever do one thing, and sometimes I don't feel like going on an emotional journey just because no one wants to hang out. I need less exhausting hobbies."

"What emotional journey?"

"I—I write music. Um, I think I told you that."

"Oh, right. Yeah, I remember that. I didn't know you still played the guitar."

"I just do it for me. It's not a big deal, but uh. Yeah." If only Laith knew half the lyrics were about him. "So, what else do you do besides partying and researching?"

A soft hum traveled the space between them, indicative of Laith's deliberation. He stood with his hip pressed against the counter, right hand resting on its surface. "Well, I go to the gym a lot and I like to cook, but when I don't feel like doing anything, I'll just lie in bed and drink all day. I don't know. I hang out with my neighbors sometimes, but I realize that's not the advice you're looking for."

The drinking comment turned his blood into ice. His lips promptly parted to ask after it, but at the last second, his mind decided to say something else. That would've just ruined the moment. "I didn't know you talked to your neighbors. I mean, I guess I don't really know who else you talk to besides Emily and Justin."

"They're nice. We don't see each other all the time, 'cause our work schedules are backwards, but when they *are* home, it's impossible to miss it. They're never inside; they hang out in the doorway and talk, like, watching the hallway. I don't know how to explain this. They're next-door neighbors and I live right across, like a hotel."

"What do they do?"

"They perform at the DP. Night performances, obviously; that's where the money is. So what usually happens is, I'll work while they're home, then party while they're working. The good part is that I get to watch all their shows."

"That's fun. Maybe I should be a performer too."

"What's your talent?"

"My talent?"

"Yeah. What are you gonna perform? Are you gonna play the guitar?

Sing or dance?"

"I wouldn't play to a crowd." Not in a million years. "But I can learn how to dance."

"Yeah, if you don't already dance well, you're gonna need more than that to wow the crowd."

"I'm handsome; isn't that enough? Isn't that why they came out to see me?"

"I mean..." Laith glanced him down. "Yeah, I could see it. If you stripped on stage, the house would be full."

He grinned. "Maybe not that. I'm thinking more like, um... like an act. Magic tricks!"

"Do you know any?"

"No, but I can learn."

"Goddammit, Theo." Laith shook his head, smiling. "Just do something you're good at."

"But I'm not good at anything."

"That's not true. What do you do all night besides playing the guitar and watching TV shows? Our talents are in the stuff we do when we don't have to do anything."

"Well." He cocked his head aside. "In high school, I used to study a lot, even when I didn't have any exams coming up, but none of the subjects I have now are interesting. I hate all of them, actually."

"Oh, so you're one of *those* people."

He scowled. "What people?"

"The *huge* nerds. You know, the ones who do equations at home 'cause they think they're fun."

"Shut up! You spend all day *researching*—" His hands quoted the air. "—like that's not the same thing."

"It's not. What I read about is important."

"Math and science are important too."

"Yeah, but they make you a nerd."

He playfully shoved Laith on the chest, just barely able to hold back a smile. That put a big grin on Laith's face, laughter bubbling in his throat.

"Oh, so you're a nerd *and* a bully."

"No, I'm not!" He raised his voice for impact, but every word was spoken with a grin.

Done with the dishes, they ended up going to his room. That was the only part of the apartment they hadn't been to yet and the next logical step too, since they didn't feel like eating anything else or watching another movie. Even though the invitation had been innocent, Theodore couldn't say the thought of taking tonight to the next level hadn't crossed his mind. He knew that had crossed Laith's mind too, even if nothing was said, all in favor of preserving the atmosphere. Laith just took a seat on the bed, closer to the end this time, while Theodore took the desk chair once again, turned so they could face each other.

Under the dim yellow light that shone from the floor lamp, they spoke of what they liked to do and the places they liked to visit. Laith told him of all the nooks and crannies in the Dead Ponies, the music and the shows, the performances and the services. Everything that the body craved could be satisfied, be it carnally or intellectually; their facilities ranged from brothels to clubs, to open mic stages, to concert avenues, to VR arenas, to movie theaters and more. They had absolutely everything. Two of those places sounded familiar, names Theodore had heard before—the Vapid Beasts and the Queen Bees. The latter was where drag queens performed, with multiple rooms for all kinds of talents, many of which happened at the same time. The crowd was just that big.

The Vapid Beasts, on the other hand, was a much different place. Hwan had mentioned working there for a while, up until his boyfriend's tragic demise and the bloodbath surrounding it. In his description, Laith didn't mention any of that. He said the Vapid Beasts was the home of the Hollywood boys and some of the other well-known faces around, just verging on the line between prostitution and legitimate flirting. Services were offered, but that didn't mean every schmuck with a wallet could get a turn. There were both a dance floor and a stage, so people could either show off their bodies dancing, or seem distant and unattainable while sitting at a booth watching the performance—a singer, a dancer, a talent show. Obviously, the Hollywood boys were the latter.

The way Laith spoke of that place was so dreamlike that it brought into question whether he even knew what had happened there, if he knew he was essentially romanticizing his brother's burial ground. Theodore would never ask.

"Do they ever have problems with bigots ruining the fun? I feel like places like those, openly accepting, would have a lot of assholes coming in."

"Sure they do, but those are very rare occurrences. The DP is such an empire that the homophobes can't really afford to say anything about it. Only the ones from the surface ever try anything."

"What's the biggest scandal that's ever happened?"

"I'm not sure. Shit goes down all the time, but I don't really know anyone who goes there for fun. No one I know can afford it."

Okay, so Laith either didn't know at all, or he was deliberately keeping it out of the discussion. Those were the only two explanations Theodore could come up with.

Their conversation jumped from topic to topic. As enthralled as Theodore was, he still couldn't help splitting his attention between the words that came out of Laith's mouth and the way he leaned back on a hand, feet locked at the ankles. The question as to why he'd dressed like a rat tonight when he usually dressed down to visit the surface practically lived in Theodore's head, but never made it out. Not so much because he didn't want to potentially spoil the mood as much as he knew his father was the reason, one way or another—he was the only variable that had been changed.

Doubts regarding the inner workings of the DP and to what extent Laith worked under Henry were also plenty common, although none were expressed in fear of overstepping his boundaries. Laith was being so charitable, spending time with him when he didn't have to, that the mere thought of pushing him away was terrifying enough to keep Theodore from trying anything. The only good it did was bring him the self-awareness to match Laith's benevolence.

"You know, you can smoke, if you want to. I'll open the window for you." He jerked a thumb to go with the offer.

Green eyes followed it to the window. "Do you want to?"

Oh, that wasn't what he'd meant, but then again, who was he to refuse such kindness?

"Yeah, sure."

Watching Laith shift around to fish out his wallet, Theodore thought of the desk drawer directly next to him. His lips parted with the information that he had weed, actually, and didn't need Laith to share his, but his words got all tangled up in his mouth, unable to come out. Laith didn't even know he'd picked up smoking; nobody did—how would *that* conversation go? Memories of last night froze his blood in his veins, Henry's voice a hammer in the back of his mind, pounding his brain into a wet, quivering pulp.

Laith pulled a joint out and offered it. Their fingers touched as it exchanged hands—Theodore made sure of it.

"I actually have a lighter." His confession burst out of his chest in lieu of much more incriminating material. He just had to bring it up.

Dark eyebrows bounced, a hint of delight on Laith's face. "Yeah?"

"I found it on the street." He pulled the desk drawer open. The first thing that slid over was the baggie, closely followed by the cigarette pack with only one cigarette missing. The sight erased any evenness from his pulse, heart jumping to his throat. Perfectly composed, he took the lighter out and showed it off. "It's blue."

"It sure is." Laith smiled.

Time stopped. While he could absolutely shut the drawer and get stoned without ever addressing its contents, part of him wanted this conversation to happen. He wanted to compare Laith's judgment to his parents'. How disappointed would Laith be? How much would Laith hate him? He bit his lip, heart banging against his ribs.

"What if I told you..." Words tumbled out of his mouth. His brain could barely focus on a comprehensive argument, stuck on last night, frantic. "What if, I mean, you said I don't really smoke, but what if I did? What if I picked it up?"

Laith's eyebrows slowly drew together. His lack of a comment prompted Theodore to continue.

"My parents said smoking makes me worthless, that I'm letting my friends control me and I'm throwing my life away."

"Your dad is a reactionary. He only says all that stuff 'cause he's afraid you'll fall into bad habits."

"What if I already have?"

The scowl on Laith's face grew deeper. "It takes a long time for you to pick up a *habit*. It's not just smoking sometimes; it's part of your life."

"Is it a habit for you?"

"Sure. It's a habit for most of the people I know."

"How do you know it's not an addiction?"

"Oh, it's hard to get addicted to weed. I'm not saying it's impossible, just that pretty much anything else is more addicting than weed."

They held the stare.

"What is it? Why do you think you're addicted?" Laith asked.

"I smoked every single day last week."

"Really." Laith didn't sound convinced, tone flat. "How'd that go?"

"I'm serious." To demonstrate his point, Theodore took the baggie from the drawer and waved it in the air. That drew Laith's eyebrows up. "Justin gave

28

me this. I smoke overnight, then go to class really, really high. It's the only way I can sit through those lectures."

"Damn, you hate your major *that* much?"

"You didn't believe me the first time?"

"No, I did. I guess I didn't realize how bad it was."

An exhale left his lungs, shoulders drooping a bit. His back remained straight, however, muscles tense. The baggie seemed to have enough for one last joint, so he offered Laith's back to him. "Here, take it. I have enough for one more."

"Consider it a gift. Looks like you'll need it, anyway."

Surprise cocked his head aside. Really? His heart swelled with the sweetness of that gesture, warmth spreading across his chest. Multiple dissertations ran freely through his mind, all the different ways he wanted to tell Laith how much that little bit of kindness meant to him—especially at a time like this—but all that managed to leave his lips was a small *thank you* and nothing else. He slipped the joint into the baggie, too precious to be smoked, the only gift Laith had ever given him.

"Don't worry about what your dad said. You know he's only trying to freak you out."

"I know, I just... I wanted someone to agree with me, I guess. I wanted to hear you say it's okay."

"It's not okay."

Their eyes met. Too stunned to say anything back, he just stared at Laith.

"Things are obviously not going well. Smoking isn't the problem; it's a symptom. It's a way to cope without actually fixing anything. You hate your major—that's fine. What would you rather take, then?"

"Law."

That word flew out of his mouth before he could process it, the first thing on his mind. Despite how confident he'd sounded, the truth was that he didn't know if that answer was genuine or the image of himself he wanted to become. Did he actually want to major in law, or did he only think of it because it wasn't business? It could've been anything else.

"No, not law," he quickly corrected. "I don't know what I want to study."

"You can figure that out later. People like you usually take a gap year before going to college, anyway. Why don't you do that?"

"People like me?"

"Go to Europe. I hear France and Italy are popular choices."

"I don't—I'm not like that. We don't have money for that."

"How do you know?"

"Because my dad never offered it. I've never even left the country."

"Alright, then *don't* go to Europe. You said your dad wants you to work for him, so offer to work for him for a year or so. Figure out what you like in the meantime."

"You make everything sound so simple. It's really not like that at all."

"Sometimes, it is."

"Not with my dad. I've never had a single conversation with him that wasn't extremely difficult." His eyebrows drew together, noose fastening around his throat. "I'm sure you know exactly what I'm talking about."

"You're his *son*. The chances of you getting through to him are ten times higher than mine on principle alone. He cares about you a lot."

"He doesn't care about *me*." He touched his own chest for emphasis. "He cares about what I represent, how I make him look. I'm supposed to carry on *his* legacy, not create my own. It's never been about me."

"There's no way you can know that without having ever opened up to him. He's playing off the image you cast of yourself, so don't be mad if he can't see who you really are."

That stung. He didn't even know what to say, breath stolen from his lungs.

Laith's phone buzzed and cut the silence. The first thought that crossed his mind was that, hopefully, this call would kill the topic and end their conversation right here; no more theories about his relationship with his father and no more exposure on all the things he'd done wrong. He already felt like an idiot.

When Laith fished his phone out, Justin's name read on the screen— Theodore could see it glow in the low light. Laith didn't seem very delighted by it though, just short of rolling his eyes as a thumb swiped across the screen. Loud music promptly blasted into the room—Justin must be at the DP.

"Hey, man."

"Dude! Jesus Christ, I've been trying to reach you for two days! What the fuck is going on?!"

Laith passed him a glance. "I'm busy, Justin. That's what's going on."

"I know, I know; you've *been* busy. Where are you?"

"Does it matter? Just tell me what you need."

"Well." Justin hesitated. "Are you coming tonight? Emily and Ryan wanna talk to you."

"I talked to her just yesterday."

"I know, but then you blocked her again, and I think you know how she feels about that. She has a lot to say, apparently. She's—she's really mad, dude. I don't know what you told her, but it wasn't good."

Laith rolled his eyes in lieu of a verbal response.

"I've been calling since yesterday, you know. I came by to get you, 'cause you didn't show up, but you weren't home either," Justin continued.

"I never said I was going."

"Yeah, well..." Justin's tone faltered. "Are you at Theo's place?"

Their eyes met again.

The lack of an answer pushed Justin to continue.

"I know you haven't seen each other throughout the week, but he blocked me last night, you know, when you didn't show up, so I put two and two together."

Somehow, two wrongs had made a right. Justin was definitely one of the people who got lucky that way.

"If you *are* there, can you tell him he doesn't need to block me? I'm on his side."

"I didn't block you because of Laith." That explanation came straight from Theodore's heart, too sincere to get caught in his throat. "My dad said I had to stop being friends with you, so I blocked you. I don't think he'll ever see my phone, but I just didn't want to risk it."

Laith pursed his lips, tying together a look that was the combination of annoyance and disapproval.

"Rename my contact then, or better yet, delete it altogether, so if he *does* get your phone, I'll be a bunch of numbers. I just don't wanna stop talking to you. With the way things are going, it feels like I'm losing all my friends."

"I never meant for this to be permanent. I was gonna unblock you after Christmas."

"Why Christmas?"

"Because..." He passed Laith a glance. "Well, I guess it doesn't really matter now. I'll unblock you. Oh, and Laith wasn't here yesterday. I promise."

"Okay, just..." Justin sighed. "I'm glad you two are together, 'cause it definitely feels like a battleground where I am. I don't want us to fall apart."

"We're not going to," Laith reassured him. "We'll pull through. I don't know what I'm gonna do about Ryan, but I'll figure something out."

"No," Theodore cut in. "Leave Ryan to me. You take care of Emily."

Holding the stare, Laith nodded.

"What do I tell them?" The anxiety in Justin's voice was palpable.

"Tell them I'm busy." With that, Laith ended the call.

"I feel bad for him," Theodore lamented. "None of this is his fault."

"Every part of this is everyone's fault. They've been pinning it all on me, but they're just as much to blame. They're the ones making a big deal out of it when they're not even involved."

"They're worried, is all."

"Yeah, worried about *you*, like I'm going to murder you or something. Emily's known me forever; she knows everyone I've ever been with. Out of all of them, she should know how safe you are around me."

"Well, *I* know that, but maybe she forgot. Actually... it's probably Ryan's fault, to be honest. He's the one with a problem."

"Then we'll talk to him first."

"No, I told you—*I'll* do it. You take care of her."

"They live together. I don't think we'll be able to tackle them separately."

"It's okay; we'll figure something out. We have Sherry and Justin to help us."

"Yeah, sure."

That sounded very dismissive, but Theodore decided not to press on it. Instead, he turned the lighter in his hand, mind whirring. Sherry could lure Ryan out of the apartment, or vice versa with Justin and Emily, for separate meetings. Which one of the two was more suspicious? Emily, probably; she always had an eye on everyone, it seemed. Justin could coax her out then, so Theodore could see his brother.

The thought of being in an apartment alone with Ryan closed a hand around his throat and strangled it. The stairs promptly came to mind, Ryan shoving him down, followed by every altercation his brother had ever had with Henry. Ryan had put on a considerable amount of muscle ever since going to the gym—he could break Theodore's neck. His hands trembled with the thought. So maybe Sherry could be there too, if only as a moderator, watching them hash it out. Her height alone brought him peace.

"I've been trying to talk to Emily since the farm." Laith's voice was low, eyes cast off in the distance. "She just doesn't listen to me. I don't think speaking to her again will change anything. I need somebody else to do it."

"Justin could try. They're really close."

"I don't know about that. That man runs from confrontation like it's contagious."

"If you're there with him, he might feel brave enough to speak up."

"It's never been that way."

"Things could change."

"I'm thinking we both talk to them together, or we both talk to Ryan together and let him speak to Emily later."

His stomach went cold. Laith had a lot more stage presence than he did, and near Ryan, fights always broke out. He could picture it perfectly, the four of them in a room. He opened his mouth to speak, but somebody always spoke first. Whatever they said, the other would take issue with it, immediately escalating the situation to something physical. Emily would get between the two of them to break it off, while Theodore was left in the corner, unheard and unseen.

"No, no, no; you and Ryan can't be in the same room together. Let me talk to him."

"What about Emily?"

"Justin will talk to her."

"No, he won't."

"Yes, he will. Just make him do it."

"That's not how it works. You can't force somebody to do what you want; it ruins the message."

"Okay, then I'll talk to him. I'll ask him to do it—nicely."

"He's not gonna listen to you."

"Alright, alright, let me think." A sigh left his lips, on the verge of exasperation. "Okay, what if it's me, him, Ryan and Emily? That might work."

At the very least, he wouldn't be forced to stand in anybody's shadow and would be given the necessary attention to deliver the message. Not to mention that Ryan would have no reason to attack Justin at all. If anything, Emily might be the one getting hostile with him, but she wouldn't make it physical. She never had.

"What about me?" Laith asked.

"What about you?"

"They're pissed off at *me*, not you; I should at the very least be in the room too."

"No." That word practically shot out of his mouth. "No, trust me; it's better if you aren't."

"I'm not gonna let you fight this for me."

"Laith, this fight isn't *about* you. The only reason Ryan has a problem with who you're seeing is because that person is me. He has a problem with me, not you."

"He has a problem with *me* seeing *you*."

"Because I'm his brother, not because you're his friend."

"Because of both!"

He reached across the gap and touched Laith's knee. "Just let me do this, okay? I have to give it a shot. If nothing comes out of it, I'll let you handle it the way you want to."

They held the stare. Laith pursed his lips and set his jaw, green eyes piercing with disapproval. His reluctance was crystal clear, but still he yielded, even if against himself.

"Fine, but I'll be waiting downstairs."

"Deal."

Chapter 4

The girls

Now that I'm free to be myself
who am I?

- Mary Oliver, *Devotions*

Their conversations fluctuated from light-hearted to pessimistic and back, never managing to veer too far. They stood in a very precarious position, a strip of land between two pitfalls that were Ryan and Henry, difficult to ignore. The ground broke off and debris fell into the abyss, but for one precious moment, they were able to coexist. Theodore even moved to the spot next to Laith, so they could share the bed, hand on his knee. What he really wanted was to hold Laith's hand, but that level of intimacy was far more than he could ask for. He'd already gotten a hug; that should be enough. Taking Laith's hand would be pushing his luck.

At two in the morning, the girls came home. They heard the front door open, laughter and giggles loud in the foyer. The first thing Theodore did was get up and close his bedroom door. One of the rooms was just across from his; the moment Jessie and Hannah came down the hallway, they'd see Laith on his bed. Fully clothed, just chilling, but still. The implications were mortifying.

He listened through the door. Their drunken conversation traveled down the hallway, breaking apart the moment it reached the first door. Daisy and Nadia bid their goodbyes as Jessie and Hannah pushed forward. Right outside Theodore's door, their footsteps could be felt through the wooden flooring, drunk and uneven, stepping out of line. Once inside their own room, the girls closed the door.

Turning around, his eyes fell on Laith, watching from the bed. There was a hint of emotion on his face, similar to the one from before, when they'd hidden around the corner while the girls had left.

A pang of guilt drew Theodore's eyebrows upwards. "Do you..." Oh god, he already regretted this. "Do you wanna meet them?"

Laith held the stare.

"You said I shouldn't."

"I know." He swallowed. "So do you?"

"Yeah." His reply was meek and small, Laith's voice a whisper.

Theodore's pulse quickened.

In the hallway, a hand knocked on the door. Laith stood a couple of feet behind him, leaning against the door frame—he could feel Laith's stare boring into the back of his neck. Behind the door, feet shuffled as the girls giggled, saying words he couldn't make out.

"Who is it?" Jessie asked, louder than before.

"It's me. I wanna talk to you."

"We're getting dressed. I'll go to you when we're done."

Alright, then. With his heart in his mouth, he turned around and joined Laith in the doorway. The way Laith leaned on it was similar to the time on the farm, except his hands were hidden in his jacket pockets now, shoulder against the frame. A step too far into his personal space, Theodore touched the dog tags, fingertips feeling their edges. At this point, tobacco was the only thing he wanted to breathe.

"What do you wanna ask them?" He kept his voice quiet, so it wouldn't travel along the hallway. It was a whisper in the inch of space that separated them.

"I don't know. I guess I just want to see how incompatible we really are."

"They're the straight ones, Jessie and Hannah. You saw us jogging that one time."

"I remember. They're taller than the other two."

"Yeah. Hannah is the bodybuilder and Jessie is the supermodel."

"Supermodel, huh?" Laith smirked. "So she's the one who fooled around with you."

His face burned. "That was a long time ago. We don't even talk about it."

"Do you think about it?"

"No, it was terrible. One of the most embarrassing things I've ever done."

"So that's why you never did it again."

"It's not just that. I don't..." His hands flew up in the air. "It would be meaningless. We don't feel that way about each other."

Laith hummed his understanding.

The sound of the girls' door opening immediately pushed him a step away from Laith, dog tags slipping through his fingers. When Jessie showed up, she saw the two of them standing side-by-side, inconspicuous. Her eyes immediately locked on Laith, wide on her face, a breath caught in her throat. Half-paralyzed, she reached a hand back into the room and motioned frantically. In a moment, Hannah joined her at the door, eyes promptly doubling in size.

"So, um." Theodore kept his voice low, blood rushing loudly in his ears. "You guys said you wanted to meet him."

As if on cue, Laith moved away from the frame and reached a hand towards the two of them. Taking turns, they shook his hand and introduced themselves, even if unnecessarily—they didn't know that. Laith introduced himself too.

"God, if I knew you were here, I wouldn't be wearing pajamas," Jessie spoke around a quasi-smile, using humor to lessen the awkwardness that hung in the air.

It worked, or rather, Laith let it work, offering her a smile in return. "Well, I like the cat on your shirt, so."

"Thank you. I like your jacket."

As the two talked, Hannah crossed both arms over her chest and leaned against the door frame. Her eyebrows drew close together, eyes glinting with suspicion. Laith noticed it, of course.

"I'm sure you have a lot of questions going through your mind right now." Laith's tone was outwardly pleasant, a very conscious choice. "You can ask me whatever you want."

"Within reason, of course," Theodore quickly added.

"Right. Reason." Hannah squinted. "I just want to know what exactly is going on between you two. Theo says you're not dating, but you're always getting together—you're in *our* apartment. I'm just not sure I like having a stranger walking around where I live."

"It's like Theo said, we're not dating, but we *are* seeing each other."

"So you're dating."

"No, there's no exclusivity involved."

"So it's an open relationship."

Laith breathed in, chest full. "I mean, I guess—"

"Listen, you're either his boyfriend or you're not, and I don't want a stranger in my house. None of us bring strangers home. Why should you be an exception?"

Jessie touched Hannah's arm, both as an indication for her to take it easy, as well as solidarity toward the point she was making.

That word practically knocked Theodore out, eyes big on his own face, heat crawling up his neck. Breath came in laboriously. "He's not a stranger," he blurted out. "I've known him for years—*four* years, actually."

"No, I get that," Laith rebutted. "I get what she's saying. I'm a stranger to the rest of the household, which isn't fair. They live here just as you do."

"Yeah, but it's not like I met you last night and brought you home."

"You've known each other for four years?" Jessie interrupted. One of her eyebrows raised while the other scowled.

Sweat prickled at Theodore's palms.

This was a horrible idea.

"Remember how I said he's Ryan's friend? That's because we met through him."

"So you've known him longer than you've known me," Jessie remarked.

"Yeah. I mean, we only really started talking recently, but yeah, I have."

Jessie glanced back at Laith, eyebrows twisted upwards. "Have you been taking him underground?"

"No, he's been going with some other guys. I've never offered to go with him."

"Do you mean Dylan and the others?"

"Or are you talking about Justin?" Hannah added.

"Huh, I didn't know you knew about Justin." Laith sounded genuinely surprised. "It's not him, though. Theo knows some other guys. Could be Dylan, I don't know; he's just not who I'm thinking of."

"Who are they?" Both girls spoke at the same time, addressing Theodore.

There was no breath left in his throat, lips sealed. His brain couldn't even think of a word, much less put it in his mouth. All he managed to do was stare back at them without an answer.

"The guy I know isn't dangerous, if that's what you're worried about," Laith cut in. "I don't know the others, but I can tell you this one guy isn't gonna get Theo in trouble. It's fine."

"How do you know it's fine? The tunnels are a cesspool." The scowl on Hannah's forehead only deepened.

"'Cause I know Tae-hwan."

"Oh, so you *are* talking about Dylan and his friends." A sigh left Hannah's lips, shoulders relaxing.

"Am I?"

"Yeah, some of them used to go to our high school. We've met."

"Wait, so if Theo's going down anyway, why don't you go with him?" Worry furrowed Jessie's brow.

Laith shrugged. "I guess I could do that."

"Would you mind giving us your number?" That was the nicest Hannah had sounded this entire time. "I'd like to be able to reach Theo when he's not around."

"Which is a lot, by the way." Jessie met Theodore's eyes, despite clearly addressing Laith. "He's never around anymore. I guess he prefers Hwan to us."

"You sound like my mom," Theodore blurted out. "You two do, actually."

"If you're going to live with us, we need to know what kind of stuff you've been doing and the people you've been bringing over." Just like that, Hannah was back to her strict self. "If you didn't lie to us, we wouldn't resort to this."

"Hey, it's fine," Laith interrupted. He took a step in between the two, holding his palms up. "I'll give you my number."

Suddenly, Theodore's chest burst. "*They* can have your number, but *I* can't?"

"You can have it too. This isn't worth fighting over." Laith stood in a way that allowed him to glance back and forth between the two parties. "We're all on the same side here. Your friends are just worried about you."

"I don't understand why you lie to us so much." Jessie's voice was soft with emotion, eyes fixed on him. "And it's always about the stupidest things too. We just want to know you're okay."

"You don't—" Oh god, this was it. He could feel the floodgates open. "You don't get it. I'm still figuring stuff out for myself and I need to do it alone. I'm afraid to tell you everything, because I don't know most of it either. I have a lot going on and I just—I don't know how to talk about this stuff. Nobody taught me how. I don't know what to say and what *not* to say. I don't even know what you're looking for."

"We just wanna know the real you."

"I don't know who that is!" His lungs worked way too fast, hyperventilating. "Man, if I knew, I would've told you already!"

"Tell us who Laith is to you," Hannah cut in, softer than before.

"You *know* that. He's—" He could feel Laith's stare burn into the side of his face, eyes trained on Hannah. "He's everything to me."

"What about Dylan and the others?"

"I barely talk to him. I don't talk to him or to V. I'm friends with Hwan and Marquis."

"Have you guys made up?" Jessie interrupted, blue eyes glancing between the two of them.

"Have we made up?" Laith's confusion cooled Theodore's blood.

"Yeah. Didn't you guys have a fight last weekend?"

"Everything's fine now," Theodore quickly cut in, lungs devoid of air. "We're okay. We're friends again."

Laith scowled at him. "What did you tell them?"

"Not much," Jessie answered for him. "We know very little about you, but we *do* know about you. Last week, there was a fight—you ran into each other at a club and argued. A few days before, Theo stood you up. Before that, we didn't hear anything, so I'm assuming it was fine. The first time—"

Fuck no.

"Listen," Theodore spoke over her, sweat budding on his forehead, "I just told them very, very vague stuff. I thought it was fine. I didn't really say anything *about* you, just how the evening went. You know, drinking and partying. Is that bad?"

"No, it's fine." Laith shook his head, eyebrows drawn the slightest bit together.

"Can we know you a little better, though?" Hannah's friendly tone almost sounded like it'd come from a completely different person.

That question veered the conversation to much less inflammatory topics, but only because Laith was the one handling it. He told them very basic things about himself, that he lived in the tunnels and partied a lot. Naturally, the girls egged him on to keep talking about the underground, which completely removed the spotlight from him—smart. It was very easy to see how Laith shaped the conversation without letting them realize he was doing it. While explaining one thing, he mentioned something else, without actually going into it—a bait that the girls took time and time again, going in circles about the tunnels and everything they offered without actually ever learning anything about Laith at all. The only personal question they asked was about his neck tattoo, which he used to talk about his tattoo artist and the tattoo parlor that he went to rather than anything about himself. Watching his tactics in action, Theodore realized he'd fallen for them too.

Late into the night, the girls grew sleepy. They wanted to keep talking, but their eyes became too heavy to remain open for much longer and their heads began to nod. That was when Laith cut the conversation short with a very friendly observation that he'd stop wasting their time and let them go to bed. Hannah didn't let him slip away without giving out his number, though. Laith reassured her that he hadn't forgotten about it, and Theodore believed that was true—he'd been distracting them in hopes *they'd* forget about it. Cornered, Laith gave out his number, speaking it out loud so they could all punch it into their phones.

Theodore refused to do it. With his heart burning in the pit of his stomach, he crossed his arms and waited. They all noticed it, but nobody said anything. When Laith was done, the girls bid them both goodnight and walked back into their room. They held their stares a little too long on Theodore before closing the door.

"What is it?" Laith lowered his voice, so the girls wouldn't hear him.

That only prompted Theodore to pass him a glance, no reply. Instead, he started for his own room. That trajectory involved crossing the hallway in front of Laith, which allowed him to hold an arm out and block Theodore, repeating the same question with different words—*what's going on?* Still disinclined to answer, Theodore simply took his arm and dragged him into the room, chest consumed by flames. A very intense emotion choked him with a fist and filled his lungs with the urge to punch something. Frustration, probably—he wasn't sure. He'd never felt it like this, so strong, all-encompassing.

Back inside his room, he shut the door. His first instinct was to slam it, but his hand grabbed the knob just in time and closed it softly. He had no idea where this had come from, only that he hated it. Hated what? His head immediately thought back to the girls saving Laith's number into their phones, hands closing into fists. He'd hated *that*. He'd spent so long trying to get that number, jumping through hoops, playing Laith's little games and for what? For those girls to get it at the first request. How many times had he asked for it? How many times had he asked other people for it? It was supposed to be special. Now, everything he'd gone through had been completely fruitless.

"Theo."

Laith's voice got a squint out of him, eyebrows drawn into a scowl. In his mind, they'd been building up to something far more meaningful than this, the moment Laith would finally let him have his number, the moment he'd finally proven himself worthy. He wanted to scream. Instead, he held the scream in his throat and threw his hands up in the air, frustrated. Heartbroken. Fuming. So many emotions fought for dominance that he wasn't sure which one to feel.

"I thought..." He swallowed the confession—*I thought this was supposed to mean something.* What he needed to get through his thick head was that he wasn't special, never had been. Why should he deserve anything meaningful? He was just an annoying little rich kid who couldn't leave Laith alone. Idiot. "Whatever." He sighed, shoulders drooping. "It doesn't matter."

"I'm curious now. What were you thinking?"

Their eyes met. The fire that had consumed him a minute ago had suddenly vanished, leaving the hearth empty.

"I thought you'd make it harder for them too. Getting your number— reaching you."

Laith cocked his head aside, considering that. "You think I'm an asshole, huh?"

"I'm just wondering what I did to deserve it."

"What?"

"The tricks and games."

Laith's shoulders drooped, eyes softening. "Theo, the truth is that... I didn't want you to contact me. I didn't want to give you an opening to get close to me, 'cause I knew Ryan would have a problem with that." He reclaimed his seat on the bed, this time turned around to face Theodore. "The fact that we got close anyway, despite everything I did to avoid it just solidifies what we have. It was gonna happen regardless—I just made it take longer than it should."

The hearth in the bottom of Theodore's chest grew warmer, no flames, no smoke. It felt like bedding around his heart. Meekly, he walked over to the bed, hands hidden behind his back. Laith watched him take the seat on his left, close enough that their knees touched.

42

"You never wanted to talk to me, did you?" His eyes remained downcast, staring at his own shoes.

"I did, actually, which was why I tried so hard not to, but ended up failing anyway."

"Do you hate me?"

A hand touched his chin, fingertips soft on his jaw. Laith's eyes were the heart of a forest.

"I really don't."

Closing his eyes, he let Laith kiss him.

mmermermer

Laith's sobriety was a constant reminder that everything they did, everything they said was on purpose. They kicked their shoes off and lay in bed, lit up only by the floor lamp in the corner of the room. Laith slipped an arm under Theodore's neck and held him close, head cushioned on Laith's shoulder, that arm wrapped comfortably across his back. It reminded him of how they'd fallen asleep last week, except fully clothed and perfectly awake. He traced the edges of the dog tags as Laith talked, not very interested in the topic as much as he just wanted to listen to the low rumble of Laith's voice, deep in his throat. It was nice, too nice. He never thought he'd cuddle anyone in his whole life.

The only problem was that he no longer knew the rules of this game. When Laith was drunk and horny, he knew exactly what to do, confident that reproach would never come, but with Laith sober in his bed, could he still do whatever he wanted? Laith had a lot more ground to judge him on, watchful of his every move now. If he slipped a hand up Laith's shirt, would he be angry? He couldn't even find the courage to try. Holding each other like this was nice, a different ride than anything they'd ever done, but he still couldn't help wondering if it'd go anywhere else. They'd only gotten together to fuck before; he didn't know if that was still the case. It was all he was good for, anyway.

As the sun peeked from behind the horizon, Laith grew tired; his words became sluggish and his speech stopped making sense. He nuzzled into Theodore's hair, snuggling him, and fell silent.

Still fully awake, Theodore wondered why they didn't fuck. Was Laith not interested? Maybe the appeal was only present when he was drunk and had no other option, or better yet, when Theodore started it. Since he'd been too self-conscious to make a move, Laith had simply held him and fallen asleep. Was he really that ugly? His chest trembled with a breath. Laith had complimented him before, but then again, he'd been drunk. Everything he'd ever said—save for tonight—had been under the influence. Were they still meaningful if Laith hadn't changed his mind about them? Yes, except he hadn't really complimented Theodore on anything tonight. He'd said he liked him, sure, but at this point, Theodore was looking for something else.

On the brink of losing his mind, he fished out his phone and tapped on the group chat with Hwan and Marquis.

How did you guys know you were in love?

A moment later, Hwan replied.

For me, it was the realization that I wanted to be with him every day of my life. That I wanted to bring him home to my parents and call him family.

That was really moving, but the mere thought of bringing Laith home almost made him throw up. He couldn't even picture it, Laith walking through the front door with him. Unimaginable. His mother would scream while his father took the gun from under the stairs. Well, he didn't know if that was still where Henry kept it, but the sentiment remained. Plus, Laith would never want to be there for The Talk; Theodore had been advised to bring his long-term boyfriend instead. To Hannah, that was who Laith was, but he'd rather not think about that word too much. Wishful thinking had already ruined him once, regardless of Sherry's influence.

What if what you have still isn't everything you want?
It just feels like nothing is enough.
Are you talking about Laith?
He's literally cuddling me right now but I still feel empty. I want more than this. I want this every day of my life and far more too. I wanna come home to him and hold his hand on the street and tell everyone that he's mine.
You want a relationship, Theo. That's what you just described.
Do you do all of that with Marquis?
Yes.
How does it feel like?

Fulfilling.

He'd never been more jealous of a single word before. On an angry whim, he locked his phone and squeezed it, hand resting over Laith's chest. He watched the rise and fall of his breathing, unperturbed by the fist that lay on him, dog tags smeared over with light, the reflection of daylight from the window. Slowly, his hand loosened, fingers touching Laith's shirt. They traced the collar until it hid under the jacket—only then did it hit him that Laith had fallen asleep in his clothes. How common an occurrence was that?

Laith's right arm rested across his own stomach, hand close to Theodore's waist. He could touch it. The thought ceased his breathing, heart banging against his ribs. Leaving his phone on Laith's chest, he moved his hand over.

Fingers touched Laith's knuckles, following the bumps up and down, very lightly, barely there. Could he hold them? He brushed the side of Laith's hand, nervous. An image came to mind right then, Marquis taking Hwan's hand while straddling their guest, and Hwan holding it back. His heart sank. Choking, he took his phone and left the bed entirely. Laith stirred at the disturbance but didn't wake up.

In the kitchen, he filled a glass with water and brought it to his mouth. Two of them rushed into his stomach, lungs breathing in deep. What was wrong with him? Why couldn't Laith find fulfillment in him? He couldn't wipe the image of Marquis' and Hwan's hands from his mind, jealousy like acid on his tongue. God, he hated them. No, he hated what they had. No, he *wanted* what they had. He wanted Laith to rail him and hold his hand at the same time. What a dream. The lake promptly came to mind, the only time they'd ever held hands, swiftly followed by his knee in Laith's stomach. Sometimes, he wondered if that was what Laith had wanted out it, to sink and sink and sink.

Trembling, he flipped his phone over and tapped on Hwan's contact. His fingers called him before he could even process what he was doing.

"Hey, Theo."

"Why doesn't he do boyfriends? Why doesn't he date anyone?"

"What?"

"It can't be me, because he doesn't date *anybody,* so what is it? I know he doesn't believe people fall in love with who they *really* are, only a fake image in their head, a reflection—is that it? Does he really think he doesn't know me?"

"I have no idea what you're talking about."

"I'm obviously talking about Laith. I really want him to date me, but I don't know what would make him change his mind about that. Like, I don't even know how to approach it. *Hey, so I know you don't think love is real and that dating is a waste of time, but maybe we could try it anyway?* He'd never speak to me again."

"I had no idea he felt that way. We've never talked about that."

"Are you kidding me? That's like, the biggest thing about him, that he's a slut who doesn't date anyone."

"He wasn't always like that. He'd only ever had one kiss before he left; everything else must've happened much later on."

"Emily." That word left him like the answer to everything. "Of course."

"Who's Emily?"

"I'll call you back." He hung up. In a frenzy, he tapped onto Emily's contact and called her. The line rang a million times before she answered.

"Hello."

"Okay, first of all, I'm so sorry for the way I spoke to you last week; I was shooting in the dark when I said what I said. I really didn't mean to come for you the way I did. I'm really sorry."

"Theo, it's six thirty in the morning."

"I'm sorry for waking you up too. I'm such a piece of shit; I have no excuse for this. I just really want you to talk to me."

"What is it? You sound manic."

"Why doesn't Laith do relationships?"

"Oh, goddammit. You have to let this go."

"I just wanna know!"

"I told you he's no good. I told you not to fall for him; he's only gonna break your heart. You have to move on from this."

"Just tell me. Is it because he doesn't believe in love? Is it to make a statement? Is it because he thinks relationships only start to end?"

"No, he's just too trusting. He sees the good in everyone, he falls in love with everybody; he's the perfect target to get hurt. He doesn't date to protect himself."

"I'm not gonna hurt him."

"You don't know that. You couldn't possibly know that."

"I have no intention of doing it!"

"Nobody does. People don't get into relationships thinking of all the ways they're going to break up with their partner. Don't be stupid."

"He could give me a chance, don't you think? I could be just what he needs."

"He's too old for you."

"He's twenty-three."

"Why are you even thinking about dating, anyway? You have so much ahead of you, parties to go to and people to meet. Go experience the world."

"What if I wanna do all of that with him? These things aren't mutually exclusive."

"He's already done that. Are you really gonna make him do it all over again?"

"Yeah—he hasn't done it with me. It'll be different."

"Why do you think *you're* so different?"

"I don't think that; I don't even know what the standard is. I just wanna give it a shot. What's so wrong with that?"

"Look, he's been through a lot. I know you just want somebody to hold your hand at the movies, and while I'm sure he could do that, he's just not someone you wanna be around for long periods of time. I've already told you this—his lows are *very* low. Do you really think you could handle them?"

"I don't know... Probably not, but isn't that why he has you? You and Justin, I mean. If he ever does get with me, it's not like you guys are going to disappear. Plus, I feel like he can handle himself, even when he's going through something."

"You'd think that, because he's never called you in the middle of an episode. Theodore, he's too much for you. I know he's charming and he looks like a dream, but that man is a ticking time bomb. Every once in a while, he goes off on himself and there's nothing you can do to stop it."

"He said he was okay now."

"Now is the correct word."

He frowned. "Does he really think I'd hurt him?"

"Why don't you ask him yourself?"

Ugh.

"Emily, I know about the hospital; he told me last week. I know he's self-destructive and that he drinks too much, but we all have something fucked up about us. Whoever I end up dating—if it's him or not—won't be perfect either, because nobody is. I just want to give it a shot with him."

"Does he feel the same way about that?"

"I called you because I wanna know the answer to that. What can I tell him that would make him consider it rather than reject me outright?"

"Just ask him, Theo. There's no tiptoeing around it. If you want him, tell him you do, but don't expect him to say the same back."

That last part cut right through him.

"Is that why you're so angry at him? Because he wasn't supposed to have said yes to me the first time?"

"Of course. We had an agreement."

"That I was off-limits."

"That any of our siblings were off-limits."

"Why?"

"How would you feel if your best friend started dating Ryan? If everywhere you two went together, Ryan would be there. That you'd have to see them hold hands and kiss all the time. It'd be weird, right? Uncomfortable? That's how he feels about you."

"We've never even done anything in front of him."

"The knowledge that you have is bad enough."

"God, shut up. That's such bullshit."

She scoffed. "You think I'm making this up?"

"No, you're sugar-coating it. Ryan hates me because I'm taking his fucking boyfriend away. He doesn't want me near anything that's his."

"Then why are you so obsessed with what's his? I saw the way you looked at Sherry last week, how you couldn't stop staring at her chest. Embarrassing, really."

His face burned, brain unable to answer.

Emily continued. "Why don't you play with your own toys for a change? Stop going into his room just to take what's his."

"He doesn't own people. I can date whomever I want."

"Sure—those two people just happen to be in your brother's pants. No correlation, right?"

He hung up.

Chapter 5

Breakfast

Night by night
I let you eat me alive
I want you to eat me alive

- Glass Animals, Your Love (Déjà Vu)

Back in the room, he crawled into his old spot, adjusting Laith's arm over his shoulders, similar to how it'd been before. Regardless of what Emily had said, the fact of the matter was that Laith was here with him. Not in her apartment, not in Ryan's bed, not in the club with some stranger—with *him*. Right now, he had to celebrate that. It was easy to forget how much he actually had when his eyes were always on the prize, always wanting more. Sometimes, he had to look back and appreciate how far he'd come. A week ago, he would've never imagined cuddling Laith like this. It'd seemed like an impossibility.

Despite not being tired, he managed to fall asleep. It was a short nap, or it felt like one. Movement woke him up soon enough, the rocking of a ship, turning to the side. Something touched his face, soft like a pillow, warm. When he breathed, his lungs filled with amber. He pictured Laith on a ship, leaning against the taffrail with a pirate hat and a white blouse on, unlaced at the chest. The way he crossed his arms squeezed his pecs together, puffy sleeves, sun shining over his skin.

A hand ran up Theodore's back, palm flat over his shirt, riding it at the bottom. Fingers brushed hair out of his face as the very top of his head received a kiss. Decently awake now, he opened his eyes. The only thing he could see was Laith's chest, and with his nose buried in it, he let his eyes close again—seeing was pointless. He touched Laith's back with a hand, feeling the pattern etched into the leather, the three-headed snake. No thoughts formed in his mind, blank with peace, lungs big in his chest.

"Good morning." Laith's voice, spoken into his hair, was almost as quiet as silence itself, as if trying not to break it.

In response, Theodore placed a kiss between Laith's pecs, then another on the collar of his shirt, and another one further up, this time on his skin. He trailed up Laith's neck, kissing over the fern leaf, all the way to his jaw. Still in Laith's hold, the arm that once held him across the waist now rested over his hips, fingers touching the waistband of his pants. He opened his eyes to the sight of two emeralds staring back at him. "Good morning."

The smile on Laith's face was quickly covered up by a kiss.

He wasn't sure what it was that did it, his eagerness or his interest, but Laith rolled on top of him and deepened the kiss, open-mouthed and messy. It traveled straight between his legs. That happened to anything Laith did though, be it effortless or thoughtful, or in this case, something so practiced that Theodore couldn't even tell. His hands pushed the jacket off Laith's shoulders, dog tags brushing him on the chest, hanging between them. Laith didn't immediately take it off, but slipped a hand under Theodore's shirt instead, feeling him up. Goosebumps followed his every move, palm warm on Theodore's skin, soft over his stomach. It ran up to his chest and grabbed it, thumb swiping over his nipple. That surprised him—his body jerked a bit, but since he managed to keep quiet about it, he hoped Laith wouldn't notice.

A much more pronounced tug on Laith's jacket got the response Theodore had been looking for. Laith begrudgingly pulled away and knelt between Theodore's legs, chest puffed out, hair a stylish mess. With two shrugs, the jacket slipped down his arms. In the meantime, Theodore made himself useful and took his own shirt off, tossing it aside. By the time his head was free again, he caught sight of Laith doing the same, skin soft under the glow of the daylight, dog tags glistening over his breast. Theodore only managed to get one good look in before Laith was back on him again, kissing down his neck. Then again, one good look was all he needed.

Teeth tugged on his skin as a hand popped the button on his pants, not as a distraction, but to save time. He got that as soon as Laith pulled his pants off, eager to get going, biting into his neck. That brought him back to last week, the bite when Laith had pushed inside him—that memory shook his shoulders with

50

a shiver. God, he wanted it; he'd wanted it ever since. Hwan and Marquis had been good, but the experience had been different, impersonal, too far from what he actually craved, from what he *needed*. Once his pants hit the floor, Laith pulled his boxers down.

"Give me a hickey." That was supposed to be a request, but it did *not* come out as one. It almost sounded bitchy.

Luckily, Laith didn't mind it, grinning into his skin. "You want a hickey—is that what I heard?" His voice was so low it resembled a growl, hands tossing Theodore's boxers off the bed.

He swallowed. "Yeah."

Was that a bad idea? Well, it didn't matter now; a hand closed around his cock just as Laith bit into his neck. His hips jerked with surprise, stomach swallowed by flames. Somehow, the way Laith sucked on his skin was a perfect match with the hand that stroked him, a synchrony that led his mind into putting two and two together—Laith's mouth on his cock. He couldn't find the words to say it, enraptured by intermingling feelings. He quickly found that he didn't have a problem with it, breathless anyway.

When Laith pulled back, the hand on his cock left it as well. He immediately opened his mouth to protest, to get Laith back on it, but then he realized that Laith had pulled back to look at what he'd done. Was it noticeable? Was it big enough? Laith had practically eaten him alive, so his guess would have to be a resounding yes. Yes, it would be there all day long, or however long hickeys lasted; Theodore had no idea.

"Is it terrible?" he breathed, chest moving with it.

Their eyes met.

"It's the worst." Laith shaped every word around the filthiest smirk he'd ever seen. Absently, he mirrored it.

The dog tags rattled as Laith moved up again, knees digging into the mattress, back straightened. Theodore took the opportunity to burn his body into the back of his retinas, every tattoo and every muscle, skin practically golden. Laith's hands did quick work of his own pants, pulling them down, boxers included, elastic band tight around his thighs. He could crush Theodore's skull between them.

"What's in that nightstand?"

His question drew Theodore's eyes up to his face, mind drawing an immediate blank. Oh, the nightstand; *his* nightstand. Yeah, nothing.

"Nothing you're looking for."

"Nothing?" That sounded more like a surprised exclamation than an inquiry, eyebrows up on Laith's forehead.

"Unless you're looking for tissues and a phone charger."

Laith tutted. A hand slipped into a pocket and pulled out a condom straight from his pants, not even stored in his wallet. Was that how often he needed them, that keeping them in a wallet was just too inconvenient? Wow. Laith dropped the condom on Theodore's stomach. "Put it on me."

Just like that, his face caught on fire. Okay, he could do this; it couldn't be *that* hard. Two edges of the wrapper were straight while the other two had little zigzags all the way down. He quickly discovered that the straight ones didn't tear; only the zigzags did, and pulled the condom out. He held it very carefully in both hands, pinched between his fingers. As soon as he motioned to put it on, Laith took his wrist, stopping him. The gesture was small, but it spoke volumes—he'd already made a mistake. His heart jumped out of his mouth. A hand came down to pinch the very tip of the condom, the little bit of plastic there. "Do it like this."

The anxiety that rushed down his veins wanted to shake his hands, but god forbid it even tried that right now—he'd chop them right off. Focused very hard on keeping them steady, he pushed the condom onto the head. From there, he rolled it down the shaft with no issue, hand fisting Laith all the way to the base. That got a positive reaction out of him, hips leaning into the touch, pushing forward—encouragement throbbed between Theodore's legs. Afraid to pull the condom off by accident, he decided not to jerk Laith off, but took the encouragement to heart, a real compliment.

Laith touched his shoulders. Their bodies had developed a whole new language by now, entirely non-verbal; just like that, Theodore knew he was supposed to lie down. He followed Laith's every move, back lying on the mattress, hands on Laith's sides. Fingertips felt the bumps of his ribs and the softness of his skin, palms flat over his waist, holding him. It wasn't a technical hold as much as it was an emotional one, keeping Laith close—he could do that now. Sure, the rules of the game had changed, and while he didn't think he could still do *anything* he wanted, he knew this was okay. The time they'd spent together last night, talking to each other, coupled with the hug in the hallway had brought them a sort of closeness that Theodore would've never imagined. Laith had let him hold him then—why would that change now? It wouldn't. His theory was only proven right when Laith dived for a kiss.

Their lips pressed hard together, not enough of a distraction to keep Theodore from noticing just how far his thighs had spread, Laith's waist nestled between them. His knees brushed Laith's ribs. The lower Laith positioned himself, the higher his heart jumped, excitement curling his toes. This was it. Again, this was it. Incidentally, how come Laith was the only one who could give him this feeling, the kind of anticipation that stole all air from his lungs and slowed time down to a crawl? He hadn't felt that way with Marquis and Hwan. They'd been good, but he hadn't looked forward to the threesome as much as he'd looked forward to this.

The head pushed against the entrance, guided by a hand, knuckles brushing his skin. He hated how embarrassing that was, face radiating heat, stomach all tensed up. Laith teased and rubbed, making to do it but slipping past instead, once, twice, three times. It drove him insane, already panting. When a command came up his throat, the head went in, pulling a breath through his nose, sharp and surprised. Laith pushed, filling him up, stretching him out—it didn't compare to anything else. He moaned into Laith's mouth, hands grabbing his back, feet rising into the air. It wasn't all of it, but just enough for comfort.

Laith's hips drew an easy pace, slow at first, to get him going. A hand closed around his cock and matched the tempo, successful in getting his back to arch off the bed, or at least try to. Laith's weight kept him pinned to the mattress, but god, every part of him just wanted to squirm.

Laith picked up the speed soon enough, staggering Theodore where he lay, bedframe grazing the wall. It was a dull noise in the back of his mind, barely registered at all, buried under the fire that ate him up from the inside out.

Laith pushed in a lot deeper than he'd done before; not all the way, but not nearly as shallow as the first time either. The practiced way he did it, hips following that arch like second nature, told Theodore that *this* was how he usually slept around, nice and deep. It was good, too good—he muffled himself quiet on Laith's tongue, hands squeezing his sides. Sober, Laith was a lot quieter, groaning very sparingly, moaning here and there. Theodore had even stopped expecting it, so when a sound did come up Laith's throat, it shot straight into his bloodstream.

At one point, a hand grabbed his arm and pulled it away from Laith's body. An instruction followed, spoken against his lips, that he should hook his arms under his own thighs and keep them locked. Okay, no problem, but was there a reason, or did Laith just not want scratches on his back? Theodore wasn't even doing that. He couldn't promise that he wouldn't, only that he hadn't—yet. Still, he complied, no questions asked.

The moment Laith pushed in again, easier, deeper, he learned the reason. This angle shot stars into his eyes, a moan pulled from the back of his throat. Laith picked up the pace, hips moving expertly, thrusting fire into his stomach. A hand touched his head and drew him nearer, fingers tangled into his hair, forehead touching Laith's chest. It wasn't an embrace, or not a proper one, but his heart still swelled, warm with affection.

Near the edge, he reached a hand between their bodies and closed it around himself. He didn't think it'd be a problem, but couldn't even manage two strokes before Laith swatted his arm away, claiming that *he* should be the one to do it. Theodore didn't mind that at all, face buried into Laith's pecs, thighs trembling under his own hands.

Laith jerked him tight and fast, keeping up with his own hips, a maddening combination. When Theodore was just about to cum, moans escaping his lips, body squirming, Laith pulled out completely. It felt like he'd just been shoved off the side of a cliff—a gasp fell into his throat, eyes snapping open. No words could reach his mouth, brain completely empty.

Laith promptly latched onto his neck next, kissing down to his collar bones, messy and hungry. His arms loosened around his own legs, mind still reeling as Laith kissed down his chest.

"No," he breathed, eyebrows drawn up. "Why did you do that?"

Green eyes passed him a brief glance, mouth speaking over his stomach. "You're not coming just yet."

An exasperated sigh left his lips, head falling back on the mattress. Hands touched his thighs, holding them apart, fingers pushed onto soft skin. At this point, it was impossible to keep them from trembling. His hip joints and knees ached, but he still didn't move, toughing it out for now.

As soon as a tongue touched his cock, his body started, eyes slipping closed. Laith dragged it all the way up the shaft and took him in.

Laith's expertise sucking him off, coupled with how fast he could do it, pulled a moan from the back of Theodore's throat. The pit of his stomach burned, pressure rising in his loins. He wished Laith could do this while fucking him. Marquis came to mind again, the way he'd sat on his crotch as Hwan had stood between his thighs, but that had been different, unemotional. What he wanted was Laith's attention splattered all across his body, a representation of his diligence. He wanted to see the face of Laith's dedication and find himself looking back, the shape of it, the first who came to mind—him and nobody else.

A couple of fingers pushed into him and his back arched, lips pressed hard together, muffling a sound. Laith kept to the tempo, pushing up while going down, assiduous and thorough. For as insane as that drove Theodore, he couldn't help wishing for those fingers to stretch him out even further, the way only Laith could do, his cock at the forefront of his mind. As his fingers picked up speed, that was the only thing Theodore could think about, obsessed, no longer capable of processing anything else. His thighs twitched, stomach tensing up. He was close.

"Please." That word slipped out of his mouth straight from the heart, breath coming in short. Just as he was about to cum, Laith pulled back again, except this time, the betrayal immediately lit a fire inside Theodore, closing his hands into fists. He groaned his frustration, eyebrows furrowed into a scowl. The emptiness that gnawed at his stomach felt like a million miles long.

"No," he whimpered, utterly powerless.

For as much as he wanted to punch Laith in the face, he knew this man was the only one capable of giving him the release he so desperately craved, hard enough to make him go blind. He was about to explode.

"No, please," he mumbled.

"Please what?"

His eyes opened to see Laith reclaiming his place above him, noses a mere inch apart. The hunger that clouded Laith's eyes held a breath in his throat, excitement running down his veins. That look told him everything Laith would do to him, just as depraved as he was. He could barely wait for it. A hand touched his face, jaw pinched between Laith's thumb and two fingers.

"Please what, Theo?" Laith's voice was down to a whisper, malicious.

They held the stare.

"Fuck me."

He could only catch a glimpse of the smirk that curled Laith's lips before they were on his own again, faces pressed together. Laith's weight between his thighs was welcome, very welcome, since he could no longer hold them up, arms shaking. A hand kept one of them up, hips still in place as Laith pushed back in. God, the feeling alone sent precum down his cock—he felt it against his own stomach.

The kiss was soft and sloppy, an afterthought as Laith's hips fell into that arch and worked against his own, filling him up, rocking him into the mattress. He touched Laith's back, arms no longer useful, noodles at this point. With his eyes closed, he let himself get lost in the swirl of emotions that burned his bones to cinders.

It didn't take long for him to get close again, not with how good Laith felt, buried deep inside. Laith must've noticed that, because a hand soon found Theodore's cock and stroked it, just as fast as Laith thrust into him. That shook his entire body, moans pushed into Laith's mouth, tongue on his palate. His legs relaxed, thighs spread as much as possible, arm holding Laith across the back. He was so close that he could cry, meowling into Laith's mouth, eyebrows pushed hard together, up on his forehead. The hand on his jaw held his face down so Laith could break the kiss.

"C'mon, baby," Laith whispered, breathless, "make it pretty for me."

He couldn't concentrate on any of that, mind stuck on the word *baby*, body trembling like a leaf. That was just enough to push him over the edge, that word in Laith's mouth, addressed to him. His feet shot up into the air, toes curled, stomach so tense that it hurt. Pleas spluttered out of his mouth, begging Laith not to stop, cock pulsing in his hand. Fire burned his skin as cum shot over his own stomach, pulling a moan from his throat. He grabbed Laith's arm, nails digging into it, but couldn't stop the fist that stroked him through every throb and every shot. He squirmed, back arching off the bed, whimpers on his lips. The intensity that pulsed through him was unlike anything he'd ever experienced.

With a groan, Laith pushed in deep and held the position. He'd been bottoming out this whole time; Theodore had just been too far gone to notice it. He knew the intensity had eventually turned up to eleven, but hadn't been able to pinpoint exactly what had done it. That had been it.

They breathed together, Laith's cock pulsing, hips locked. The hand on his face loosened the grip as Laith leaned down for a kiss, lazy yet full of feeling, that warmed his heart. He touched Laith's face and buried fingers into his hair, pulse slowing back down, muscles trembling with exertion. Laith carefully pulled out, allowing Theodore's legs to stretch and lie on the mattress. They hurt like hell.

A hand brushed some hair out of his forehead, slick with sweat, glued to his skin. When the kiss broke, their eyes met.

"God, I love waking up with you."

That comment tugged his lips into a smile, heart wrapped in velvet. He knew that wasn't as sweet as it'd sounded, that Laith had meant he liked fucking him first thing in the morning, but it still warmed him up inside.

"Who did you fuck last week?"

And just like that, his blood turned cold. Shock widened his eyes, body petrified, unable to move. He couldn't even think of a reply, because all that ran through his mind was *how did he know?* Hwan and Marquis hadn't left a single mark on him.

His reaction cut a smirk across Laith's face. "So I'm right." Laith pulled away, moving to leave the bed. "That explains why you were so easy today."

That slipped a hand down Theodore's throat and manually pulled all breath out of his lungs. Still in shock, he moved to a sitting position, aided by a hand against the mattress. It propped him up. "Is it bad?"

"Of course not." Laith redid his own pants, perfectly nonchalant. His tone was as conversational as if they spoke of breakfast. "Just means I could really give it to you this time."

Heat burned through his face. Speechless, all he could do was watch Laith get dressed.

"Have breakfast with me?"

Laith's question almost failed to register in his brain.

"Yeah, I just need a minute," he practically stuttered.

"Alright. I'll be in the kitchen." With that, Laith left the room.

In a daze, Theodore grabbed some tissues from the nightstand and wiped himself down. So he'd been easy, huh... What did that mean? Hwan hadn't mentioned a thing. It might just be the difference between his very first time and any other time after that. Since Hwan had only slept with him once, he didn't have a frame of reference. How come Laith knew he'd slept with someone *else* instead of this just being the byproduct of sleeping with him the first time? How could he tell? It could've been a shot in the dark, but it'd been such a bullseye. Theodore's cheeks burned.

He needed a shower.

Throwing the used tissues in the trash, he caught sight of the condom— it wasn't smart to leave it in there, under the desk. What if somebody saw it? He didn't know who would be rummaging through the trash in his room, but paranoid about the possibility, he took the trashcan with him.

Outside his room, he had a view of the entire hallway, which allowed him to catch sight of both Daisy and Nadia sitting at the counter, facing the kitchen. The girls talked; he could hear their voices, a jumbled mess muffled under the scream that echoed in his skull—they were in the kitchen. *Laith* was in the kitchen. They were in the kitchen with Laith. What were they talking about? Why were they laughing? He froze three steps away from his own door, clutching the trashcan to his crotch. His mind could barely even process the fact he was completely naked.

Daisy absently passed him a glance. She had a big grin on her face, seemingly on the verge of more laughter. Somehow, he knew they were talking about him. "Well, look who decided to show up. Did Laith eat your clothes too?" There was humor in her voice, friendly teasing. It still curdled his blood into ice though, even if her joke had been harmless, in good fun—he felt targeted. He could picture it just fine, Laith telling them about him, making them laugh. The girls snickered in response to Daisy's comment, sending his pulse flying—he couldn't be here anymore. Caught in the hallway like a deer in headlights, he rushed into the bathroom and locked himself in.

What had Laith told them? The possibilities were so harrowing that breath failed him completely, coming in short gasps. His arms felt like jelly; the trashcan slipped from under them and fell on the floor. The world darkened at the edges, growing more intense with his light-headedness, ears muffled. His forearms met with the counter and held him up, head hanging low, practically in the sink. He panted.

What were they saying about him? The snickering at Daisy's little remark was very incriminating; he couldn't picture a scenario where they *weren't* talking about him. Laith must have told them what had just happened. With his eyes closed, he breathed. No more thoughts, nothing on his mind, just a very conscious attempt at calming down. His arms shook.

When his head was no longer lighter than air and his legs didn't feel like dropping him to the floor, he moved to glance at the mirror. He looked like shit, as pale as death itself with huge bags under his eyes and hair messier than the result of a hurricane, matted with sweat. Low on his neck, near his collar bone, was a colossal hickey the color of an ugly bruise. Was that what Daisy had joked about? At least it'd be easy to cover up; a hoodie would do wonders.

After the shower, he wrapped a towel around himself and fled down the hallway. The goal was to be so fast that no one would see him do it. He didn't look back to make sure of that. Disappointment wasn't an option.

Locked in his room, he put on his skinny jeans, a t-shirt and the black hoodie from Diesel. The hood itself was big and fluffy, and the way it fell over his neck covered the majority of it, hickey included. Next, he fixed his hair, combing it first, then running his fingers through, so it wouldn't look too perfect. He knew Laith didn't use a comb at all, hair too straight to get tangled up, but that wasn't *his* reality. In decent shape, he took a big breath and left the room.

Daisy and Nadia went back and forth between the counter and the dining table, bringing huge containers full of food, plates, glasses and silverware to the dining room.

As Theodore approached, he could make out the conversations going on inside the kitchen itself, their thoughts on diner food versus restaurant food. It didn't really matter exactly—the point was that they weren't speaking about him anymore.

In the kitchen, he saw Hannah drying her hands on a dishrag, Jessie wiping the oven clean and Laith closing a couple of overhead cabinets, the ones everybody had trouble reaching, except for him, apparently. They all glanced at him as soon as he approached, conversation momentarily suspended. The girls both grinned while Laith glanced him down. "You look nice."

The compliment lit his face like a furnace, genuine in the soft tone of Laith's voice, a quiet observation. If Theodore commented on it, he'd only make it worse for himself, so he decided to go with something else, despite how much it was appreciated. "How can I help?"

"We got it," Daisy informed him from the counter, picking up the last of the glasses there. "You can all come over now."

Since the table only had five chairs, the girls had brought one of the stools, lowered all the way down, to make for a sixth seat. Since Nadia was the shortest of them, she took it.

At one in the afternoon, this was lunch rather than breakfast. They passed each other bowls of pasta and cartons of juice, talking of random topics that Theodore barely paid attention to. What mattered was that they didn't speak of him, or Laith, or what they had together. Every time someone opened their mouth, his heart jumped with the fear that they'd bring any of that up, but they never did.

The friendly atmosphere was very surprising, with none of the judgment he'd expected out of this encounter—the girls meeting a rat. It was true they knew Hwan and the others, but those two groups weren't very close, while Laith was a recurring appearance. Theodore knew he'd been a topic of conversation while in the shower, but other than that, he had no idea what else they'd discussed. If they'd gotten to the point of frivolities, then that meant all the personal stuff was out of the way. Laith's dodgy answers must not have yielded the girls much information, though, only the illusion of getting to know him. Still, it must have been good enough if they'd moved on from that.

Once everyone had finished eating, the girls began the process of taking everything back to the kitchen. Hannah and Jessie only helped with the transportation, not the actual washing, since they'd cooked. Those were the rules—they got to rest now, sitting on the couch, watching TV. They invited Laith to join them, but he informed the room that he was on his way out.

Theodore promptly halted at the kitchen archway and turned to face him, dirty plates in hand. "Why? You can stay. You can't—you can't be busy on a Sunday."

"No, but I need to go home. I need a change of clothes, at the very least."

"I'm sure Theo has something that could fit you," Jessie tried.

"Thanks, but that's really not the point."

"Then I'm coming with you." Theodore set the plates on the counter, eyes fixed on Laith. "If you'll let me."

"I mean..." Laith cocked his head aside. "I guess."

"You're not skipping the dishes," Daisy stated, elbows-deep in the sink.

"Yeah, that's fair. I'll just wait for you downstairs," Laith suggested, taking a couple of steps toward the door.

"Will we see you again?" Hannah's tone was difficult to read, not mournful or poignant. It didn't imply that she'd miss him in any way, far more concerned that he'd slip into the shadows again, an unknown figure that continued to roam her home.

"Oh, yeah. I'll be around."

Chapter 6

A shark in the ocean

What I would do to get under your skin
Behind your secrets and all of your sins.

- Greta Isaac, *You*

Across the street, Laith held his phone to an ear. He kept close to the wall but was only partially under a shadow, not long enough to cover anything past his legs, hair bright in the afternoon sun. The way it backlit his head made it look like a messy halo, gold-wrapped strands falling over his forehead.

As Theodore approached, he could see the scowl there, digging into Laith's face, above his black mask. The call ended just before Theodore crossed the street, unable to catch anything that was said, but if Laith's expression was any indication of how it'd gone, then it hadn't been good. The moment he stepped onto the sidewalk, Laith passed him a glance and started down the block.

"Is everything okay?" He knew it wasn't, but couldn't think of a different way to ask.

"Yeah."

He squinted, even if Laith couldn't see it.

Laith's legs were much longer than his and strode along very quickly while he practically ran to keep up, falling an inch behind despite himself. It was that midway speed, where if he walked, he'd be left behind, but if he ran, he'd shoot straight ahead, so he had to walk very fast and skip every now and then to keep pace. That call had changed everything about Laith; it'd extinguished his good humor and added urgency to his day, no longer a lazy weekend. If Theodore had to guess, he'd say one of Laith's friends had been on the other end of the line.

Laith took the stairs down into Cantaloupe. Early in the afternoon, not a lot of people hung around the entrance, but the ones who did all passed Theodore a good, long glance as he followed Laith down.

The fact that he'd never entered the tunnels with Laith wasn't lost on him. He thought of when he'd first gone down, V asking him if he minded being seen with a bunch of Poison Darts. Did people know who he was and associated him with Poison Darts? If so, then were they interested because Laith was an Alvorada or because Laith was the Great White? Realistically, they probably stared because Laith was accompanied. That was all.

Laith took the stairs all the way down to the subway. This station was very similar to the one near Hwan's place, with the two train tracks, one at each side going in different directions. They took the train on the right—Theodore drilled that into his mind. It wasn't nearly as full as he'd seen them last time, with plenty of space right in the middle. Laith crossed the wagon to lean against the metal wall by the back of somebody's seat, in a sort of cabin of his own. Theodore stood in front of him, holding onto the pole that ran up the seat and met with the other ones overhead. Doing his best to appear nonchalant, he took out his phone and noted down everything they'd done so far, keeping close tabs on the directions to Laith's house. If he couldn't have his address, then he'd take note of it himself.

When he looked up again, he found a few heads staring at him from a good few feet away, people that sat on benches or stood by them, almost everyone at one end of the wagon. To confirm his suspicions, he glanced at the opposite end only to find the same scenario staring back at him. It creeped him out. With his heart in his throat, he reached back towards Laith, eyes still locked with a stranger's. He grabbed the lapel of Laith's jacket and tugged on it, semi-paralyzed. In response, Laith shoved his arm away and moved closer. As soon as they stood in each other's personal spaces, the stranger broke the stare to glance at Laith next, then immediately averted his gaze. In fact, everybody in the wagon stopped looking.

"You're okay," Laith reassured him, voice small in the gap between them. He lay an arm over the backrest behind Theodore, where nobody sat. It didn't touch him at all, but it was still close enough to make a statement, that they were together in some way.

The whole time Laith rode next to him, no one stared.

They hopped off at Blaze, a densely populated station much like the ones Theodore had been getting accustomed to. This was what came to mind when he thought of the tunnels now, hordes of people crammed into dimly lit areas with neon glossing over their hair and the leather of their clothes.

In the hustle and bustle of the crowd, they took the stairs up one flight. It seemed to come out deep into what looked like part of the guts, where a stream of people traveled east. That wasn't to say no one went against the grain, only that they weren't the vast majority.

With no hesitation, Laith jumped into the crowd and followed it almost all the way to the end. Close enough to it that Theodore could catch a glimpse of the other side, wide and massive, Laith took a left. Before doing the same, Theodore took a moment to glance around himself, looking for a reference point that would set this hemorrhage of stores apart from the rest that looked just like it. What he found was a sign, hanging from the ceiling, that pointed to the Dead Ponies up ahead and listed some businesses off to the left. One of them was called Forest Fire, which he drilled into his mind before taking the exit.

If the tunnels were a human body, then the guts would be the main arteries while hallways like this one would be smaller veins, spread around for better circulation. Only a fraction of the crowd from before walked down this path, but that was still a significant number of people. At the very end, it merged into a T-intersection, which Laith simply crossed for the building directly ahead. It was one of the more inconspicuous ones, just a door on the wall and balconies on both sides, from the second floor up to the fourth. The people who lived on the first floor only had a row of windows.

The door led up a few steps into a long hallway that cut sideways, so Theodore had to glance left and right to see its entirety. Straight ahead, crossing it, the path forked into a choice to take the stairs up or simply continue forward to what seemed yet another sideways hallway, where he supposed more apartments resided. That put a sideways H in his head. Laith took the stairs up one floor and turned right.

Traversing this place was in no way different than any portion of the guts, with people coming back and forth, speaking loudly to each other. It was a mess; Theodore had no idea how anyone slept in here. The doors must be soundproof.

As they walked down the hallway, he spotted two people chatting, each in their own apartment. The doors were open, so they could lean on their respective frames and talk that way, watching the hall, just how Laith had described. The two neighbors promptly caught sight of them. Conversation halted with their approach. Eyebrows were drawn up with delighted surprise, lips curled into smirks.

Laith motioned vaguely between them. "Girls, this is Theo. Theo, these are my neighbors."

Girls?

One of them reached a hand toward him, the way royal women did in the movies, with the back of the hand up, as if showing off their rings. It definitely looked that way, since she wore a big green jewel on that hand. Was Theodore supposed to kiss it? Unsure how to proceed, he took her fingers and tugged on them a little bit, going for a sort of handshake. He had absolutely no idea what he was doing right now.

"Ms. Intervention. That's my stage name, but I'll let you use it." Her voice was deep with a feminine touch to it, intentional. She was about as tall as Laith himself, but at least twenty years his senior, bald with very thin eyebrows. Her body was lean and androgynous, skin three shades darker than Laith's. She wore a simple dress that hung from her shoulders all the way down her legs, blue and green, arms bare. A belt wrapped around her waist gave her a stunning silhouette, polished and regal. She reminded him of a queen.

"I'm D'angela," the other neighbor jumped in, catching Theodore's attention next. She didn't give him a hand to shake or even moved away from her door frame, so he simply nodded his acknowledgement. She clearly didn't want to be touched.

About the same age as her neighbor, D'angela was a little shorter than her and just as white as Theodore. Her hair was short and dark, like a crown at the height of her ears, bald at the very top, eyebrows shaved halfway off. She was bigger than Ms. Intervention, but held herself in much of the same way, feminine and poised. Her dress had ruffles on the shoulders and ended just above the knee, covered in a pastel pink floral pattern.

"Well, aren't you a sight for sore eyes," Ms. Intervention commented. "Are you a model, by chance?"

Theodore felt his cheeks heat up. "You think I could be one?"

"Absolutely," both women spoke over each other.

"Look at you!" D'angela motioned up and down. "Style personified. You'd make a gorgeous woman."

"Oh, stunning, but I'm not sure that's what Shark's looking for."

Ms. Intervention's remark drew a scowl onto Theodore's face.

A soft creaking sound came up behind him, indicative of Laith's disinterest in letting this conversation continue. "Okay, we'll catch up later," he spoke hurriedly, one hand holding the door open for Theodore.

"We have a *lot* to talk about," Ms. Intervention added.

"We'll hold you to it!"

"Glad you're doing better, by the way. You're sober today."

Huh. Theodore opened his mouth just as a hand found his arm, closing gently around it.

"Okay, thanks."

That was his obvious cue to leave, hand tugging on his arm, yet he didn't want to. These women clearly knew a lot about Laith, information he'd been dying to know, but would never be able to ask right in front of the subject himself. He'd have to come back later, while Laith wasn't home. That reminded him to take note of the path they'd taken after the subway—he'd do it out of Laith's sight. Hopefully, he'd get a moment alone.

Laith's apartment was small, like a hotel room with a kitchen in it. The front door opened into a small foyer with the bathroom on the right—door left wide open—and a sitting area on the left, together with a circular table and a bookshelf, the kind built into the wall. Up ahead was the double bed, the main focus of the entire place, since everything else was placed around it. The headboard was against the rightmost wall with a TV mounted across from it, which allowed just enough room for a passage between the two, along the foot of the bed. Pillows and sheets were strewn all over, a mount over the mattress, as if Laith had gotten up during a fever dream and tossed it all into the air.

Laith rushed further into the room to tend to it, throwing the pillows against the headboard and smoothing the sheets with his hands. "Sorry about the mess; I wasn't expecting anyone today. I, uh—I never am."

"It's fine, really. I don't care about that stuff."

His mother clearly would, but he wasn't her. Then again, she'd have far more qualms than just the mess over the bed. The more he took notice of the room, the more prevalent Laith's lifestyle became. Dozens of pairs of pants were tossed over the arm of a chair, the circular table was stacked with books, and stealing a quick glance into the bathroom, he found piles of clothes on the floor as well as a counter covered in clutter. Did Laith really live like this? Theodore could be messy at times, but he'd never taken it this far.

Finished with the bed, Laith took a big breath. "Well, uh. I'm gonna take a shower. You can..." An arm motioned to the room in general. "You know, make yourself at home."

"Okay, thanks."

He approached the bed as Laith walked back to the foyer, shoulders shrugging Qasim's jacket off. Behind the front door was a wide hanger with multiple hooks where jackets had been placed, Qasim's alongside them. Laith kicked his boots off into a corner, already populated with other pairs of shoes, right next to the door. It bore noticing a baseball bat among them, resting against the wall, shining silver, made of aluminum. The sight brought a shine to Theodore's eyes.

"Do you play?" His question came out with a breath, almost catching in his throat.

Laith turned to look at him, eyebrows drawn with confusion. In response, Theodore quickly motioned to the bat, eyes wide on his face. Laith turned once again, this time to see what he was pointing at.

"You never told me you played," Theodore continued. "What position were you?"

"Uh, pitcher."

"Really? That was Kyle on our team. I was a shortstop."

"I haven't played in a long time."

Still turned toward the door, Laith pulled his shirt off. The muscles on his back moved in the low light, tattoo perfectly visible across his shoulder blades, ship sails and masts snaking up his side. With the shirt thrown carelessly into the bathroom, he worked on his pants next. The first thing that occurred to Theodore was to look away, but just before he did, a thought crossed his mind— they'd already seen each other naked. Staring at Laith now, especially with him turned around, wouldn't make a difference. Laith didn't tell him *not* to look. Explicitly undressing right in front of him welcomed his attention, right? Yes, of course; Laith would've walked into the bathroom otherwise.

"I haven't played in a while either." His eyes followed the curve of Laith's ass, pants thrown over the arm of the chair with the others. "We could practice sometime. You'll pitch and I'll swing."

Laith disappeared into the bathroom. "When I say *a long time*, I really do mean a long time." The size of the apartment didn't muffle his voice very much, still just as audible from where Theodore stood. Not closing the bathroom door helped too. "Five years, at least," Laith clarified.

"Since high school?"

"Yeah."

"Me too. I wish there were clubs where you could play without having to enter a championship or compete with anyone. That was the part I hated."

Water echoed within the bathroom, loudly hitting the tiles. That probably meant their conversation was over. In silence, Theodore turned around, eyes on the kitchen across the bed. It looked incredibly neat and tidy for someone as messy as Laith, without a single pot in the sink. The counters extended along the back wall, with cabinets below most of them, except for the last few, where stools had been pushed beneath them, just two. Was that where Laith had his meals?

Taking a seat on the edge of the mattress, Theodore faced the foyer again. From here, he could also see the wardrobe, doors wide open. Inside, piles of black clothes spilled from the drawers, empty hangers on the rack. What even was in there? If the pants were on the chair, the jackets were behind the door and the shoes were on the floor, then these must be the shirts. Were the boxers in the drawers or were they part of the pile? He decided to stop looking, lest his curiosity took the best of him.

As it turned out, Laith's apartment was one of the ones with a view, balcony doors right next to the wardrobe, window next to the stools in the kitchen. The curtains were drawn, sliding doors open a gap. On this side of the bed was a nightstand covered in empty bottles and an ashtray that overflowed with cigarette butts. The sight alone seized his heart in a hand, breath pulled from his throat. Had this been a particularly bad week, or did Laith just drink this much? He'd mentioned being bored and drinking all day—Theodore's blood ran cold.

On a whim, he grabbed as many bottles as he could and walked over to the kitchen, eyes looking for a trashcan. He had to open a few of the cabinets below to find it. Two trips back and forth cleaned out the nightstand, ashtray included. That pulled wind into his lungs, hands fishing out his phone. Now, he could jot down the path they'd taken after the train.

As the hands on his watch turned, his mind went back to the women across the hall—were they still there? His foot tapped, fingers fidgeting. Would Laith care if he left for a moment? He promptly got up and approached the bathroom door, hand touching the frame as he peeked in. Steam fogged up the glass in the shower, but he could still see Laith through it, a vague shape that moved under the falling water. The floor was clear now, clothes put away, hidden somewhere, probably under the sink. A freshness permeated the air, reminiscent of mint.

He stepped into the doorway. "Hey."

His voice was just loud enough to grab Laith's attention over the sound of the falling water, green eyes finding him through the mist. A hand wiped the glass so they could see each other better, soap on Laith's skin, hair slicked back.

"Do you mind if I leave for a minute?"

"Are you sure you don't wanna join me?"

His pulse skipped—should he? He didn't even know that was an option. That wasn't why he'd interrupted at all, but it didn't mean he should disregard the invitation either. His mind promptly went back to this morning, how he'd felt under Laith's touch, burning alive, hands on his thighs, kisses down his neck, the hickey there. Would Laith give him another?

"Do you want company?"

A slow smirk cut through Laith's face. "Yeah, I do."

He swallowed dry, hand squeezing the door frame.

"But if you have something better to do, you can leave," Laith added, shoulders bouncing. "I'll just see you later."

"Well, I mean..." he replied a little too fast, pulse skipping a beat. How could he even say no? A tongue swiped over his lips, hand motioning vaguely in the air, meaningless. He hesitated. Shit, shit—fuck it. "I guess I could stay."

Laith's smirk widened.

Undressing under Laith's gaze added a thrill to something he'd never really thought about before. Realization dawned when he pulled the hoodie overhead and found Laith staring back at him, eyes in silent revere. His heart jumped, even though this shouldn't be surprising; he did the same to Laith all the time. He'd just never thought he'd be on the receiving end of it one day.

Sheepish, but still flattered, he placed the hoodie over the mess on the counter and started on his shirt next. He tried to take it off how Laith did, even if there were no muscles to flex or anything to show off; he knew Laith could find something there. The multiple comments on his appearance were proof of that, despite his inability to see what Laith saw. The one argument he'd agree on, however, was that he was pretty good-looking. He'd even go so far as to say his face was his best attribute. No, wait—he had nice thighs too. Yeah, that was fair. Everything else could be scrapped, though.

His shoes came off next, kicked under the counter. While undoing the button on his pants, he thought of how to make this enticing. Maybe he could turn around... unless that was too obvious. Would it be too obvious? With his eyes down, he turned anyway. If he took his boxers off too, then he could pretend this had all been out of shyness. Yeah, that worked; two birds, one stone.

With his jeans tossed on top of Laith's own, he threw a glance over his shoulder. The way green eyes burned, low and intense, let him know his little performance, however amateur, had worked just fine. The effort had paid off.

Light caught on the falling water like a cascade of crystals. It reached Laith through stained glass and warm fog, casting small shadows over his chest, a picture of the droplets that clung to the glass, growing thicker before slipping down. They drew moving patterns over his skin, rain on the window of a car.

He looked like a painting, a study of light and shadow, the way water rippled down his abs, light bouncing off his pecs. A strangely holy feeling fell over Theodore as he stepped into the shower, reverence in the pews of a church, a reminder that he was in the face of something divine. That word bounced around in his mind like the voices of a choir, accompanied by a figure chiseled out of marble, unrecognizable; Moses on a throne, Michelangelo's talent on Laith's body, sculpting details into his skin.

He approached Laith the way a Christian neared the altar—worship kept his head low and his gaze downcast, unworthy of looking his god in the eye. First, he touched Laith's sides and kissed his neck. Water lapped his face, drenching his hair, the introduction to his baptism. He went down willingly; his lips dragged along Laith's body, kissing the ripples of his stomach, glued to the image of his religion. On his knees, he accepted Communion.

He'd never been god-fearing, but this could change his mind. His dedication to Laith was enlightening; it gave him purpose, it carved a path. This was what he was meant to do. He worked the head with more diligence than he'd ever seen from himself, application born out of piety.

Laith could make him believe in anything.

When a hand grabbed his hair, he understood what Laith had meant when he'd said that there was cruelty in love. He'd never felt something like it. Surprise paved the way to shock, which paralyzed him, unable to breathe. He sunk nails into Laith's thighs as his body stiffened, eyes shut, watering.

A minute later, the hand let go.

Chapter 7

The intervention

I feel so fucking numb
It hits my head and I feel numb.

- Glass Animals, *The Other Side Of Paradise*

*His heart choked him, hands trembling—he felt like an idiot. Why couldn't he do any-*thing right? At this point, he'd take anything; *one single* thing, but no. All he was good for was disappointing others, especially the ones he wanted to impress the most. He could punch himself. His eyebrows furrowed, teeth clenched. His parents must already know he had a propensity for failure, which was why they kept such a tight leash on him, turning him into the best version of himself he could be, free of error. Taking into account everything Ryan was, then fucking up must run in the family.

"Emily called me earlier." Laith's voice rescued him from the depths of his mind. The lack of emotion in that comment kept him from judging the nature of that call. Then again, if it'd been good, he was pretty sure Laith would've projected that. Plus, it *was* Emily, so yeah, it was probably bad.

Sitting in silence, he watched Laith put a shirt on, black to match his jeans, no tears over the knees this time. He let himself get distracted, taking notice of how dapper Laith looked in those pants, hoping that would help fill his mind with something less upsetting. Still, he failed to ignore the sinking feeling in his chest.

"What did she say?" He tried to sound nonchalant, like the content of that call wasn't worrying. His eyes dropped as he spoke, hands putting socks on his feet.

"They wanna talk to me. Right now, like as soon as I can get there.

They're waiting for me at her place—all of them."

Wait.

"Isn't that what we wanted?" Suddenly, his mind raced. "To have them all in a room so we can talk to them—so *I* can talk to them. I'm assuming Sherry is gonna be there too."

"What are they gonna think if *you* show up when they're expecting *me*?"

"I don't care. It doesn't matter; this is our chance."

Laith stared at him, eyebrows pinched the slightest bit together.

"Trust me," Theodore pushed. Emotion propelled him forward. "I can do it."

"And if you can't?"

"Then you'll go up."

A long exhale left Laith's lungs, displeased.

"We've talked about this," Theodore softly continued. "We shook on it. This is exactly what we've been waiting for."

"Doesn't it strike you as a little too convenient, though? They're all right where you need them to be."

"No—an intervention's been in order since the farm. I'm actually surprised it took this long."

Laith damn near rolled his eyes. Even if he ultimately stopped himself, it still stabbed Theodore clean through, throat closing—no, not right now. With a scowl on his forehead, he got up from the bed.

"Let's just go."

mmmmmmm

The time constraint didn't allow him to stand around and talk to Laith's neighbors, but the look on their faces told him everything that went through their minds. Their stares scanned him from head to toe, ending in a squint—they knew exactly what had happened in that shower. While the wet hair had definitely given it away, he had a feeling they would've known regardless.

He wished he could spend the day here, in this hallway, telling those women everything they wanted to hear—or maybe everything they *didn't*—in favor of all the answers that ate him up inside. They knew who Laith was; they had to. *Somebody* had to.

He should've skipped the shower.

It was difficult to leave the hallway; walking away from them felt like letting something important slip through his fingers, an opportunity unlike any other. It filled him with dread.

He really wanted to be wrong about that.

mmermlmln

Emily and Ryan lived on the fourth floor, turning right out of the elevator. Laith told him to skip the doorbell and just walk in, since that was what he usually did, thus what the group expected. It definitely seemed strange to simply barge into an apartment Theodore had never been to, but he wasn't *him* right now—he was Laith, who'd been here multiple times. Puffing his chest out with his back straight helped him build the confidence necessary to do something like that, at Ryan's place, no less. It was insane, but he tried not to overthink it.

As soon as the door swung open, conversations reached him, everyone's voices as clear as day. His heart hammered, hand carefully closing the door. Luckily, no one could see him and vice versa; the entrance hall was small and empty. At the very end was a door, while the left wall opened to what he assumed was where everybody resided, probably the living room.

Before he could move, Emily's voice rose above the others. "Laith?"

He froze. If she happened to walk over and blow his cover, it'd be much worse than a grand reveal, so this was it. He had to do it. He had to do it *now*. Without further hesitation, he walked through the archway.

Just as suspected, this was the living room, with a couch against the wall and one door at each side of it. In his current state, he couldn't bring himself to glance around the rest of the place, fixated on the people who sat on the couch.

The first one he saw was Emily, already up, standing in the middle of the room, clearly on her way to the front door. Her eyes widened with surprise, eyebrows up on her forehead. Behind her, Ryan sat on the couch with Sherry on the arm next to him. He had a combination of shock and anger on his face, while she looked delightfully surprised. The last person in sight was Justin, off to the left, who leaned against the wall by himself, arms crossed over his chest. His eyes were wide, eyebrows up, but other than that, Theodore couldn't read anything else.

Suddenly, the room was dead silent.

"Oh." Emily sounded beyond disconcerted. "Theo. We weren't expecting you."

"I know; I was with Laith when you called. We thought it'd be better if I came up instead."

"So you've *been* seeing each other," Ryan interjected. Before Theodore could rebut that, his brother immediately turned to Justin with a finger pointing at him. "I told you! I fucking told you! They've been seeing each other this whole goddamn time!"

In response, Justin simply recoiled closer to the wall. He looked extremely uncomfortable, unable to meet Ryan's eyes. The way he cowered looked like he was trying to merge with the wall and perhaps disappear.

"No," Theodore cut in, "this is the first time we've met since the farm. This whole week, I didn't see him at all, but you're right—we've *been* seeing each other. Not just that, but I've been frequenting the tunnels too. I have friends down there, people I met without your help. My life is not so different from yours."

Ryan stared at him, shocked. He could feel the others staring too, eyes boring into his skull.

"You're going down?"

"Yeah, and before you blame Laith, he has nothing to do with it; I've been going on my own. I've wanted to since you started telling me about it. I knew I had to see it for myself, so I did. I'm far more capable than you give me credit for."

Ryan's features slowly twisted with disgust. "Well? How do you like it?"

"The tunnels are everything I've ever wanted them to be."

Ryan scoffed. "No, they're everything I told you they were. They're my home."

"You don't even live there. You think you're so disenfranchised that you belong with the rats that have nowhere else to go, when in reality, you're a rich piece of shit just like me. You belong in fucking Crestwood with our parents, idiot. Being adopted doesn't change that."

"I'm not fucking adopted," Ryan spat. Anger burned through his words. "Mom had me first. It's not my fault Henry came in later and decided to have *you*. I'm not the one in his will, you are. I'm not getting a single cent, so yeah, I might as well get used to my surroundings, 'cause that's where I'll end up anyway."

"Bullshit. You're acting like you didn't grow up in a suburb and go to one of the best schools in the city. Do you really think not inheriting money later in life makes you the same as a rat who's never had anything to begin with? You literally have the same opportunities as any other rich white guy around. Stop playing the fucking victim when you're not one."

"Oh, *I'm* playing the victim. I'm just playing, huh. Okay, uh, remind me again how many times you've gotten whipped. Right, that's zero; Henry's never even laid a hand on you."

"So you're oppressed 'cause your dad beat you when you were young. Are you fucking kidding me?"

"You have no idea what that was like. It ruined my life."

"No, it didn't. I know it was horrifying, and I'm sorry you had to go through that, but Ryan, Jesus Christ; you're acting like someone murdered your entire family and left you in the woods. You're putting yourself down on purpose."

Suddenly, Ryan got up. "I don't have to listen to this. You're in *my* apartment, telling me that everything I went through *because* of you was meaningless. That I should just fucking forget about it and move on. Well, Theo, I'm trying to. I've *been* trying to, but you're not letting me. Everything I've done so far was to get as far away from my old life as possible and carve myself a new one, but you just *have* to follow me everywhere, don't you? All I've ever wanted was for you to leave me the fuck alone. Now, how's *that* my fault?"

His throat closed, dagger slicing it in half. "I'm not going to be in your life if you don't want me to. I just happen to be friends with people who are also your friends."

"People who were my friends *first*. People I fucking introduced you to!"

"Yeah, and? They became my friends out of their own free will. So what? Can't we have friends in common?"

"That's not it. You're in the space I've been creating for myself. I need you to get out of it."

"Okay, that's not fair," Emily cut in. She held out a hand, eyebrows drawn together. "We can be friends with both of you. We can be friends with whoever the fuck we want to. We're not a commodity, Ryan; we're people you know."

"You're the friends *I* made!"

"So is Theodore. He's not the issue."

"No, but god, I've carried him all my life! I fucking raised him! I know it's not his fault and I'm not mad at him, but Jesus, I just need a break!"

"Okay." Theodore's throat hurt. "I'll give you your space, but I'm not giving up on my friends."

"They're *my* friends!"

"Why can't you both hang out together? What's the big deal? I thought Laith was the one fucking this up for us." Emily sounded extremely confused.

"He's another problem entirely," Ryan explained. "He doesn't give a fuck about me. All those warnings we gave him, all those rules we made; we might as well not even have wasted our breath. He ran to Theo the first chance he got. Traitor." Dark eyes found Theodore's face next, Ryan's brows drawn into a scowl. "You can keep him. He's worthless to me."

"Don't say that." Emily's voice practically trembled, quiet with fear. "You two are so close."

"We're really not. I mean, not *anymore*. I'm just—I'm just trying to find where I belong, you know? My place in society, surrounded by people who care about me. That's obviously nowhere near my parents, and Theo—he reminds me of everything I never had. Watching him grow up was so fucking painful 'cause I didn't have that. I couldn't do that."

Here, Ryan turned to glance at Theodore again.

"I never told you this, but after mom came home with you, she was a completely different person. She was distant, like her eyes were open but she wasn't there. You were in the bath, underwater, and she just stared at you like— like you were a broken plate, not a baby. It freaked me out. I was so scared and so confused; how come she was just watching you drown? So I pulled you out and shook you until you cried. That sound—Theo, you cried so fucking much. For years, you wouldn't stop; it drove me insane. I couldn't stand it. When I look at you, that's all I think about, how much of a shit job I did at raising you. How that's what I spent my entire life doing while kids played in the backyard and swam in the pool." Ryan took a couple of steps back, eyes fixed on his brother's face. "I need to be away from you. I need to move on from this."

With that, Ryan walked to one of the doors by the couch and disappeared behind it. The soft click it made against the doorframe held the same emotional impact as if Ryan had slammed it outright. Actually, this felt worse.

Unable to breathe, Theodore just stood there, staring at the door. His body shook from head to toe, trying hard not to fall apart, at the edge of a precipice. Piece by piece, the world around him came undone, eager to bury him in debris—he had to keep it together. He could do it; he knew he could, despite the eyes that burned stares into the sides of his face, witnessing his struggle. That raised the stakes significantly; if he failed, they'd all see it.

His eyes filled with tears, throat shut tight. No. He fought the urge right away, heart beating on the roof of his mouth. Oh god, not now. Please, not now. If he cried, it was over.

Sherry got up from the couch. Her height forced him to stare straight into her face while he kept his eyes up to stop them from leaking. Hopefully, she wouldn't notice the unshed tears there. If she did, nothing was mentioned. She walked into his personal space and wrapped both arms around him, squeezing him into a hug. That simple act of kindness broke him into a million pieces scattered across the room. He was a cracked porcelain figurine, only held together in that one delicate position. As soon as she touched him, the pieces crumbled. He sobbed, muffled against her skin, heart stabbed a thousand times over. It hurt. Every tear felt like a cut.

Much of what Ryan had said had been expected, yet hearing it from his mouth just how miserable Theodore made him was a sort of pain he'd never experienced before. He thought he'd been prepared for it, that he would've been able to handle the confirmation of his suspicions, except this had been a lot worse than he'd ever imagined. He'd already robbed Ryan of his childhood— how much more was he willing to take? His boyfriend, his girlfriend, his friends?

Last weekend came to mind, Ryan crying at the counter, uttering the words *what we built—it's gone.* He'd destroyed Ryan's friendships just like his father had done years prior. He remembered how angry Henry had been that day, calling Ryan's friends all sorts of names, equating him to the lot of them. Thinking back, that might've been when his parents had finally given up on him. That was what the lack of commentary on Ryan really was, why they'd stopped berating him for what he wore, what he did and what he said. In a way, Theodore wasn't too different than them. After all, he was just as cruel.

Sherry's comfort was undeserved. She should be following Ryan into the next room over and hugging *him* instead, the one who needed it most. With a fist squeezing his heart into a pulp, Theodore pulled away from her. His hands promptly rubbed at his eyes and wiped his face clean, still wet, a huge mess. He couldn't even look at her.

"You should go to him." A sniffle ate around some of the words, nearly incomprehensible. It was difficult to breathe through his nose. "He needs you more."

Two fingers touched his chin and tilted his face up, eyes drawn back to her. Sympathy lined the bed of her eyes, caramel like the setting sun, practically gold. It was the kind of look that not only saw him, but opened him up like a book and read every page. Her tenderness was comforting. He desperately wanted her to embrace him again.

"Does he?" she asked.

His lips trembled without an answer.

"None of what he went through was your fault," she softly continued. "Still, it hurts, doesn't it? Being related to that kind of wound, unable to mend it."

The room stood still. Under the touch of her fingers, Theodore could only hold the stare, submerged. Her image trembled.

"We both know Ryan's going to be okay—he has all of us to look after him—but what about you? Who do *you* have?"

That question hurt more than anything Ryan could've ever said. His eyebrows scowled upwards, tears slipping down his cheeks.

"Who's *really* there for you?"

He couldn't answer.

The hand under his chin moved to his head, drawing it close for a kiss planted right on top of it. "I love you, but you know I can't be there for you. Justin and Emily might, though. If they can... stick to them. Stick to the ones who love you, who you know will put you first. Stop choosing yourself second." Her voice was quiet, muffled into his hair.

That last part didn't seem right. He'd always thought he was extremely selfish, putting his own interests before anybody else's, shoving his friends and their worries aside, ignoring everything Laith had ever expressed to him, taking his parents and all their privileges for granted. He wasn't who she thought he was. It was true, however, that when it came to Ryan, the older brother, the loud one in the family, Theodore got lost. It'd always been that way; Ryan had a lot more problems than he did, thus he deserved a lot more of their parents' attention. At least, that was how Theodore had always seen it.

Perhaps breaking away from Ryan had driven him to overcompensate for all the times he'd come second, and now, he could only come first—to an overwhelming fault. Was it really so bad, then, to want to be friends with Ryan's friends? He'd never meant to interpose. If anything, what he'd really been looking for was a way for Ryan to like him, to finally let him in. Of course, now he knew that wasn't possible.

Sherry pulled away to look into his face. "Where do you think you fall amid Laith's priorities? First or twentieth?"

Unfortunately, he knew the answer to that, but still understood what she'd meant by it. She wanted him to put their involvement into perspective, to compare how much of themselves they each put into it. The point was for him to realize Laith wasn't matching his efforts, and therefore, didn't deserve him.

Except he already knew that. He'd known that going into it. Even before making the first move, he knew this wasn't a level playing field—it was a challenge. That was the whole point, to win Laith over and gain his affection as a prize. He'd never expected Laith to put a single ounce of effort into it. He hadn't even been one of Laith's priorities until they'd started seeing each other—he'd carved himself a spot. He'd been climbing up the list with everything he had, and from what he could see, it was working. Just last week, Laith had confessed to wanting to choose him. This afternoon, Laith had taken him to his place. Things were changing. Theodore knew he'd at least made it into the top three by now and that he could make it even higher.

As her questions hung in the air, Sherry left through the same door Ryan had disappeared behind. It probably led to his room. Her exit prompted Justin to venture closer, no longer pushed against the wall, freed from his anxieties. Theodore knew he wasn't big into confrontation, but the way he'd cowered when Ryan had pointed at him, coupled with his physical distance from everyone brought that to a completely different level. Laith's certainty that Justin wouldn't confront the others—not even Emily—made a lot more sense now.

An uncharacteristic awkwardness hung about him, shoulders stiff, hands hidden away in his pockets. It was strange to see him so out of place. "Uh, I hope you know you can count on me. I'll be there for you."

Theodore smiled. "I know that. Thank you."

Justin's shoulders relaxed, looking like a shrug. He must've been really tense. A breath filled up his chest, eyes glancing at Emily next, who still stood by Theodore, just out of sight. Theodore turned to look at her only to find both arms crossed over her chest and dark eyes cast down with thought, introspection written all over her face. That explained her silence.

"Emily?"

Her name caused her to meet Theodore's eyes first, then Justin's, only now seeming to take notice of his presence.

"What's going on?" Theodore asked.

They held the stare for a moment.

"I need to know what's going on between you and Laith. Did you ask him to date you?"

That call from earlier hit him harder than a bus. It'd been a moment of weakness, a manic episode; it hadn't meant anything. His cheeks burned with betrayal. "No, I—I was just curious. I wanted to know why he wouldn't do it, you know, to tell myself it wasn't my fault. That I wasn't the problem." A bold-faced lie. He was good at those.

Emily's features softened, eyebrows pointing upwards the tiniest little bit. "I gave some thought to it. I pretty much stayed up thinking about it, and—well. I changed my mind; I don't think you'd hurt him. Actually, I was more worried about *you* getting hurt than the other way around. I got caught up in everything Ryan had told me about you, how young and innocent you were, inexperienced about life, growing up in a bubble. I thought Laith would hurt you as badly as he'd hurt me, but I was wrong. You're nothing like what Ryan said you were. You told me that time and time again, going out of your way to show me all you could handle, but I'll admit it took me a while to see it. Ryan just had me in the palm of his hand."

Relief released a breath from Theodore's lungs—was this real? The back and forth with Emily had felt like hitting his head against a brick wall. It'd worn him out to the point of giving up. There was nothing else he could do, nothing else he could say to change her mind. She'd only snapped out of it because of the one who'd brainwashed her in the first place. Ryan was his own undoing.

"You guys talked last night?" Justin glanced between them.

"Yeah." That was all Emily was willing to say, eyes locked on Theodore's face. "I just need to know you're okay," she continued. "That you were ready for everything you two did together. I don't want you to do anything you're not comfortable with just to prove a point."

"I'm not trying to prove anything; this is just who I am."

She slowly nodded. Her eyes fell into thought again, not really looking at anything. A moment later, she turned to her friend. "Justin, can I have your phone? I need to call him."

Before he had a chance to comply, Theodore spoke. "Laith's downstairs."

Two sets of eyes stared at him.

"Let's go, then."

Chapter 8

Reconciliation

*I was so frightened that
I became even quieter inside.
For it seemed to me that
I was finally going to have to feel*

- Clarice Lispector, *The Passion According to GH*

Outside, the first thing Emily did was throw both arms around Laith for a big hug. As the shortest in the group, she pillowed her head on his chest, squeezing his midsection. Surprise petrified him, eyes wide, hands up in the air. First, he glanced down at her, then at the other two that approached soon after. It was clear this behavior wasn't normal for her, or he would've taken it much more naturally.

His eyes questioned both Theodore and Justin, but instead of opening their mouths, they just grinned. A hand plucked the cigarette from Laith's lips while his free one hugged Emily back, very similarly to how he'd hugged Theodore at the farm, loose and detached. He was definitely not used to this kind of physical affection.

The knowledge that Theodore was one of the only people Laith had ever *actually* hugged filled him with pride. He was important enough that Laith had wanted to hug him back, *really* hug him back. Soon, he'd be so important that Laith would even want to hug him first. Ideally, that'd come to Laith as naturally as when their bodies met over a bed.

"Emily, what's happening?" Laith barely moved his lips, paralyzed.

In response, she not only pulled away from him, but shoved him against the wall as well, for good measure. Now, *that* he took a lot more in stride, seemingly relieved by it. She was back to her idiosyncrasies. "Can't I hug my best friend? I feel like shit for the way I treated you this week. I was a dick!"

"Yeah, well." Laith shrugged, fixing his jacket with a hand. "Can't say that was too far from the norm."

"Idiot." She grinned. "I owe you an apology."

"It's fine."

"No, it isn't. I shouldn't have said half the things I said to you. I called you an abuser, dude. It was fucked up."

Another shrug bounced Laith's shoulders, eyes off to the side. "Whatever."

"Laith." She touched his arm, a lot more serious now. "I'm sorry."

"Okay." His tone was dismissive, reply spoken without eye contact, desperate to end the topic. Suddenly, he found Theodore's face, catching a breath in his throat. "So everything's fine now, right?"

"Ryan's still upset." Emily was fast on the draw, beating Theodore. The way Laith had asked it had caused him to believe he'd been addressed, but her answer was as good as his. "He's up in his room," she added. "There were some disagreements, all very emotionally charged, so it might take him a while to calm down, but he'll be alright. Sherry's there with him."

"He doesn't wanna see me anymore," Theodore jumped in, heart painfully squeezed. "Emily said you guys wouldn't stop being friends with me because of him, but I don't know how we're gonna do that."

"We can hang out with you two separately." Justin's tone was both gentle and matter of fact. "I don't think that's gonna be a problem."

"Yeah, we'll just have a schedule. Fridays are usually reserved for Ryan, so we could see you on Saturdays. How does that sound?"

Emily's idea was good; it'd be the answer to all their issues, not to mention it was the one thing Theodore had been trying to achieve this entire time, but still, his first thought was how he'd remained in second place anyway. Even after all of this, they'd see Ryan first and hang out with him after, the main course and the leftovers. He forced a smile despite the ache in his chest, hands stuffed in his pockets. A nod was his answer, non-verbal; if he said anything, he'd probably choke on it.

Laith didn't buy it. Theodore saw the squint in his eyes, feet moving closer for inspection, eyebrows furrowed with suspicion. They stood across the circle from each other. "Why don't you like that?"

"I *do* like it." His heart jumped, hyperaware of this newfound attention. "It's a good idea."

Laith simply held the stare, smoke blowing out of his nose. Somehow, that was a stronger push to keep Theodore talking than anything he could've said.

"I just feel like..." Sweat budded on his forehead. "Well, you guys are always gonna be Ryan's friends first. I'm just his little brother."

Emily frowned behind her mask. Her eyebrows gave it away. "That's not how we feel about you at all."

A tut turned Theodore around to glance at Justin next, watching him take a step closer. Justin clasped a hand on his shoulder, so heavy it shook him a bit. There was humor in it though, in the hidden smile that rounded is face, eyes shining over his mask. "C'mon, I think you need to party. Ryan's got you down, so let's make you feel better. That's what friends do."

Hope quivered in Theodore's chest. Really?

"Yeah, I think you need a shot," Emily cheekily added.

He could barely believe his own ears. "I thought you hated seeing me drink."

"That was Ryan in my head again. I know you drink already, and at your age, we were all drinking too. I'd be a hypocrite if I had a problem with *you* when I didn't have a problem with any other friend of mine. I *was* a hypocrite— and I'm sorry."

"That doesn't mean we'll let you get completely wasted, though," Justin jumped in.

"No, just buzzed. A nice kind of buzz."

"Yeah, like you'll still get enough rest to watch class tomorrow morning."

"We'll stop drinking early, so by the time class rolls around, you won't be hungover. I'll remind you to drink plenty of water."

"No mixing drinks either."

"Just beer, water and *one* shot."

The way those two coordinated their thoughts about him, what he could or couldn't do at the party, reminded him of his parents, but in an ethereal way, disembodied, if his parents were young and cool. He remembered how considerate Justin had been when they'd first smoked together, concerned to be there with him, to watch him through the high. As for Emily, she'd always been accommodating, a shoulder to cry on. She'd kept her tenderness and care even when he'd spouted the most hateful, most vile stuff on the phone and hung up in her face.

They'd both always cared about him a lot. He might not come first in their list of priorities, but he knew he was up there anyway.

"Is there a party going on?" he asked.

"There always is."

The hand on his shoulder moved to the other one, Justin's arm hooking him across the neck to pull him along. He didn't know where they were going, but followed Justin regardless, starting down the block.

"We're close to Streisand's," Laith remarked. "I haven't been there in ages."

"Oh my god, you're right. Man, I haven't heard that name in years!"

"But you live here," Theodore cut in. "How come you don't go there anymore?"

"I don't know. The crowd at Streisand's is made up primarily of college students, so when Ryan and I graduated, I guess we ended up moving onto something else. We've been hitting underground clubs a lot more nowadays."

"Streisand's is like a rite of passage," Justin explained. "Once you're done with college, you're pretty much done with it too. At least, that's how it goes for most of us."

Huh. That'd explain why Dylan and the others only ever went there to chaperone for his brother.

The weight of this moment only hit Theodore in full when the house came into view, with drunk people sitting on the front lawn and muffled music echoing across the street. He was at Streisand's with Laith and the others. He'd *party* with Laith and the others. They'd partied last week too, but the farm had felt more like a hangout than a party. If he had to point to a reason, he'd probably say his hangover, too sick to drink. He supposed that drinking together was what came to mind when he thought of a party, so not being able to do it coupled with arriving late, when everyone was already drunk, had pretty much ruined the experience. That was also what made this so exciting—he'd finally get to drink with these guys.

On a different note, it was weird to be here in the daytime. Young people drinking on a Sunday afternoon was a common sight, since nothing was open and options were limited, but he'd just never started drinking this early. He was usually asleep at this hour too.

"Holy shit." Emily's voice gathered the group's attention, eyes set straight ahead. In her enthusiasm, she even grabbed Justin's hand. Theodore saw Justin glance down at it too, eyebrows up with surprise, before meeting Theodore's face, entirely by accident. Neither one of them spoke a single word, unnecessary; that look had said it all. "Remember when I barfed all over the yard? Right there, where that guy is standing. Laith and Ryan were doing cartwheels, trying to show each other up, while I pretty much turned myself inside out."

"I almost threw up too." Justin grinned. "It was the tequila."

"That awful tequila, cheap as hell. God, that was bad."

"I didn't see any of that," Laith contested. "You must've thrown up like the fucking exorcist, 'cause when I looked at you again, the grass was already blue."

"You were doing cartwheels for a long time."

"No, I wasn't. It was just the one."

"It wasn't just one."

"Bro, you were so out of breath you almost passed out. Don't you remember that?" Justin jumped in.

"You're making me look bad. I destroyed Ryan that day."

"Then almost stepped on the sick."

Emily laughed.

"Yeah, but I didn't," Laith defended.

"'Cause I shouted at you!"

"I remember that."

Letting go of Justin's hand, Emily started up the stone path that crossed the yard. "The only time you ever shouted," she added.

In response, Laith simply tutted.

mmemmemmemm

Once inside the house, Emily went straight for the kitchen. She handed each of them solo cups and took a tequila bottle from behind the kegs. Theodore had never seen anyone drink from those bottles before, but if they were out in the open, then it must be okay to do it.

"You just told us of when you threw up with this, and now you're having it?" he asked.

"It's tradition." She smiled. "You'll be okay if you don't have too much." One hand poured the equivalent of a shot into her plastic cup as she spoke, eyes down to measure it. Then, she brought the bottle to Laith, but before anything could fall into it, he moved his cup away.

"I'm not drinking tonight," he explained. "I'll stick to water."

That comment struck something within her. She didn't move, eyes twice their original sizes, glued on his face. "Are you...?" She never finished that question and he never answered it, either. Instead, he simply turned to fill his cup with tap water. Still in a state of shock, Emily reached across the circle and passed the bottle over to Justin. "Can you finish pouring the shots, please?"

"Yeah, yeah."

She took Laith's elbow and made to leave, a clear indication that he should follow. That wasn't lost on him, of course, but he refused to move nonetheless, not budging from the sink. Her efforts weren't forceful; it was supposed to be a discreet signal, so when he remained perfectly in place, she was forced to stare up into his face and address it. "I'd like to talk to you."

"There's nothing to talk about."

"Yes, there is."

"Then say it here."

The two held the stare. It was curious to see how Laith went from a pushover to stubborn in such a short amount of time. Theodore supposed it depended on how much he cared for the topic at hand, how far he'd go to stick to his ideals. Either that, or Laith was just different with him, much more lenient. The special treatment felt nice, even if he'd only noticed it now.

His attention was on the quarrel, watching it openly as Justin moved out of view. Theodore didn't have to look at his friend to know he was pouring himself a shot, just like Emily had asked him to.

"Do you want one too?" Justin's voice was quiet, trying not to disrupt the discussion by the sink.

Theodore nodded.

Emily passed the other two a brief glance before speaking, clearly addressing Laith. "Are you back in touch with Fred?"

Who was Fred?

"No." Laith practically spoke into his cup, sipping from it shortly afterwards.

"Okay." She stared into the side of his face, eyes no longer on her own. "How are you feeling?"

"Fine."

Justin moved away from Theodore and placed the bottle back where they'd found it. Laith saw that, and in response, raised his own cup for a toast.

"Welcome to the gang, Theo."

Despite the weight of the atmosphere, Theodore's heart still summersaulted, lips curling into a smile.

"To Theo!" Justin added, mirroring Laith.

They all touched their cups together before downing the tequila in one go. It burned like hell, but it was nothing Theodore hadn't already experienced. Still, he grimaced to keep it down. Horrible.

Emily was the first to fill her empty cup with beer. Justin followed, and while he was busy with that, Theodore watched her cross the room for the archway. Rather than walk through it, she stopped with a hand on the frame, face hidden away. It'd been sudden enough that he guessed something must have crossed her mind, a surfacing thought. "When you called me the other day…" Here, she turned to glance at her best friend. "What did you do afterwards?"

Instead of answering her, Laith walked out of the room. Naturally, she followed.

"The keg's all yours," Justin remarked. His voice broke through Theodore's focus just as effectively as a bucket of cold water. He even flinched.

"Right, thanks." He placed his cup under the tap and twisted the knob.

"Don't worry about those guys. They always get carried away with each other."

He glanced up to meet Justin's eyes. "Who's Fred?"

"Laith's old therapist. He stopped seeing him a while ago."

"Why?"

"He said he was doing better and didn't need him anymore."

"Was he?"

"I think so. I believed him, anyway."

"So he told you about the therapist but not about the hospital."

"You think they were related?"

"Did they happen around the same time?"

"I mean…" Justin moved his head, weighing his thoughts. "Probably. I don't really remember; it's been a while. He doesn't tell me much, you know. Everything he talks about is usually a joke, which is how I get to know some stuff, but not a lot. He only talks to Emily."

"Right."

With his cup full, Theodore left the kitchen, Justin in tow.

Emily was just now figuring out that Laith hadn't been doing well. Theodore didn't know too much about it himself, but last week, Laith had mentioned the mental strain he'd been in, stressed out by the scenario Theodore had put together and Ryan and Emily had perpetuated, like actors in a play. He hadn't meant for it to go that far; he'd just wanted the others to know, or rather, for *Ryan* to know. Demonizing Laith hadn't been part of the plan.

This week, his father had decided to become a problem too, as if Laith didn't already have enough on his plate. Again, because of Theodore. Actually, everything could be traced back to him and how stupid he was, doing whatever he wanted, disinterested in the consequences, which had all ended up falling on Laith. Theodore had even driven him to take pills, whatever his prescription was for. If he had to guess, it probably combated stress.

How long did they last, by the way? Laith had been on them all night; he couldn't possibly still be under their influence. Since he still refused to drink, he might've taken another one in his apartment, while Theodore had busied himself with something else. They must be stored in the bathroom.

His guess that Emily and Laith had moved to the backyard soon proved correct; on the back porch, he saw them cutting through the crowd. Emily seemed to be the only one talking, leaning forward to stare into Laith's face, following him with effort. If Theodore already had trouble keeping up with the man, then he couldn't imagine how much harder it was for her. He followed a few feet behind, so they could have their privacy, unable to make out what it was that she so avidly conveyed. The two stopped by the back fence, away from the crowd, in their own space.

Streisand's backyard overlooked a dense patch of the woods, thirty or so feet from the fence. At five thirty in the afternoon, the sun hadn't technically started setting yet, but it'd grown close to the very top of the trees. Summertime always stretched the days out for way too long.

As soon as Theodore and Justin joined the other two, their previous conversation seemed to be done. Emily downed her entire cup of beer in a single go and left. The group watched her walk back to the house in a dumbstruck daze, wordlessly surprised. The suddenness of it was what got Theodore the most. She must not be happy with the end of that talk.

"Everything is fine now, right?" He addressed Laith with a fixed stare. "You're friends with everyone again and the thing with my dad is settled. No one's giving us trouble anymore, yeah?"

"Yeah. It'll be fine."

"No. I'm asking if things are fine *now*."

"They are. We'll work something out with your dad and it'll be fine. I'm in charge, remember?"

The absolute peace that radiated from Laith filled him with confidence. Whether it'd come from the end of their problems or the pills didn't really matter; things were finally under control.

"The stuff with your dad," Justin jumped in, thoughtful, "you know, I'm still thinking about it. He freaked me out when we met in the office, and even more when you told me he's—you know, but I've been thinking and... I just don't think he'd be able to know when we hang out. Like, unless one of us tells him, he won't know. He *can't* know."

"Yeah, Laith's his spy, or he's supposed to be, but he's obviously not saying anything."

"We have it figured out," Laith added. "We're fine, and if you're worried about him running into us, don't be; I know his schedule."

"You do?" Wow, Laith had a much stronger hold on the situation than Theodore had given him credit for.

"Yeah, pretty much. I know when he's underground, and when he isn't, I know the kind of places he goes to. Streisand's isn't one of them."

Theodore scoffed out a laugh. "The whole reason he assigned you to me was so he wouldn't have to come to places like this."

Laith nodded.

"I hope you unblocked me," Justin commented sheepishly, voice disappearing into thin air.

In response, Theodore took out his phone, unlocked it and unblocked his friend right in front of him. "There. Friends once again."

Justin smiled.

Chapter 9

And I like large parties. They're so intimate. At small parties there isn't any privacy.

- F. Scott Fitzgerald, *The Great Gatsby*

When Emily came back, she had a bottle of rum in a hand and a full cup of beer in the other. Despite whatever had happened earlier, she seemed to have put it behind her, grinning from ear to ear now, her cat-like lipstick stretched black across her face. The hand with the bottle shook it up in the air, contents swirling around. "Now we can play truth, dare or shot. We haven't played with Theo yet."

"Truth, dare or shot? I don't think I've played that version."

"I'll teach you." She took a seat on the grass, legs folded under herself, tilted sideways. Her dress was very short, like an oversized t-shirt with the sleeves ripped off, big enough to fit Ryan, but the leggings that she wore under it didn't require her to sit so modestly. She probably just wanted to. It'd been getting chilly enough that she couldn't walk around with her bare arms out anymore, so she'd thrown a jacket on, even if she didn't wear it right; she carried it over her elbows, as if it'd slipped down her shoulders by accident, but it was very intentional.

Theodore sat across from her, legs crossed, with Justin and Laith at each side. One of Justin's legs rested on the ground while the other was propped up, bent at the knee. Laith, on the other hand, sat longways, similarly to Justin, except he leaned back on a hand, not on his own knee.

"Let's say I'm the one who spins the bottle first," Emily started, placing the bottle in the middle of the circle, so it lay on its side, "and it lands on you. I get to choose whether I wanna give you a truth or a dare, and you get to choose whether you wanna play along or take a shot from the bottle. Then, it's your turn to spin."

"Oh, it's not so different from truth or dare, then."

"Not at all; we just turned it into a drinking game."

Theodore passed the circle a glance. "Wouldn't it be better with more people, though?"

"Sure." She shrugged.

"Call your friends over," Laith suggested. "Hannah and the others."

Theodore's heart jumped. Should he? "You think it'd be fun?"

"Hell yeah."

"Are you talking about the girls who live with him?" Justin asked, blue eyes fixed on Laith's face.

"Who else would I be talking about, dumbass? We don't know a single Hannah."

"So you've met them."

"Yep, just last night. They're really nice people."

"How?" Theodore cut in, perplexed. "All they did was attack you. Before lunch, I mean. Hannah was relentless."

"Nah, she's sweet. She cares about you a lot. All of them do, actually."

"Are they hot?"

The circle stared at Justin.

"Theo called one of them a supermodel, so." Laith shrugged. "I guess she's hot."

Theodore's eyes widened. "She—that's not what I meant! We're just—!" He couldn't even finish that thought; his brain was such a mess that if a Minotaur happened to fall in it, he'd have to call it a maze.

Laith smirked at his frustration. It made him want to punch him.

"Which one is that?" Justin asked.

"Oh, you'll know when you see her."

"Okay, since we're being nasty," Emily glanced from Justin to Laith, "any blondes?"

"One, but she's taken."

"How do you know?" That question flew out of Theodore's mouth. He was going insane.

"She told me."

"What?"

"Apparently, two of them made their relationship public yesterday, but you weren't there."

"Why didn't they tell me over lunch?"

Laith sounded out the equivalent of *I don't know,* a mumble accompanied by a shrug. "I guess it didn't come up."

"You—" He couldn't form a single thought. "Why did she tell *you?*"

"'Cause I asked. They were being gay, so I pointed that out and they told me."

"I can't believe it. They've never been gay in front of me."

"Do they know you're getting your back blown out on the reg?"

Justin's question made Laith burst into laughter so hard that he started wheezing. It put a big grin on Emily's face, while Theodore only felt the wind that whipped past as he fell off a cliff. He couldn't even breathe.

"I mean, you pass. If I hadn't caught you staring at Laith like a schoolgirl, I would've never known—that's why I'm asking. Like, they know Laith's gay; you look at him and you know, but maybe they don't know about you. I'm just saying, maybe it's not intentional. They were gay in front of him 'cause they know he's one of them, that's all."

Laith hiccupped.

"They know about me." Theodore's voice was small.

"Damn, really?" Justin clicked his tongue, moving to pull his wallet out. "Then I don't know."

"To be honest, it's pretty hard *not* to be gay when Laith's around," Emily argued. "They might've gotten pulled in."

"That's true." Justin plucked a joint between his lips. "Even *I* feel like hitting on men when I'm around him sometimes. I mean, just look at Ryan."

"Oh my god," Laith breathed in deeply, hand wiping a tear from his eye. "I'm gonna kill you."

"Bro, I'm already dead." The joint muffled Justin's words, eyes down at the flame that burned the end of it.

"I mean, Jesus Christ; Ryan was already bi when I met him."

"I know that; I'm goofy, not stupid. What I'm saying is..." Here, Justin toked on the joint, lighter put away. He breathed out before continuing. "Even the most passing of gays come out around you. Ryan would've never hit on me if you weren't there."

"Man, I don't know what the fuck your point is."

"Theo's friends are probably too straight for the couple to feel comfortable with PDA." Emily accepted the joint from Justin.

"Yes, that's what I'm saying!" Justin practically shouted. "Thank you!"

She winked at him, joint between her lips.

"They know about you, by the way." Laith's voice dripped with mischief, smirk cutting across his face.

"Me?" Justin pointed at himself.

"Yeah, you. They brought you up last night."

"What'd they say?"

"Nothing; they just brought up your name. I have no idea what Theo said about you."

"I didn't say anything!" Theodore rebutted. "They know you have a farm and that you smoke weed. That's it."

"Shit, you told them I smoke? Now they think I'm a fucking junkie."

"You used to be," Laith practically mumbled, eyes cast aside. With the joint in hand, he blew smoke off into the breeze.

"So did you!"

"Yeah, no shit. Why do you think we're friends?"

"Well, I have a few theories," Justin mused, moving to sit upright, "but you're not gonna like them."

"Alright, give me the worst one." Laith passed the joint to Theodore.

"The worst one, huh? Okay. You only started talking to me 'cause I deal to the Hollywood boys."

Theodore took a drag as they talked, lungs warm with smoke. The more he did it, the easier it became. This time, his throat barely even itched.

"Bro, if I was trying to use you, why have I never asked you to introduce us?"

Justin shrugged. "Like I said, those are just theories. I've never really gone into too much detail."

"Yeah, but that's not the worst one," Emily interjected, eyebrows furrowed upwards.

"Tell me the worst one, then," Laith urged.

Justin stared at her, lost.

"That you only started talking to him 'cause you wanted to pick him up."

"Oh." Justin clicked his tongue, hand reached toward Theodore. "That's not even a theory."

"You're right; it's the truth." Laith shrugged.

Justin stared at him, wide-eyed. "Are you kidding me?"

"Nah, dude, you're hot. If you were into it, I woulda fucked you right when we met."

Emily pointed at her best friend with a hand, a gesture that said *I told you so* without words.

"Is that why you asked me if I had a girlfriend?"

"That's generally why people ask other people if they have a girlfriend."

"Oh my god, Justin." Emily laughed. "Are you dense, man?"

"I'm sorry, I was confused! I just thought he was a client like everybody else."

"Do all your clients hit on you like that?" Laith scowled.

"I mean…" Justin's shoulders bounced. "I've heard weirder shit. They're usually drunk when they come to me, so crazy talk is expected. I thought you were just being weird."

"Can't blame you for that." Emily raised her eyebrows, piercing glinting under the last rays of sunshine. "Now smoke that shit or I'll take it from you!"

"Okay, okay, sorry."

As Justin toked on the joint, Laith glanced at Theodore. "Are they on the way?"

"Oh, uh." Heat rushed up his neck, hands fishing his phone out. "I'll text them right away."

"I can call them, if you want."

"Since when do you have their number?"

"Hannah texted me this morning. She wanted to know if we were in the room."

Holding the stare, Theodore could feel two sets of eyes bore into the side of his face. He had to make sure they didn't get the wrong idea here. "While we slept in, you mean."

A slow grin pulled at Laith's lips. "While we slept in, yeah."

Somehow, that just made it worse. The way Laith had said that had completely negated his previous statement, like a very badly kept secret. Shit.

"Damn, you guys spent all night *and* all day together?" Smoke blew with each word, joint pinched between Justin's fingers, an offering to Emily. She wasted no time taking it.

"Uh, yeah. We met up around eight last night."

Keeping his silence, Theodore simply turned to his phone and opened up the girls' group chat.

"You must be exhausted." Emily's tone was far too casual for the weight of that comment. It burned right through Theodore's face, fingers trying to type out a text. Not watching them was a good call; he didn't have to look to know the size of Laith's grin.

We're at Streisand's right now.
Do you guys want to stop by?

"I'm more resilient than you think."

"Resilient... isn't that when you don't like change?"

Jessie replied within the minute.

Like, right now right now?

"No, that's resistant. Like, resistant to change."

Yeah, right now. We wanna play truth or dare.

He didn't have to tell her about the shot part. Let it be a surprise.

"Resilient is when you cum, and then five minutes later, you're good to go again," Emily explained. That froze Theodore on the spot. "That's what he means."

"You just ruined the joke."

Four different reiterations of the same text flooded the group practically at the same time agreeing to be there as soon as possible. Great.

"He didn't get the joke! What was I supposed to do, *not* explain it?"

"Isn't there a word that's like, irresistant?" Justin asked.

"No," she quickly answered.

"You might be thinking of irresistible, which is also true about me."

Emily scoffed. "If you don't dismount, I'll push you off your high horse right now."

"Are you gonna bring a ladder for that?"

Emily and Laith moved in Theodore's peripherals, but he preferred not to watch. She was probably just shoving him, anyway. He locked his phone and slipped it back into his kangaroo pocket.

"Dude, careful!" Justin's concern prompted Theodore to glance up just in time to see the other two disengage from whatever scuffle they'd just had. Rolling a shoulder, Laith offered the joint back to him. The acceptance was wordless, fingers touching as it changed hands.

"Man, you almost dropped it!"

"But I didn't," Laith defended.

"But you could have!"

"But I didn't."

"Justin." Emily touched her friend's arm. "I bet you have enough on you for another three joints, so even if he *had* dropped it, it would've been fine."

Theodore's throat burned with smoke.

"That's not the point. It's a principle—you don't waste it!"

"I didn't waste it."

"I know, I'm just telling you to be careful."

"I am careful. Theo, tell them about last week."

Theodore exhaled. "What about last week?"

"What part of last week do you think I'm talking about?"

"Uh." He passed the joint over to Justin, mind whirring to come up with something relevant to this conversation. "The bong rip?"

That was the best he could do. Still, Laith rolled his eyes.

"You know." Justin muffled his words on the filter, voice strained as he held smoke in his lungs. "*I* was the one who taught these guys how to use a bong. I'm important."

"That's true," Emily corroborated. "If it weren't for you, I would've lived the rest of my days unable to use one. Now I can get high *and* look cool while doing it."

"Justin is a man of knowledge. An erudite, if you will. He can give you information on the most obscure of topics, but if you ask him what rice is, he'd tell you it's a vegetable."

"Isn't it?" Justin blew smoke into the air.

"Oh, honey." Emily grinned, taking the joint from him. "It's a grain."

"Isn't that just a subsection of vegetable?"

Suddenly, Theodore wasn't sure anymore. *Was* grain a subjection of vegetable? If so, then would vegetables be a subsection of plants? Was everything technically plants? The circle shared a confused look.

"No, that's not right." Laith scowled. "They're different things. When you think of vegetables, you don't think of corn and beans, do you? You think of carrots and lettuce."

"Okay, but aren't they all plants?"

"I was just thinking that too," Theodore confessed.

"Yeah, but they're not all the same thing just 'cause they're all plants. You're essentially equating hide to meat."

"How are they different?" Justin squinted.

"They're from different parts of plants! Grain is like—grain is seeds, while vegetables are the tasty part. Like, you could just pull a carrot from the ground and eat it, but you wouldn't do the same to fucking beans."

"Okay, so fruits are vegetables too."

"Fruits come from flowers, dog! They're not vegetables!"

"Okay, guys." Emily passed Laith the joint with her free hand up. "Let's not get too heated about plants here."

"You just proved my point, anyway." Laith stuck the joint between his lips and took a long, *long* drag.

"Since when are you Mr. Botanist?" Despite the humor in Theodore's question, it was still a genuine one. "I had no idea you knew so much about... grain."

Laith breathed in sharply, a maneuver to trap smoke in his lungs. "Bro, it's high school stuff. You just finished it; you should know."

"Okay, then I get a pass," Justin jumped in. "I've been out of high school for seven years."

"Wait." Theodore counted on his fingers. "You're twenty-five?"

"Yeah, and I'm a Taurus."

"I don't know what that means."

"It's my zodiac sign. You know, the star alignment stuff."

"No, I *know* what the zodiac is; I just don't know what any of them mean."

"Emily could tell you more about it. I only know about my own."

As Justin talked, Laith passed Theodore the joint, smoke dissipating in the air.

"I don't know very much either," Emily clarified. "I just think it's fun to read the horoscope and see if my day matches with what it says."

"What's my horoscope?" Theodore brought the joint to his lips.

"It depends on your sign. When's your birthday?"

He couldn't exactly answer with smoke in his throat, so a hand came up to signal for her to wait.

Laith ended up answering for him. "February fourth."

Huh, so he remembered. Theodore stared into the side of his face, holding a breath. When Laith met his eyes, he turned and exhaled.

"Okay, February fourth. It looks like you're an Aquarius."

"What does that mean?"

"It says here that you're a nonconformist rebel who hates authority and dresses weird. Is that you?"

"No, I look good all the time."

Laughter filled the circle.

"Alright, maybe you don't dress weird. By the way, your horoscope for today is caution. People are gonna try to sabotage your day—are you gonna fight or are you gonna ignore them?"

Hm. Who could have tried to ruin his day? The obvious answer would be Ryan, but then again, Ryan had either tried to or succeeded in ruining his day pretty much his whole life.

"That could be true for literally any other day," he argued.

"Yeah, I know. These are all vague and could apply to anyone here; that's kinda the point. I just find it fun to figure out what they're telling me, whether it's true or not."

"Do me next," Justin cut in, accepting the joint from Theodore.

"Okay, Taurus. It says here that you should get some friends together to help you fix your place up, like clean and do yard work."

"Wack." Laith tutted.

"Guys, I have an incredible proposition for you," Justin joked, joint poking out of a grin.

"Is it yard work?" Theodore asked.

"I'll tell you when we get to my place."

Emily giggled. "Okay, mine tells me to work hard and get my shit together."

"I know the *perfect* place for hard work—it's in my yard."

Justin's comment made Emily laugh.

"What sign are you?" Theodore asked her.

"Scorpio."

He blinked. "These are so random. Is there any logic to them?"

"Of course there is!" Justin loudly mumbled, joint between his teeth. "The stars are kindly telling you what your destiny brings!"

"That someone's gonna try to ruin my day? *That's* my destiny?"

Justin toked quietly, ignoring Theodore's question.

"There's a sex chart too, you know."

The circle stared at Emily.

"Read my sex chart." Laith nodded in her direction.

"Okay, Capricorn. Let's see... Do you want the chart or the horoscope?"

"The chart. Tell me what I'm good at."

"Don't you already know that?" Justin passed the joint along.

"He just wants to hear it." Emily puffed while searching, eyes down at her phone. "Alright, here we go. Capricorn, you are a practical man. You don't think about sex as much as you simply perform it. To you, it's just another task, which you will complete to the best of your ability, putting all the time and effort necessary into satisfying your partner. Does this sound like you so far?"

"I mean..." Laith made a face. "The task part is kinda inconsiderate, isn't it? Sounds like I'm some fucking robot."

"Literally a fucking robot," Justin remarked.

"Okay, shut up; I'm gonna keep reading. You are pragmatic, extremely horny—"

"That's correct."

"—and prefer to show your affection through actions rather than words. You are a provider and want to give your partner everything they could possibly need, both inside as well as outside the bedroom. You are passionate and will try anything your partner suggests, but prefers to do things your way. You have a small number of positions you're comfortable with, because you know you're good at them, and prefer to stick to what you know rather than fail while trying something new. After that, we have the sign-to-sign compatibility."

"A small number of positions?"

"You're only good at missionary and that's it." Emily passed the blunt while Justin burst into laughter.

"Damn, they really just called me straight, huh. Who knew conversion therapy was real?" Laith took the joint and toked on it.

"In his defense," Theodore jumped in, lips parted to follow that up with

98

his case, but as soon as he noticed the weight of everyone's attention, he didn't want to say anything anymore. It was clear that they'd been waiting for this moment, eager to know what he thought of such claims. Well, his original point had to be scrapped now, but he still had to say *something*—they all expected it. "He—I mean, he *does* prefer to do things his way."

"Really." Laith blew smoke through his nose. "You're comfortable saying that."

Hyperaware of the stares, Theodore hesitated. Oh god, what could he even say here? He was in a vacuum-sealed coffin. "That doesn't mean you hate doing things *my* way; it's just that you seem much more excited to do them your way."

"Are you talking about this morning?"

"No, I—" His brain short-circuited.

"Or do you mean the shower?"

"I just mean—just, in general."

"You know I didn't mean to choke you, right?"

That comment put him back on his knees as the hand on his head tangled fingers into his hair. His breathing hitched, suddenly back in the moment, body tense. No, he was okay. He let out a slow breath.

"I mean, I *did*, but—"

"Yeah," he quickly cut Laith off, heart hammering into his chest. "Yeah, I know. It's fine. It's whatever."

"Man." Justin clicked his tongue. "*You've* been in charge? I thought Theo topped you."

His comment felt like a flying brick had just hit Theodore's forehead so hard it shot him across the yard.

Laith stared at his friend for a moment, bottom lip worried between his teeth, head bobbing the slightest bit into a nod. "Huh."

When their eyes met again, Theodore's soul exited his body. He was no longer present. Out of sheer panic, his hand brought his cup up to his face. At that point, the rest of him took over, downing the entirety of his drink before pushing it in Laith's direction. "Can you—can you get me a refill, please?"

Laith watched his hand tremble for a moment, making up his mind. Ultimately, he took the cup and got up to leave. "Next time you tell Justin about me, at least make me look good." With that, Laith disappeared into the crowd.

As soon as he was gone, a big breath rushed into Theodore's lungs, shoulders dropping. Holy shit.

"He took the joint," Justin promptly remarked. "Bastard."

"Did you actually top him or is Justin bullshitting us?"

"It doesn't matter." Breath came in quick and short, just shy of hyper-ventilating. "I can't talk about this shit in front of him."

"Are you sure? 'Cause you were *very* comfortable talking about it last week, in front of everyone. Even your brother."

"No, that was different. There were no details involved; it was just fact. It was a memo."

"Why would details matter? You know he doesn't care. He's always tell-ing us about the stuff he does in the dark rooms, anyway. It's not a secret."

"I don't—" Suddenly, a different thought changed the direction of that entire sentence. The change was so drastic that it erased his previous sentence completely and started from scratch. "Has he told you about me? Details, I mean. Stuff we've done." He knew Laith hadn't told Justin or Sherry anything, but had he told Emily?

"No. He doesn't talk about you at all."

"That's what I said," Justin cut in. "I told you that already."

"I know, but I thought—I thought maybe he'd told Emily, because, you know."

"The only times you've ever come up were because I brought you up. Otherwise, he wouldn't have said a word."

"And we all know what that means."

He stared at Justin, heart beating in the roof of his mouth. If any words had managed to escape the maze his brain had become, they would simply fail to circumvent the lump that blocked his throat, so really, nothing was able to come out.

"So when are you gonna ask him?"

That question erased every single thought he'd ever had.

"You know, despite what he looks like, Laith's a sensitive guy," Justin started. "I bet he'd love it if you did something cheesy, like ordered a cake with *will you be my boyfriend?* written on it, or took him to a restaurant and gave him flowers. He's a big fan of cuisine, so food is your best bet here."

"He'd love a grand romantic gesture too. Like, asking the DJ to play your song at the club, then screaming at the top of your lungs if he'd be your boyfriend. Better yet, tell the DJ to turn the music down at one point and announce that you have something to say. That way, the whole club will stop to see you ask him."

"I think I'd rather blind myself with sewing needles." Those words left him straight from the core of his being. The lump had been defeated.

"Okay, then what were you thinking?" Emily didn't care to hide the vexation from her voice.

"I wasn't thinking anything because I'm not doing it."

"Why not?"

"I already know the answer to that and it's no."

"So you're gonna skip the question and go straight to mourning? 'Cause that's what you're doing. By not asking, you're accepting defeat. The next step would be to get over him and move on. Have you started on that yet?"

"That's not the next step. I'm not in *mourning;* he hasn't even rejected me. I just... I like things the way they are."

"Then why did you call me at six in the morning asking me why he wouldn't date you?"

"It was a moment of weakness. I was manic."

"I think you really want him to be your boyfriend."

"Yeah, well, I can't change who he is, so." He shrugged.

"Except you wouldn't be changing him at all. He's not afraid of commitment; he's afraid of getting hurt, so tell him you're not going to hurt him."

"Oh, simple." Irony tasted foreign on his tongue. "Did you already forget what you told me? I don't know that I won't hurt him. I can't promise him that."

"You'll just have to ask him to give you a chance."

"Or I'll just enjoy what we have and not try to sabotage it, thanks."

"You wouldn't be sabotaging it," Justin jumped in. "He wouldn't mind if you asked him. That kind of stuff doesn't matter to him."

From the corner of his eye, Theodore saw the crowd part with Laith's return. He carried Theodore's cup in a hand and the joint between his lips, practically a stub at this point. His presence kept Theodore silent, hoping to kill the subject before Laith caught wind of it. Unfortunately, that thought didn't occur to the others.

"I think you should do it tonight," Emily suggested. She leaned back on a hand, lips stretching into a smirk. "Right now."

Theodore furtively shook his head as Laith sat back down.

"Right now," she repeated, dark eyes fixed on him.

"Here." Laith passed him the cup, speaking around the butt of the joint. It wasn't even lit anymore.

"Do it," Emily pushed.

Laith passed her a glance. "Are you talking to me?" He sounded genuinely confused.

"No, she's talking to me," Justin lied. That got a look from Theodore, wide-eyed. "She wants to give me a dare, but the game hasn't started yet. I told her she should wait."

"Yeah, save that one for later." Laith reached an arm across the circle, roach between his fingers. Justin took it and stashed it away.

"I don't know, it's kind of embarrassing," Emily admitted. Her tone was somewhere between teasing and mischievous, eyes locked on Theodore. A hand came up to touch the spikes on her choker, playing with them. "Should it really wait for everyone else?" she asked.

Theodore dropped his gaze at the cup and drank from it.

"Depends," Laith commented. "What's the dare?"

"Uh, for me to be brutally honest for two minutes straight," Justin answered.

Emily glanced at him. "I said five."

"Sorry, five."

"Then yeah, you should probably do that now," Laith concluded. "You don't know any of Theo's friends, so the brutal honesty would just make you sound like a dick. Do only the three of us."

Wow, Justin must really like Theodore for such a sacrifice. He'd have to pay him back in full.

"C'mon," Emily urged. "Read us."

"Okay, okay, uh. Well..." Justin cleared his throat. "Who wants to go first?"

"Me."

Laith and Emily both spoke over each other.

"Alright, Laith goes first."

"Why? *I* gave you the dare, so do me first."

"Okay, uh. You're, um... Laith, are you timing it?"

"I can."

"Then let me know when the countdown starts."

"Alright." Theodore glanced up to see Laith pull out his phone and fiddle with it. "Okay... now."

Justin nervously cleared his throat. Theodore could tell from the way he sat, back perfectly straight, shoulders tense. "Emily, you're beautiful, and you're also kind of a freak."

That made her burst into laughter.

"I mean that in a good way, though! Like, you're cool. Your makeup is freaky in a cool way and you're kind of terrifying, but in like, a nurturing way, you know? Like, you could kick my ass, but I also know that, if I'm going through something, I can talk to you."

"When have I ever kicked your ass?" she spoke with a bright grin.

"Well, you've never kicked *my* ass, 'cause I've been staying out of trouble, but I know you could. You've kicked Laith's, so really, you could kick anyone's."

"Okay, okay, me next," Laith urged.

"No, I'm not done talking about her."

"Bro, you'll never be done talking about her."

"Just give me a minute, alright?" Here, Justin turned back to his addressee. "Emily, I consider you a really good friend of mine, and I want you to know that this next part comes from the heart, okay? I know you care about us a lot, but sometimes, you go a little crazy about it, especially with Laith. Like, I get it — *I get it* — but it feels like, sometimes, you forget he's an adult."

The expression on her face was utterly unreadable.

"Don't hate me," Justin continued, palms up in the air. "That's just how I feel about it. I think you should trust him more, 'cause he can definitely handle himself. We both know he can." With that, Justin turned to Laith. As soon as their eyes met, Justin's shoulders relaxed, breath leaving his lungs. "Man, I don't even know what to say to you."

"Aw, c'mon. Read me to filth."

A hand motioned vaguely towards Laith. "I don't know. You're a mess, dude."

That got a scoff in response, Laith's lips curled into a small smile.

"I mean, I don't think I could make a point that you aren't already expecting from me. You're loud and unapologetic; you do what you wanna do and you don't care about what other people think. That's really admirable."

"But...?"

"But you're also a dumbass."

Laith grinned.

"I know it's on purpose, but I feel like I had to point that out anyway. Here's the thing about you, dude—it's *all* on purpose. Everything we think about you is what you want us to think about you, so I don't really have anything subversive to say. Even when you're constantly fucking up and being a huge mess, I just have this feeling that it's all part of the act, like it's intentional."

"Everything we do is intentional; it comes from our *arrière-pensée*, conscious or not. You do it too."

"Sure, but... I don't know. You've definitely put a lot more thought into it than I have. I guess that's the point I'm trying to make."

"I'm not sure I'd say that."

Justin shrugged, turning to Theodore next. "As for you, Theo, I think you're a really sweet guy. You have a fire under your ass that I don't think a lot of people can see. You're caught in between two completely different worlds, trying to find where you belong, and I just hope that place is with us."

"You talk like you're in love with me," Theodore joked.

In response, Justin smiled. "Maybe I am. Who knows? We might elope before the day's over."

Theodore laughed.

"You know, Sherry doesn't think you put yourself first, but I think you do," Justin continued. "She's only really seen you around Ryan, so I don't blame her; you're different when you're away from him. Better, I think."

"I think we're all better away from him," Theodore confessed. "Especially Emily."

He saw her drop her eyes to the beer cup between her hands, no response in her mouth. She must know he was right.

"How much longer do I still have?" Justin asked.

"One minute."

"Damn, this shit's rough. I already want to apologize to everyone. I feel like such a dick."

"Well, that's what the dare entails." Emily shrugged, eyes up at him now. "I asked for it, didn't I?"

They held the stare. Theodore could tell Justin was having a hard time keeping his mouth shut about the lie. The need to apologize and come clean screwed a frown into his face, eyebrows up with guilt.

"Why don't you read Ryan next?" Laith suggested. "He's not here to hear it."

"Oh, I'm not reading him. That's a hard pass for me."

"We're not gonna tell on you, dude."

"I know, I just—it doesn't feel right."

"C'mon, I bet you have some piping hot takes on him."

"Man..." Justin threw his hands up. "I'm not gonna do that. This is already hell."

Laith's phone buzzed. It seized Justin's attention immediately, eyebrows up with hope.

"Am I free?"

"You are free." The reluctance in Laith's voice was practically palpable. He put his phone away with vexation pursing his lips, eyes just shy of rolling.

Chapter 10

*And when you kiss me
I'm happy enough to die.*

- Florence + The Machine, *I'm Not Calling You a Liar*

*By the time the girls arrived, it was still light out, despite the sun's gradual disappear-*ance. With his back to the woods, Theodore couldn't see it, but he knew it'd been setting behind the trees; the shadows proved it, stretching halfway across the yard, long and pointy. His watch read 7 p.m.

He saw the girls first, since his spot faced the crowd. They all had jackets on and solo cups in hand, eyes darting back and forth, looking for him. He promptly sprung up to his feet to greet them, which welcomed the rest of the circle to do the same. Walking ahead of the others, Daisy soon caught sight of him and led the girls over.

With butterflies in his stomach, Theodore introduced them to Emily and Justin, but failed to mention their names, so Laith ended up doing it for him. He felt silly; there was no way those two would magically know the girls' names. It'd just slipped his mind to introduce them like that.

"So what's this about a truth or dare game?" Jessie asked, openly excited.

Everybody sat back down as Emily explained the game again. Each of the girls ended up sitting between one of the rats, so the circle had to be expanded over the lawn.

"Who starts, then?"

Jessie's question prompted Emily to offer her the bottle. She'd taken the spot between Emily and Laith. "Why don't you do it?" The way she said that was suspect. It was in the tone of her voice, way too soft, way too nice, with a tilt in her words. Was she flirting?

"Okay, here we go!"

The bottle spun over the grass.

"Jessie, are you still straight?" Theodore's question received a strange look from the circle. His addressee stared at him with furrowed eyebrows and a big smile on her face. "I'm just making sure," he clarified.

"Uh, yeah. I am."

A tinge of disappointment pursed Emily's lips. So she *had* been flirting.

The bottle stopped on Hannah.

"I choose dare for you." Jessie grinned. "I dare you to arm-wrestle Laith."

The two involved shared equally surprised looks.

"Really?" Hannah asked.

"If you want to." Jessie's shoulders bounced. "You could always have the shot otherwise."

"No, no. I'll do it." Hannah scooted closer to the center of the circle. The jacket she wore made it difficult to tell whether she even had any muscle at all, so Emily and Justin's confusion was perfectly understood. She lay on her stomach and propped her elbow up on the ground.

"I'll have you know," Laith started, moving to mirror her, "I've never arm-wrestled anyone in my life."

"And I've never lost a match." Hannah smirked.

In response, Laith passed the circle a glance. "Remember me as I lived."

"Tall and handsome?" Jessie tried.

He gave her a wink and a nod, tongue clicking. The only thing that was missing was a finger-gun, but that hand was currently busy locking with Hannah's. The two stared at each other.

"Jessie, count us down."

"Okay. Three... two... one... go!"

They struggled. Their arms trembled, elbows pushed into the grass. First, they leaned to one side, then to the other, back and forth in a show of strength. Eventually, Laith managed to get a bit of ground over Hannah, just enough to take her down. In close calls like this, Theodore supposed the smallest advantage could make a huge difference. Laith let go of her hand with a big grin on his face.

"One for one!"

The crowd clapped and cheered as Hannah rolled her eyes. There was no ill-will behind it, though; she got up with a smile and offered Laith a hand, which he graciously took. "Beginner's luck," she commented, pulling him up.

On his feet, he bowed. "It was an honor."

She rolled her eyes again, smiling wider now. Back in her spot, she spun the bottle. It stopped on Emily. "I actually don't know anything about you," she confessed, "so I'll give you a truth. What are some things you like to do?"

"That's too easy!" Theodore remarked.

"If you'd told us anything about her, I wouldn't be asking this question."

The circle oohed. That comment was enough to shut him up.

"Thank you, Hannah; that's a lovely truth. My favorite thing in the world is to have fun. I enjoy long walks at the graveyard and playing bass for the ghosts. I also like seeing my friends and dancing to good music."

Hannah smiled. "You're a goth."

Emily leaned back on a hand, playing coy. Her fingertips touched the spikes on her choker. "What gave it away?"

The crowd snickered.

She took the bottle and spun it. Daisy was her victim, sitting between Justin and Theodore. "Please tell me you're a lesbian. That's your truth."

Daisy placed a hand on her own chest, eyebrows apologetically drawn. "I'm taken."

"Shit!" Emily's outburst was comical, not serious at all. In fact, her whole demeanor was very playful.

Daisy's spin landed on Theodore. "I dare you to kiss your boyfriend, right here, in front of us."

That word sent Theodore's heart up to his throat. "He's not my boyfriend," he immediately retaliated.

"We've been over this," Hannah interrupted. "He either takes the title and visits our apartment, or he can never show his face there again."

He felt the burning attention of the circle focused on him. When had that conversation taken place? He didn't remember it at all. He remembered Hannah arguing with Laith about it, but he hadn't exactly accepted those terms. Unless, of course, they'd rehashed it in the kitchen while Theodore had showered. He didn't dare move his eyes away from her, in case Laith was watching. He'd rather not know.

"Is that how it went?" His voice was small, but it didn't quiver. It took a lot to keep it steady.

"That's how it went."

His eyes bounced over to Justin. Surprisingly, he didn't find Justin looking back at him, but staring at Laith's end of the circle instead. He swallowed thick.

"So you two *are* together," Emily jumped in.

Theodore couldn't look at her.

"It's a conversation," Laith explained. The awkwardness in his tone was crystal clear to Theodore, but he knew the others might not be able to tell so easily. He'd just grown accustomed to the way Laith covered things up, mainly how he really felt. "We haven't decided anything yet," was Laith's verdict, which brought to mind the simple fact that, as far as Theodore knew, there wasn't anything to decide.

"I thought you liked him." The pain in Hannah's voice perfectly mirrored how Theodore felt about the whole situation. He could tell exactly where this topic was going and knew he had to kill it right here or risk bursting into tears. He'd already thought about this for way too long; Streisand's wasn't the place for this discussion.

"Okay!" His voice ended up a little too high, but all in all, it conquered the circle's attention, which was the point. With a breath in his throat, he met Laith's eyes. "Okay." This time, he whispered it.

A hand helped him uncross his legs and move up to stand on his knees, pressing gingerly over the ground for balance. Nadia was the only person between him and Laith, so the crawl to him was brief.

Laith watched him come over without a word, leaning on his right hand. He sat with his legs stretched in Jessie's direction, turned to face the middle of the circle. Theodore was mindful to keep his knees away from Laith's fingers. He carefully leaned forward and closed his eyes. The moment their faces met, his heart jumped, cheeks burning with the knowledge that the whole circle was watching them right now. If there happened to be any vocal responses to this, he couldn't hear it over the loud gushing of his own pulse. It was brief—a chaste peck on the lips just to remember what they felt like. He pulled away before Laith could do anything, specially touch his face the way he liked to. That was too private; he didn't want the others to see it.

Green eyes watched him low, staring at his mouth, but he couldn't do it, not in front of a crowd. This was enough. Breathing in, he turned around and crawled back to his spot.

It was only when he sat down that he saw everyone's reactions. His eyes first landed on Emily, who sat directly across from him, but couldn't read the emotion on her face. There *was* one, he knew that much, but couldn't figure out what it was, or if it was even good. It probably wasn't. Next to her, Jessie grinned wide. It was genuine, with rosy cheeks and hands clasped together, even if half-hidden in her lap. Hannah and Justin had pretty much the same look on their faces, small smiles that had come straight from the heart, warm and sweet. Nadia and Daisy were the only ones that he couldn't glance at without making his observation far too obvious.

He quietly spun the bottle. It landed on Justin. "I want you to kiss the prettiest girl here." That dare flew out of his mouth as the first comprehensible thought his mind could put together. It took him a full second to realize what he'd done, eyes wide. He promptly glanced at Justin, who stared back just as shocked. His lips parted to apologize and come up with something else, but nothing left them. Instead, he watched Justin pass the circle a glance.

"Does Laith count?"

His joke made the girls snicker.

"Why don't you grab my crotch and maybe change your mind about that?" Laith's eyebrows were drawn, but his response was clearly humorous.

"That's very cisgender of you," Justin remarked.

"C'mon," Jessie jumped in, ponytail moving as she tilted her head. "Don't you think anyone here is pretty?"

Justin opened his mouth to reply, but immediately closed it again. He did that a couple of times while looking for an answer, kind of like a fish out of water, speechless. Theodore could practically see the synapsis in his brain, the many thoughts that crossed his mind, all completely unspoken. When he finally looked away from her, it was to stare at Laith next, still wordless. The two shared a very knowing look that received a nod from Laith.

"She's the supermodel," Laith added.

Suddenly, Theodore couldn't breathe.

"Supermodel?" That word curled Jessie's lips into a hesitant smile.

"Yeah. I called you a supermodel earlier, but it didn't stick 'cause Justin didn't know you," Laith clarified. "Now he does."

A big breath left Theodore's lungs; he couldn't be more relieved that Laith hadn't ratted him out. Then again, he didn't think Laith would; that just didn't seem much like him. The only person Theodore had ever seen him shit-talk was Ryan, who'd definitely deserved it.

"That's so cheesy, it sounds like a pickup line." Jessie's tone was so humorous that she practically laughed her words out. "If you were straight, I would've slapped you."

"If I were straight, I would probably have liked that."

The two grinned at each other. This wavelength was really strange to witness.

"Okay, I'm going to kiss girls now," Justin quickly announced, holding his palms up in the air. "But just so y'all know—I'll kiss your cheeks."

"That's a chickenshit move," Emily promptly rebutted. "You can't go around kissing everyone's faces. Theo told you to only kiss the prettiest one."

"What if you're all tied?"

"Impossible. You must have a type."

"At this point, I think he's game for whoever," Laith cut in. "I've never seen him make out with anyone."

"I usually do that away from you. We all do. Have you seen *Emily* make out with anyone?"

"That's not the point. I know *she's* getting pussy, but are *you*?"

"Okay." Theodore held out his hands, sitting between the two. "I revoke my dare."

"No, you don't," Emily corrected. "It's already done."

"Then, Jessie," Justin raised his voice. The hint of frustration in it was new, something Theodore would've never guessed. "Can I kiss you?"

She grinned. "Sure."

Justin crossed the circle and planted a peck on her lips, infinitely briefer than the kiss before it. The whole thing was very quick. Within the same minute, he was back in his spot, taking the bottle for a spin. It landed on Nadia. "I dare you to tell Emily she's a cunt."

The entire circle stared at him.

"Whoa, what the fuck?" Emily scowled.

"Um…" Nadia shifted nervously, hands clasped together. Instead of addressing Emily at all, she reached for the bottle and used the cap to pour herself a shot. Her solo cup still had beer in it.

"Why? I was just stating the rules of the game," Emily defended.

"No, you're—" Justin shook his head, eyes down at his own cup. The whole time she spoke to him, he refused to meet the stare. "You're putting me on the spot." His voice was small, shoulders tense.

Emily relaxed. "I'm sorry. I didn't think a stupid game would get to you."

Especially considering nothing ever got to him. If she truly didn't know how he felt about her, then his reaction must've seemed bizarre. Theodore wished they were sitting closer, so he could try and cheer Justin up a bit.

In utter silence, Nadia screwed the cap back on the bottle and lay it on its side. Emily stopped her before she could spin it. "No, it's Laith's turn."

"No, it isn't," Laith rebutted.

Their eyes met.

"Everyone already got their chance to play, except for you. She'll give you a dare, so we can start round two."

"Part of the fun is waiting for it to happen."

"I'm tired of waiting. No one's drinking."

"What happens on round two?" Theodore asked.

Emily glanced at him next. "It's a round of dares. Every time we close a cycle, meaning all players get to play, the game gets more interesting. I want Laith to go next, so he can close the cycle."

"We could let Nadia spin and see if it falls on him."

"That's a one in eight chance."

"But it's still a chance."

They held the stare.

Clearing her throat, Nadia turned to Laith. "I want you to tell us your favorite thing about everyone here."

Well, then. She'd broken the tie.

"As a group, you mean?"

"No, your favorite thing about each person here."

Laith nodded. "Okay. Well, I've only known you for a day, but my favorite thing about you is probably how sweet you are. If you were a color, you'd be pink."

Nadia smiled at him.

Laith turned to Jessie next. "You have great tits. That's my favorite thing about you."

She shoved him on the leg, wearing a big grin on her face, nose tinted red. "You can't say that!"

"You're right, sorry." Laith laughed. "I mean you're pretty. Beautiful, even. Drop-dead gorgeous!"

The circle snickered.

"Okay, that's better."

"Emily, you're a bitch. That's *my* favorite thing about you."

"Asshole." She grinned.

"Hannah, you're a badass. Next time you hit the gym, call me up so I can show you how to lift right."

Hannah squinted humorously. "If the dare had been for me to fight you one-on-one, I would've taken you down in ten seconds."

"Good thing that's not what it was, huh?"

She scoffed.

"Justin, you sell the best weed I've ever had."

Justin smiled, eyes downcast. It was clear he was still upset, and being unable to comfort him broke Theodore in two.

"Daisy, I don't know you very well either, but I can tell you have balls of steel."

That put a strange look on her face. "What does that mean?"

"You'll figure it out. Theo."

His heart stopped. Laith glanced him down for a moment, deliberating on what to say. He held a breath.

"You're also gorgeous." Laith took the bottle and spun it.

That was... it? His shoulders drooped. Oh.

"Wait, that's *it*?" Jessie interrupted, putting his thoughts into words. "That's *all* you're gonna say about him?"

Laith passed her a glance. "The dare was to say only one thing about each of you."

"Yeah, your *favorite* thing."

"I was just saying what came to mind first."

That wasn't true.

"Then you didn't do the dare right."

The bottle landed on Daisy.

"That's ancient history." With that, Laith turned to address the crowd. "So, our goal for this round is to make everyone drink as much as possible, which means giving them dares they would absolutely never do. For example, Daisy, I dare you to choose two people to make out with you right now."

"At the same time?" she asked.

"Yeah."

Daisy glanced at Nadia first, then at the rest of the circle. "Well... I choose my girlfriend and Emily, because I think that's the only choice I have."

"Emily, what do you say?"

Her eyes bounced from Laith to the two girls and back, reluctant. "I know I'm supposed to decline this and make her drink, but I can't, in good conscience, pass this up."

Laith groaned. "Okay then, Nadia, what do *you* say?"

She held Daisy's stare. "I mean, if Daisy thinks it's okay..."

"Are you fucking serious?"

"Laith, can you take five?" Justin interrupted, back to his normal self. The humor in his voice brought wind to Theodore's lungs. "Let them do their thing, bro."

"Dude, the whole reason I said that was 'cause she's in a relationship!"

"Yeah, and now she's gonna kiss her girlfriend." Justin motioned to the girls in question. "Ladies, please."

Suddenly, Emily's demeanor changed, from highly interested to deeply suspect. She shot daggers at her friend, eyes narrowed. "Wait a minute. I change my mind." She glanced at Daisy next. "I'm sorry, but you'll have to drink."

Daisy noticed the strange atmosphere and the glares, but decided against bringing them up and simply downed her shot in silence. It caused Theodore to wonder if Justin's interest in watching the three-way kiss was genuine, or if he'd only said that because he knew it'd compel Emily to switch sides. Either way, the game was back on track.

From there, the dares only grew more outrageous. Daisy dared Jessie to make out with one of the girls, Jessie dared Justin to go skinny dipping, Justin dared Nadia to do a backflip, Nadia dared Hannah to sing her favorite song for the whole party to hear it and Hannah dared Emily to bench press her. In every instance, the receiver of the dare took the shot rather than attempt the dare, either because they were too self-conscious to do it, or in Nadia and Emily's case, because they physically couldn't.

Emily's turn landed on Laith. "I dare you to fuck a stranger in this party."

Laith disinterestedly looked around. That was definitely something he'd done before, so Theodore wasn't sure what the point of her dare was. Did she want him to leave for a while? Did she want to see him with somebody else? Did she want *Theodore* to see him with somebody else? If that was the case, then it wouldn't hurt; he'd seen Laith with a stranger before and he'd felt nothing about it. Sure, he'd been drunk and numb, but even remembering it now, all he felt was shame for having ruined Laith's evening. It *was* his signature move, but it didn't mean he had to like it.

"Right now?" Hannah asked.

"Yeah, right now."

Laith passed his best friend a glance. In silence, he took a sip of his water.

"Why aren't you having a shot?" Jessie questioned.

"I'm on a cleanse. It's a hippie thing."

"He's on pills," Emily corrected. The way she'd said that made it sound like he'd taken drugs, not prescription. "Now give Theo a dare," she urged.

Their eyes met.

"I dare you to sing us one of your songs."

Bastard. Theodore reached for the bottle and poured himself a shot.

"What kind of pills?" Jessie asked.

"Why? Are you interested?"

She shrugged.

Theodore was so numb that he barely felt the rum burn down his throat this time.

"You just don't look high."

"Oh, but I am, except that has nothing to do with it. I'm on prescription."

Her mouth opened in the shape of an O, but the surprise didn't last long. It quickly morphed into realization as she glanced at Laith's friends. "Are *all* of you high?"

"Yep. Like I said, if you're looking for good weed, Justin's your man."

Justin tugged on the collar of his flannel, proud. "I mean, I could be your man anyway, but you know. I'll be your weed man too."

"Oh, ballsy." Emily's eyebrows raised. "He thinks he has game."

"I do. She let me kiss her."

"It was a dare."

"She still could've said no, but she didn't. I'm a catch."

"I mean," Jessie cut in, gathering their attention, "you *are* the cutest one here."

"See?"

Theodore spun the bottle.

"Whatever helps you sleep at night, sweetie." Emily gave her friend a tilt of the head and a condescending smile.

"Don't mind Emily," Laith faux whispered, addressing Jessie but holding his best friend's stare. "She's jealous."

"Why would I be jealous?"

"Oh, man." Laith leaned back on a hand. "I don't even know where to start with that one."

The bottle landed on Emily.

"Emily, I dare you to make out with Justin right now."

The circle stared at Theodore.

"And I mean really give him the work; show us all you've got. I want you to make it so hot and heavy that we'll all need to take a break from this game." As he talked, Emily's brows shot up her forehead, lips curling into a wide smile.

"You know," Laith cut in, cup of water in hand, "that's actually the natural progression of the game. Round three is about dares that you want to see happen."

"So you wanna see this." Emily smirked.

"Who doesn't?"

"So this is round three?" Jessie asked. "I thought Theo had to land on Nadia."

"Nadia already had her turn. Laith closed the cycle by giving Theo a dare," Emily explained.

"Okay, so make out with him right now," Theodore urged.

"Alright, alright." Up on her knees, Emily crawled to her friend. Theodore couldn't really see her face from where he sat, only the anxiety that blew Justin's eyes wide and shot his eyebrows up into his hairline. He leaned back as she approached, terrified. She pushed his knee out of the way. "C'mon, quit acting like I'm the boogeyman. You're looking at me like I'm about to kill you."

Justin couldn't even reply. Actually, his silence halted her approach.

"What? Should I take the shot?"

"No." That word slipped out so fast that Justin practically spat it. "No, I mean..." His shoulder bounced, head cocking sideways.

That was enough for her to resume her advances. With the way he sat, she had to lean over him to reach his face, holding herself up with a hand by his hip, flat on the grass. The other one held him by the back of the neck as she closed the gap between them. His eyes slipped shut, body frozen otherwise. There was tongue, a quick flash before it disappeared into his mouth. He followed her lead, mirroring the movement of her jaw, meeting with her every time. The crowd hollered as they kissed, whistling loud, fingers snapping.

It was wild. Watching those two, Theodore kind of wanted to make out too. Not with them, though. Well... no, Emily was terrifying.

When she was done, she pushed Justin away with a hand and turned around. First, she wiped her face and fixed her hair, then crawled back to the spot directly across from Theodore. Their eyes met as she sat down and the look she gave him chilled him to the bone. It wasn't malicious, but mischievous with a smirk to really drive home the fact that, if the bottle ever landed on him, he was done. He was *fucked*. Her smudged lipstick with the elongated corners perfectly intact only served to make her look even scarier somehow, like a killer clown on the loose. Incidentally, that might be what drew Justin to her. She was definitely a lot more unhinged than Theodore had thought.

Without a word, she reached into the center of the circle and spun the bottle. "Just to make things clear," she started, passing everyone a glance, "denying the dare this time is worth two shots in a row."

The bottle landed on Nadia. Even without looking directly at her, Theodore could see how her body straightened up.

"I want you to tell us your wildest sex fantasy. It might not be something you'd ever actually do, but it's something that fascinates you. If anything, something you'd love to watch."

Theodore turned to see Nadia's face grow beet red.

"Um... I guess..." She threw her girlfriend a quick glance. "Double penetration, I think is—is a mystery to me. I don't know how they do it."

"How the two guys stack up on each other?" Emily asked.

"No, like... how someone could even handle that. It's just so crazy."

"I can't say I have any experience with it, so I'm not of much help, but if anyone is..." Emily trailed off, shoulder bouncing.

The circle stared up into space, thoughtful.

"Practice, probably," Laith suggested. "Sex is always about practice."

"Yeah. I bet if you start small and work your way up, you'll be able to do it too," Jessie added.

That comment set Nadia's face on fire. "I don't wanna do it! I just think it's crazy!"

"I'm just saying." Jessie shrugged. "Laith's probably right."

"Yeah, he *would* know something about that." Emily stared at him.

"Are you talking specifics? 'Cause I do know a lot about that, but I thought it was obvious."

"Oh, it's just that taking someone's virginity shares the same concept. That's what I mean," Emily explained.

Theodore felt all air leave his lungs. Paralyzed, he watched Laith's eyebrows slowly furrow while the rest of the group stared at him. Laith was the only one who didn't, thus the only one he could look at.

"I don't think I've ever done that," Laith told her.

The circle glanced between Theodore and Laith. Even Emily, indicating her point to Laith.

"Oh. No, he had a threesome the day before."

Every pair of eyebrows lifted while Theodore's soul exited the current astral plane. He no longer existed at this party.

"Are you serious?" Emily spoke with a big, yet shocked grin.

"Yeah. We ran into each other in the dark room."

Oh god, Laith didn't know. Oh my god, he didn't know. Theodore's heart hammered into his ribs.

The group responded with shock.

"Your first time was a threesome?!" Jessie practically shouted.

There was no way he could answer that, especially as the target of everyone's undivided attention. He could barely even breathe.

"Wow, who would've thought." Emily grinned.

"Couldn't be me," Nadia commented.

All the other girls agreed with her.

"I didn't..." His brain scrambled to make sense, pulse racing in his ears. "They weren't both on me; I was in the middle."

"Of course." Laith raised a shoulder.

"How do you figure?" Jessie asked.

"He was with a couple. It's etiquette."

"Do you know them?"

Laith glanced at Theodore, but as soon as their eyes met, he looked away. Everything about this was a nightmare. "I know everyone, Jess."

Theodore touched Nadia's arm. "Please, spin the bottle," he whispered.

She gave him an understanding look before doing it. Unfortunately, as it spun, the group continued to talk.

"We know you two slept together last week," Daisy pensively commented. "Which means the threesome happened on Friday, then."

Laith nodded.

"Well, I remember when Theo told us about it, just before leaving for Justin's farm. He told us he'd run into you."

"Yeah. It was, uh… unexpected, really. I didn't think I'd see him there."

"He was with Hwan and Marquis."

The circle went silent. The bottle slowly landed on Daisy, but Theodore and Nadia were the only ones paying attention to it. She failed an attempt to cut the conversation short by addressing her girlfriend; Daisy held a palm up in the air, clinging to her train of thought. "He never told us he'd slept with them."

Theodore was about to throw up.

"Yeah, I remember that," Hannah added. "He only talked about sleeping with *you*. If I recall correctly, he even mentioned something about all of us being even now, like, no longer virgins. He said that after you."

"He probably didn't want you guys to know about the threesome."

Okay, so Laith was in denial. Thank god for that.

The girls weren't, though. They all looked very confused, unsure what the truth was. Unable to speak a single word, Theodore touched Nadia's arm, which prompted her to turn to Daisy and speak up again.

"I dare you to tell me what kind of things you like in the bedroom."

That worked like a charm. It severed Daisy's thought process with surprise, dark eyes quickly finding her girlfriend, wide. She had much bigger fish to fry now, unrelated to Theodore's virginity. "I'm sorry?"

"What kind of things you like," Nadia explained. "You know, what your favorite things are."

"Like…?"

Nadia shrugged, cheeks growing warm. Nothing else left her.

"You can say oral," Emily jumped in. "It's okay."

Both girls stared at her wide-eyed. In response, she simply grinned.

"Disgusting." Laith clicked his tongue. "Spin the bottle, Daisy."

"Oh, shut up." There was so much humor in Emily's tone that she almost even laughed. "We've been talking about butt sex all day!"

"So why change the subject?"

"She hasn't even answered," Nadia defended.

"You really wanna hear this." Daisy sounded perfectly surprised. "Okay, well, besides what Emily said, I like to make you feel good. I like to see you enjoy yourself."

Nadia cast her eyes down in embarrassment, smiling a bit.

"You too, huh." Laith smirked.

"What can I say?" Daisy shrugged, reaching for the bottle. "I'm a giver."

"And you have every right to be," Emily added.

"You're—" That word left Theodore's mouth without any thought attached to it, an impulse spewed out into the universe.

The circle stared at him, but he had nothing else to say. His brain was currently engulfed in fog; he didn't even know what he'd intended to bring up in the first place.

"Are you talking to me?" Laith asked, sincerely confused.

"No."

The bottle landed on Justin.

"I dare you to tell us what you thought about that kiss. You seemed... put off by it," Daisy told him.

Oh, he remembered it now. His non-thought was suddenly fleshed out before his very eyes, the continuation of his unspoken accusation—*you're* not *a giver.* If he didn't count the last couple of times, it was very clear to him that *he* was the giver; the one who always started it, who got his hands dirty and actually made it happen, while Laith just sat back and relaxed. It'd been different today, and of course, when he'd first asked Laith to top him, but for the majority of the time, Laith had been a real bottom—in spirit, of course; he'd only literally bottomed that one time.

Wait, *was* it the majority? That time on his bed and the one on his couch made two, plus topping him made three, which—wait a minute, it was a tie; three to three. Only if that very first time even counted in his favor, when he hadn't even made Laith cum. Shit, was Laith a lot more involved than he'd thought? Had Laith been giving him an easier time due to his lack of experience? He didn't want that. He wanted the Laith who fucked strangers in the dark room without asking their names first. On second thought, that was probably the Laith from today, who'd lain him down, turned him around and later fucked his face. Damn, maybe Laith *was* a giver after all.

Justin talked, but Theodore couldn't understand a single word that left him. He looked nervous, moving his beanie with a hand, avoiding eye contact. It reminded Theodore of that time in his truck, when they'd talked about his massive crush on Emily. Oh, right—Daisy had just asked him about the kiss. Theodore blinked, trying to focus through the high.

"—someone so fierce before. She's definitely uh, passionate."

"It's okay to say I'm the best kisser you've ever had." Emily proudly grinned.

Justin's lips curled up, but never actually formed a fully-fledged smile. "You'd be right to say that."

The girls d'awed.

Before anyone had time to say anything else, Justin spun the bottle. He kept his eyes on it the entire time, watching it land on Hannah. "So apparently, you're a bodybuilder," he commented, facing her. "I would've never known."

"I'm not a bodybuilder; I just love martial arts. I've been taking Okichitaw for almost ten years now."

"I'm guessing that's a type of martial arts."

"Yes. It's from the first nations in Canada where my dad's from. He teaches it in his gym."

"Shit." Justin's eyebrows bounced, eyes half-lidded with his intoxication. "He must be really strong. You two probably are; you've only ever lost at arm-wrestling once. You're incredible."

She shrugged, not in an attempt to downplay her own strength, but to avoid showing off.

"Can you bench press anyone here?"

His question prompted her to glance around the circle, appraising everyone's measurements. "Daisy, Nadia and Emily would be easy, since they're so small. Theo would be next, then you, then Jessie. I don't think I could do Laith."

"So Jessie's your limit."

"I guess. I'm assuming she's heavier than you and Theo, because you two are twigs, honestly."

"Hey, I'm all muscle!"

She glanced him down. "How much can you lift?"

Justin held the stare, unable to answer the question. He clearly didn't hit the gym. Theodore didn't either, but he wasn't about to make a joke out of himself and pretend he did. It was evident that most people could knock him out without having to try very hard.

"Yeah, that's what I thought." She clicked her tongue.

"Bench press Laith, then. That's your dare."

She squinted. "I'll do Jessie instead." With that, she leaned over to catch a glimpse of her friend, who sat behind Emily. "Is that okay with you?"

"Yes! I've actually wondered this for a long time, but I've never had the balls to ask."

Hannah grinned. The two girls got up in unison.

"Okay, fine; I'll let you do Jessie, then," Justin commented, as if that would've changed anything.

As Hannah instructed Jessie on how they'd go about it, a movement in the crowd caught Theodore's attention. People came and went all the time, but one of them seemed to stop dead at the foot of the stairs, which was what stood out to him. When he glanced over, he saw Hwan standing in the middle of the crowd, staring at Laith. Theodore didn't know why, but Hwan's presence compelled him to get up and excuse himself. Ironically, he had to step over Laith's legs on the way, and as soon as he did, Hwan's eyes moved to him instead.

Chapter 11

Rats in the backyard

The feelings start to rob
One wink at a time.

- MGMT, *Little Dark Age*

*Hwan wasn't here alone, of course; he just happened to have fallen behind. When Theo-*dore joined him, he caught sight of the others up ahead. They were close enough that the sound of his voice caused them all to turn and greet him. "Hey, guys!"

"Hey!"

"Theo!"

"And the prey escapes!"

V's comment put a funny look on his face, confused. He cocked his head as she toked on her cigarette. "What do you mean?"

"You're the talk of the tunnels," Marquis explained, speaking around a smirk. "We all know about your little ride with the Great White this afternoon. They say you went somewhere private after the subway."

The group's attention grew heavier. On the one hand, having the un-derground take notice of his involvement with Laith was weirdly validating, but on the other, it made his sex life a lot easier to be scrutinized.

"They're calling you prey now," V added. The look in her eyes was a lot more malicious than anything Laith had ever done to him.

"Wow, news travels fast." He could feel sheepishness seep into his tone. "That happened only a few hours ago."

"Is that why he's here?" Hwan asked, eyes locked over his shoulder. Theodore didn't have to look to know Hwan still stared at Laith. "'Cause he doesn't come here anymore—or he *didn't*."

"Yeah, we were in the neighborhood. He hasn't been here in a while."

"You know he sold his soul to the Ponies, right?" Marquis squinted. Theodore stared at him. "Yeah, he works for them. You know that."

Everybody knew that; it was the birth of Laith's notoriety. Marquis must be referring to something else.

"That's not what I mean; he's branded. He gave up on the Alvorada."

Branded... Was that in reference to his tattoo?

"That's just what he does." Hwan's voice was low and bitter. "He doesn't know loyalty. He'll switch sides until he drops dead."

"Is that what branded means?"

"He's probably gonna be loyal to the Ponies now," V remarked, practically speaking over him. She addressed Hwan with sharp eyes, fingers flicking ash off her cigarette. "Actually loyal, or he wouldn't have gone through the trouble of getting branded. It's the first time he does it."

"He's only loyal to himself. Yeah, the mob is paying his bills, but that doesn't mean he's suddenly loyal to them now. He's only on their side as long as they're of use to him. It's just gonna be a much harsher parting when he finally decides to do it."

"If he can," Marquis added, "which is unlikely."

"I didn't realize that's what that was," Theodore spoke absently, engulfed in thought. His mind wrapped around a clear picture of Laith leaning against the door frame on Justin's farm, showing off the dead pony on his upper arm. "That he was switching sides."

"Well, the Ponies are different from other factions," Dylan explained. "We all have access to their goods and services, so they don't really have a community, just clients. Branded Ponies are the people employed by Burman."

"That's why he's still hanging out with the Alvorada," Marquis jumped in. "He doesn't have a new family; he just switched his old one for cold corporate greed. Branded Ponies don't last long in their old social groups. At least, the ones I've heard of."

"Emily would never give him up."

That pulled Hwan's attention, eyes staring at him now. "Who is she? You mentioned her earlier, over the phone."

"You guys called?" Marquis asked.

"Yeah. Theo wanted to ask me about Laith."

Just as Theodore opened his mouth to answer, a thought crossed his mind, that Laith might not want him to do it. He remembered their conversation on Justin's porch, how worried his friendship with Hwan made Laith, afraid he'd expose too much of his personal life. He still had to say something, though, so he turned around to point at Emily; it was the alternative he found not to expose her relationship with Laith.

The circle sitting on the grass watched as Hannah powerlifted Jessie over her head, except for Laith, who stared at Theodore and the others instead. Meeting Laith's eyes all across the yard felt like being struck by lightning.

"That's Emily," he mumbled, unable to move.

"I've seen them at the DP together," Marquis commented. "The two of them and the redhead."

"Justin," Hwan added.

That prompted Theodore to turn back around. "You know him?"

"We've never talked, but he's dealt to Qasim and the Hollywood boys. Probably still does."

"Does Laith know that?"

"What, who he deals to?"

"That he dealt to Qasim."

Hwan shrugged, eyes locked over Theodore's shoulder.

"I think I made out with her once." V's tone was absent, a thought spoken out loud.

"With Emily?" Marquis asked.

"Yeah. She looks familiar."

A hand touched Theodore's arm, but V wasn't looking at him. "She's a lesbian, right?"

"Bisexual."

"Huh." V's hand dropped, eyebrows drawn hard together. "So that's her name."

"You didn't know?"

"I didn't remember; it was a while ago. A month, at least. She was alone."

"Yeah, they split up to meet people, like you guys do."

"Right."

A long, heavy sigh left Hwan as he turned his face aside, eyebrows furrowed with vexation. Before Theodore could ask what the problem was, somebody came up next to him, towering over the entire group. The rich scent that hung around Laith confirmed his suspicions. Laith stood with his shoulders pushed back and his hands in his pockets, staring fixedly at Hwan first, then glancing around the circle next.

"You guys seem to be having fun." Laith's tone was friendly, non-confrontational. "Can I join?"

Still, Hwan refused to look at him.

"We were talking about Emily," Theodore quickly explained, before anyone else had the chance to. "Apparently, V knows her."

"I don't *really* know her; we just met at the DP once." V shrugged.

Laith briefly glanced her down. "I wouldn't be surprised, I mean, if you were more her type, I'd think she thought you up."

Huh, funny he should say that because, staring at the two of them side-to-side, Theodore noticed just how much they had in common. Besides smoking and dressing the same way, of course; most of the rats did that. No, their similarities ran deeper; they were both tall with sharp light eyes and a tough air about them, intimidating, even if they were really nice people on the inside.

In response to Laith's comment, V scoffed. "Cute, but I don't think she needs a wingman."

"I've never been her wingman. I'm just saying I believe you."

"Did you need something?" Hwan cut in, finally staring at Laith. Actually, he shot daggers at him, while Laith simply shrugged.

"I'm just hanging out, bro."

"Don't—" Hwan bit his tongue, head shaking. "Don't talk like that."

"Like what? I've always talked this way."

"No, you haven't." Dark eyes narrowed under a scowl, sharp with pain. "You didn't talk like that at all."

"When I was twelve, you mean?" Laith's tone was finally harsh, eyebrows furrowed. "Man, you've got a good memory, 'cause I don't fucking remember what the fuck I sounded like back then."

"I can tell you you didn't sound like a shitty impersonation of somebody else. You sounded like *you.*"

"A twelve-year-old who didn't even have a personality yet."

"You still don't."

"Hey," Theodore jumped in, holding out a hand as his heart hammered, "we're playing truth or dare over there. Why don't you guys join us?"

"I'll pass," Hwan mumbled, no longer looking at Laith.

"How about we have some beers and then meet you guys later?" Marquis suggested. His tone was very obviously trying to be friendly, words spoken around a forced smile.

"That sounds good." Theodore mirrored his smile. "We'll be right there, in the circle."

"You mean the circle that's coming straight for us?" V asked.

"What?"

She signaled what she meant with a bounce of the brow and a nod, eyes fixed over his shoulder. Before he could turn around, he first heard the girls' voices, much closer than they should be. Then, he immediately found himself swarmed by a crowd of his own friends, who rushed to Hwan and the others with excited greetings and exaggerated hugs.

They must have noticed his prolonged absence, plus Laith's, and had decided to come over. Even Justin and Emily were here, despite their lack of connection with these guys. Justin stood next to Laith, not really seeming to know anyone—which made sense, since they weren't the Alvorada—while Emily stared at V with a slight scowl on her forehead, a look that almost recognized her. V held the stare perfectly straight.

This party was much different than anything Theodore had ever experienced. He'd never been surrounded by so many people he knew, who also knew each other. Laith and Hwan clearly didn't see eye to eye, but in the middle of a crowd, they didn't have to exist near each other; Hwan moved to one end of the circle while Laith stayed in the other. It was obvious that neither one of them wanted to make a scene, or they already would have.

The girls came and went in the crowd, moving according to the conversations that went on around them. Jessie was the only one who spent most of her time with Justin and Laith, even if she did go to Hwan and Marquis to ask them if they'd had, in fact, slept with Theodore. They didn't respond, but glanced at Theodore instead, waiting for his input. Stricken breathless, he couldn't unscramble his brain for an answer, so his friends both turned back to Jessie and said yes. She—and some of the others around—could barely believe it. They buried the couple in questions, some of which were answered, but most of which weren't. The fanfare didn't last long, though; as soon as they noticed their questions were being ignored, they changed the subject.

At one point, Emily approached V. She crossed the circle from the edges, outside of the crowd. Catching sight of her, V left the tumult as well. They spoke near Hwan, so Theodore couldn't really hear them. Still, he watched her stiff shoulders as she talked; with her back to him, that was all he could really see. V stared at her with much softer eyes than usual, head tilted down, hands in her pockets. She didn't say much, but the little that she did say managed to relax Emily's shoulders, bit by bit. Seeing that, part of Theodore wanted to rip the two apart, while another part of him wanted them to kiss.

Jessie, Justin and Laith ended up getting along very well. The synergy between them was strangely nice; they shared the same type of humor and bounced off each other with incredible ease. Theodore had never really seen Laith and Justin hang out by themselves, but assumed that, when Emily and Ryan weren't making things weird, they got along just fine. Justin had said that Laith didn't get deep with him, or anybody for that matter, which was evident in his humor and general silliness; he was all jokes and dumb antics. Jessie's predisposition to have fun helped their conversation flow; she built on Laith's jokes and kept the laughter coming. Justin was the only one who didn't make jokes per se, because the stuff he normally said was already humorous; he was funny without even realizing it.

Theodore moved around a lot. Since he knew everyone, it was easy to get roped into on-going conversations that happened with or without him, about him or not. He came and went as his friends called for him, pulling him by the arm for a question or two, tapping him on the shoulder for his opinion on something or other. It was the most included he'd ever felt in absolutely anything.

Emily eventually came back, not to hang out, but to tell them it was time to go. Laith and Justin promptly rebutted that, saying it wasn't nearly late enough, which Theodore confirmed with a quick glance at his watch—9:30 p.m. Sure, they'd been here for almost five hours, but the night was still young. Plus, Jessie and the others hadn't been here for nearly as long. Emily brushed that off and announced her departure, because apparently, Ryan wanted to speak to her. That name killed the mood.

Without another word, Laith and Justin turned to bid Jessie goodbye. She clearly didn't understand what was going on, but decided against arguing it. Despite growing up just two houses away from Ryan, she'd never really met him, too young to be in high school with him. Still, his reputation had been rancid enough that most parents in the neighborhood had used him as a cautionary tale, so the seriousness in everyone's demeanor when his name came up must not have surprised her.

She gave the three boys parting hugs and threw in a kiss on the cheek for Justin. "You should call me, you know." She tilted her head, ponytail swinging behind her.

Justin stared at her. "If you're serious, I will. Like, I'm not kidding."

She held out her hand. "Then give me your phone."

As he scrambled to comply, Emily made a quiet exit. If there was any emotion on her face, Theodore couldn't tell; he just watched her leave the crowd for the side of the house. When he turned back to the others, he saw Jessie hand Justin's phone back to him.

"If you're not too busy tonight, maybe we could hang out." Her voice insinuated a lot more than just that, which promptly set Justin's face on fire.

Laith clasped a hand on his friend's shoulder with a big grin on his face. "C'mon, my man. Let's go."

Chapter 12

When a door closes

Forget what I need
Give me what I want
And it should be fine.

- Allie X, *Prime*

The walk to Emily and Ryan's apartment was anything but quiet. Justin buzzed with excitement, talking the entire time. Despite his feelings, he was still very aware that Jessie was Theodore's friend first and made sure to tell him he wouldn't pursue anything if Theodore didn't want him to. That line of reasoning didn't make any sense, though; Jessie was her own person. If she wanted to fool around with Justin, then who the hell was Theodore to object to it? That should be *her* decision to make. The fact that Theodore had introduced the two of them didn't change anything; she owed him nothing. Justin's argument would've only held any water if they were together. "You know you don't have to ask my permission to date her, right? That's weird."

"I just don't want things to be weird between us. Like, if you don't feel comfortable with this, I won't even text her. You're my main guy, you know that. Your friendship means everything to me."

"So do you have a crush on her or on me?" he joked, squinting.

That put a big grin on Justin's face. "I love you, man." A hand ruffled Theodore's hair, which he reacted to by shoving Justin on the side, all in jest. They both laughed as Justin tripped, stumbling drunkenly.

"When's the last time you got laid, bro?" Laith's question was friendly, despite its contents.

"Ah, man, it's been a while. Months, at least."

"Hope you didn't forget how to do it."

130

Justin tutted and shoved Laith on the arm, face red with embarrassment. Laith's sobriety kept him from stepping into the street.

"Can you guys shut the fuck up?" Emily called from up ahead, whipping around to glare back at them. "You're acting like fucking idiots."

"Sorry, Em." Justin's voice was small, eyes down at the sidewalk.

During the rest of the walk, the three of them kept to a different topic— a conscious decision. It was clear that Emily didn't like the previous discussion, a little too jealous of her friends, even if she didn't openly say it. Justin had claimed she wasn't possessive, but Theodore had to disagree; her behavior was crystal clear. As much as she didn't trust anyone with or around Laith, she didn't seem to trust anyone with or around Justin either. It could be because she felt something for them, but it could just as well be her fear of losing them. She was very similar to Ryan in that way, treating her friends as family.

Back home, she told everyone she'd only be a moment and entered the building. The three of them ended up hanging out at the entrance, talking on the sidewalk while waiting for her.

As soon as she was gone, Justin brought Jessie up again, how funny she was and how much fun he'd had at the party. Laith teased him for it, the way anyone teased a friend over a new crush, in good fun. Justin teased him back a bit, poking at his involvement with Theodore, careful not to take it too far. He was gracious, of course, which turned it into a nice time; they talked and laughed as if resuming the antics from the party, only without Jessie now.

Laith casually slung an arm across Theodore's shoulders and pulled him close. He did it as they talked, without so much as a glance, eyes fixed on Justin, who went on and on about a funny joke or a silly anecdote—Theodore wasn't sure. The moment Laith pulled him in, his ears popped and his lungs froze.

The first thought that crossed his mind was a still from last week, when Hwan had done the exact same thing to Marquis. He remembered just how much he'd yearned for that, a nonchalant move that meant absolutely nothing, but had the potential to mean everything. Playing Marquis, he hugged Laith around the waist, arm loose and casual despite his heart rate. He could barely believe this was happening. The incident in the subway had been much different than this, Laith sticking around to make him feel better before a crowd, but maybe not completely unrelated. They must've been growing a lot closer than he'd thought. Certainly not close enough that he could take Laith's hand whenever he wanted, but that he could half-hug him in public and it'd be okay. He had to fight back the urge to snuggle into Laith's side, leaning against him instead, lungs brimming with amber.

"Are you actually gonna call her?" he asked. His question ended whatever topic the other two were talking about; he didn't know what it was and didn't care to know.

Justin glanced at him with a big grin on his face. "Yeah, yeah, of course!"

"I thought you said you were shy. You don't seem very shy about that."

"What?" Laith practically spluttered. "You said you were *shy?* You're the most outgoing motherfucker I know!"

"I'm shy sometimes."

"No, you're not!"

"I'm shy with people I like, okay?"

"No, you—I've literally seen you walk up to a girl, hit on her and come back *very* satisfied with yourself. You're the opposite of shy. I don't even think you know what that word means."

"Yes, I do! *You* don't, but I do. I get shy when... things get serious."

Laith stared at his friend, eyebrows furrowed.

"Oh." Theodore's thoughts left him sans filter. "You're shy in the bedroom."

"It's not that bad," Justin quickly rebutted. "I just get self-conscious about what I'm doing. I worry too much that they're not gonna like it."

"Do they usually like it?"

"Yeah, but I'm always worrying about it!"

"Then stop," Laith suggested. His tone was so matter of fact that it could only be a joke.

Justin stared at him. "Okay, I'll stop. Thanks a lot, bud."

"Don't mention it, friend."

"I think..." Theodore's thoughts slowly came together. "If you ask them to tell you when they don't like something you do, that'd probably help, right? Then you know you're doing well."

Blue eyes glanced off to the side, eyebrows furrowing the slightest bit. "You have a point, but I don't know if I can tell them that. *Let me know when I fuck up.* Like, that's weird."

"No, don't say it like that. Maybe... ask them to tell you what they *do* like. That way, it's more reassuring, I guess."

"I mean..." Justin shrugged. "I just don't wanna make things weird."

"Make it hot, then," Laith proposed. "Turn it into a kink. A validation kink. Tell them it gets you super turned on when they tell you shit like that."

"What if they think it's weird?"

"They won't, if you're not weird about it. If you think it's hot, they'll think it's hot too. If you think it's weird, they'll think it's weird. It's all about confidence."

Justin hummed pensively.

"Plus, you can usually tell when they don't like what you're doing, anyway. You don't need them to spell it out for you," Laith continued. "It's night and day. Figure out what she likes and stick to it."

"I just get in my head, bro. It's been this way forever."

"Then let her lead you." The suggestion left Theodore on impulse, thoughts bouncing back and forth. "You can't fuck up then."

"*If* she's into it," Justin mumbled.

"It's Jessie. You might need to guide her a bit, but other than that, she's a free spirit."

The arm around Theodore's neck shook him a bit, pulling him further into Laith's wing. "He knows what he's talking about, so you should probably listen up."

He yanked the back of Laith's jacket in response, staggering him backwards. "That was literally two years ago! Can you let it go!?"

"Wait, you fooled around?" Justin asked.

"I don't even consider it anything at this point. It was nothing."

"She blew him."

Theodore stared into the side of Laith's face, wide-eyed. "Did she tell you that?"

"Yep."

"Was she good?" Justin cut in.

"It was—I don't know! I have no idea. It's literally been way too fucking long. Just—don't even worry about it, okay? Nothing even happened."

"So was she good or not?"

"Why don't you find out for yourself? It's been two fucking years!"

"Okay, okay." Justin held his palms up. "I'm sorry."

"No, I don't—I'm not upset, I just..." He breathed in. "We're just a guy and a girl who are friends. There's nothing there, I promise."

"Oh, sure." One of Justin's shoulders raised for a half-shrug. "I was just curious."

"You're a pig, is what you are." Laith smirked. "I bet she's better now, after two years of practice."

"I mean, yeah."

"I don't think she's been doing it for two years," Theodore argued. "We've only been partying and stuff for a couple of months. If she'd blown anyone in school, I feel like she'd tell me."

"Shit, I keep forgetting how young you guys are. I'm so fucking old."

"Don't girls usually like older guys, anyway?" Laith asked.

Suddenly, Justin pulled his phone out and checked it. He must've just gotten a message. "Uh." Glancing up, he slid his phone back into his pocket. "Emily wants me to go up, so..."

"Is Ryan still up there?" Laith asked.

"Probably. Why? You're not gonna talk to him, are you?"

"Of course I will. Everyone got the chance to, except for me."

"You're gonna fight." That comment slipped past Theodore's lips.

"I just wanna talk to him," Laith defended.

"It doesn't matter. You're gonna end up fighting."

"So are you two coming up with me?" Justin asked.

"I am."

Theodore hesitated. "Yeah, I guess so."

mmemmemmen

Up in the apartment, the first thing they heard was Emily's disembodied voice announcing her location, muffled by the walls. While Justin closed the front door, Laith led the way, taking the first left into the living room. It looked exactly the same as it had a few hours ago, with no sign of Ryan that Theodore could see. He might not even have left his room at all.

The group found Emily alone in the kitchen, sipping on a glass of water. As soon as Laith realized that, he turned to leave. The decisive way he did it pulled Theodore to follow, not as a conscious response, but as a thoughtless reaction to his exit, always drawn to his side. His chest squeezed. He knew this wasn't good.

Instead of leaving, Laith marched straight to Ryan's room. He'd just mentioned wanting to speak to the guy, so Theodore had no idea why he'd even thought Laith would leave. His brain was broken. When Laith ignored the living room arch for Ryan's room, an instinct inside Theodore pushed him to lean forward and take Laith's arm, holding him back. Wide-eyed, he stared into Laith's face. "I'm coming with you," he declared, only half-aware of what those words meant. Right now, his head didn't really work.

"No, you're not. You already talked to him; now it's my turn."

His lips parted to protest, but Laith was faster.

"I'm not gonna fight him, Theo. It's fine."

"That's not up to you."

"Just trust me, okay?" Laith pulled his arm free.

Theodore didn't necessarily want to let go of it, but it was very difficult to manage himself at the moment; the world wasn't steady and his thoughts weren't clear. His intention was to drag Laith back into the kitchen with the others, yet he ended up watching Laith let himself into Ryan's room instead. Foreboding closed around his throat—nothing good could come out of this. Unable to move, he stood and stared.

Sherry came out of the room still dressed in her skin-tight jumpsuit, burgundy red with a jacket thrown over her shoulders. She always looked like she was about to jump on a runway, even if there was nowhere to go. Her sight was a relief; he had no idea she'd stuck around this long. Still, he would've liked her much better inside Ryan's room with the other two. Somehow, he knew her presence would discourage Ryan from acting on his destructive impulses. Her eyes found him, hand closing the door behind her. "You seem troubled." Her voice was low and smooth, unconcerned.

"They're gonna fight."

"That's what you're worried about?" Her heels clacked as she walked, hitting the hardwood floor. A hand touched him on the shoulder. It didn't imply anything, but still he turned to follow her across the living room. "Tell me what actually concerns you, Theodore."

"That..." His thoughts vanished, and in the vacuum that was his brain, a straight line between his heart and his mouth was created. "That Laith's gonna do to him what he does to me. That he's gonna hold Ryan the way he holds me."

"Why would that be a problem?"

"Because I don't want him to think of Ryan that way."

"You know he doesn't. The possibility that he'll come out of that room in love with Ryan is zero to none."

He turned to her. "How aren't you scared that Ryan's gonna develop feelings for somebody else?"

"That's not something I can control. I know what I mean to him, and even if he does end up developing feelings for someone else, that doesn't have to be connected to our relationship. He can sleep with Laith and still be in love with me."

"Aren't you afraid Laith's gonna steal him from you?"

"People can't steal other people; the only one who can push Ryan away from me is Ryan himself. What we have is a direct result of our actions toward each other, not what anyone else says or does. I'm confident that, if he did feel himself pull away from me, he'd tell me."

His heart ached. "I wish I was confident like you."

She touched his chin. The smile on her face was joyless, somewhere between sad and condescending. "You know you're more important to him than anybody else, right?"

"Am I?"

She nodded.

"Huh." His eyebrows furrowed, gaze dropping. "I wish he'd tell me that."

✶✶✶

As it turned out, what Ryan had needed to tell Emily was that he'd be skipping town soon, or at least, that he'd been considering it. In his mind, that was the only way he could heal. That was what he'd told her, that he needed to *heal.* That was the exact word he'd used.

Staring at his bedroom door, Theodore wondered what kind of healing he meant. He felt trapped in this town, too close to his parents, crushed under Theodore's presence. Yes, *crushed*—his own words. His family suffocated him. *Theodore* suffocated him.

When Emily said that, his first instinct was to laugh, but nothing came from the tingling in his throat. Suffocated. When had Ryan gone from pushing Theodore down the stairs for Carolyn's attention to suffocated by it? He wanted to make a home for himself, to find a place where he belonged and that was fine, but making Theodore out to be some oppressive force in his life was just inaccurate. It wasn't right. The only thing Theodore had ever wanted from him was his friendship; he'd never meant for things to end up the way they had. Still, learning that Ryan wanted nothing to do with him wasn't surprising; he'd put that puzzle together a long time ago. It hurt, but didn't fundamentally change anything. Ryan had never liked him, after all.

His friends talked, but he couldn't really listen. His thoughts drowned them out.

Exactly twenty-one minutes after entering Ryan's room, Laith came back out. The entire time he'd been there, Theodore hadn't heard a single sound escape through the door.

He thought of that one time Laith had slept with Ryan, sneaking upstairs with him when he'd still lived with his parents. Had this been a rerun? He didn't look disheveled or flustered, though, so maybe not. Actually, he looked exactly the same way he had going in.

Their eyes met as Laith carefully closed the door. "Theo, I'm dropping you off. Let's go."

It wasn't nearly late enough for that, but he didn't question it. As soon as he heard the words *let's go*, he left the kitchen in Laith's direction like a little soldier following orders. Laith's voice startled the rest of the group, who approached the kitchen arch to ask him about what had just happened with Ryan. He told them he'd speak about it later and left the apartment.

The elevator allowed Theodore to run a test. It was small enough that if he stood right next to Laith, it wouldn't seem weird, and with the doors closed, he could really assess all the fragrances in the air. Breathing in deeply, the only scent he found was Laith's cologne, rich with spice, encased in amber—nothing else, not even sweat. So he really hadn't slept with Ryan. Theodore touched his jacket sleeve. "Are you two okay now?"

"We've finally reached an agreement."

The elevator chimed every time they passed a floor.

"We will no longer see each other."

That sentence, as simple as it was, lifted a thousand pounds from Theodore's shoulders, lungs free to breathe again. Relief almost buckled his knees and dropped him to the ground. He leaned a shaky hand on the wall. "Are you serious? Why?"

"I'm done trying to reason with him. This is one of those things we will never agree on, apparently. He thinks being close to you is a personal attack, that I can't be both your friend and his, and since I'm not giving you up, I'm essentially picking a side. I'm not, obviously, but if that's the way it has to be, then fine; he's not gonna see me anymore."

"You..." Laith chose *him?* That didn't make sense. His brain couldn't process it at all. "He wants to skip town, you know," he spoke on auto pilot, vomiting the information he'd been given a minute ago without giving it any thought. "He wants to leave."

"Yeah, he told me." Laith shook his head, eyes set straight ahead. "Whatever. I've done all I could, tried everything I could think of, but he just refuses to meet me halfway, so we're done. This is it."

"Are you still friends?"

"No." Laith pushed the elevator door open, passing him a brief glance. "He's cutting me off."

Theodore followed him out. "Is he gonna cut the others off too?"

"I don't know. I don't think so." A hand shuffled through Laith's jacket as he walked, legs long and fast. He covered a lot of ground very quickly, making it difficult for Theodore to keep up. "*I'm* the problem, not them. Well, okay, they're also the problem, but a different kind of problem, whereas I'm the worst-case scenario. I'm the devil torching him from the bleachers; they're the crowd tossing tomatoes. It's not the same." Laith opened the cigarette pack. Glancing inside, he stopped walking. It was so sudden that Theodore almost ran into him. There was only one cigarette left. "I really need to quit."

"So being close to me makes you the devil."

"And a traitor." Laith walked over to the nearest trashcan and threw the pack in along with the last cigarette. "And the worst friend in history," he continued. "What I did was irredeemable, but still he gave me one last chance, 'cause he's such a good guy, Ryan. He's so kind. He was willing to overlook all my faults as long as I promised to never see you again. You know what I told him?"

Theodore stared at him, heart beating out of his chest.

"I told him I'd take you home with me."

Breath escaped him, eyes wide. What the fuck?

"C'mon." Laith nodded at the street, starting down the sidewalk again. "You're spending the night at my place."

"I thought—" Holy shit, he could barely think. "I thought you were dropping me off." His voice reached him from an incredible distance, quiet in his own ears. There was no empirical evidence to suggest this *was* a dream, but still, he couldn't believe it.

"I didn't want to start an argument with the others. It's easier to break the rules and apologize later. I mean, I wasn't even lying; it's just that I'm not dropping you off at *your* place. Whatever they made of that is their own fault."

Early in the evening, the street was dark, but not pitch-black; the blue of the sky was still light, flirting with purple, the moment right between day and night. A cool breeze swept past, ruffling Laith's hair.

"Remember when I quit working for Stanley?" Laith's voice was quieter now, far less enraged. "Before I did that, I'd been working for Burman, putting on a show, getting her to really like me. I wasn't the top dog just yet, but I knew I meant something, that she liked my work and the way I carried out things, so I asked for a raise. She agreed and gave me some more hours, too. That's when my name really started going around; I was assigned more jobs, so more people talked about me. A *lot* more people talked about me. It got to the point where I *knew* it'd get to them—Emily and Ryan—so I quit the record store and told them. Justin already knew, but he's cool about that stuff; he's always known a lot more than the others. He's known my address forever; Ryan and Emily still have no idea where I live. I guess Ryan will never know."

"But... Justin said you guys don't really talk. That he doesn't know a lot about you."

"Sure, he does. We don't talk as much as he talks to Emily, obviously, but he knows stuff. It's just that different people know different things. He knows what I do underground as much as Emily knows what's going on with me."

"What do I know?"

Laith glanced at him. His throat moved with a swallow. "I guess you're about to figure out everything."

Theodore trailed beside him without a single word in his mouth.

"Then again, I think that's what you want," Laith continued. "I think that's what you've *been* after. If not since the beginning, then at least since our first date. Tell me I'm wrong."

"That was a date?" That question left him as if someone had manually pulled it from his throat. His involvement had been minimal—he hadn't meant to do it at all.

"You literally asked me out. You said, and I quote, *have dinner with me.* That's a date, my man."

"I..."

Holy shit.

"If you didn't want me in your bed, you wouldn't have brought me to it. You cancelled my plans, paid for my beer and took me to your place. I'd never received such a crystal-clear message. It's time I stopped fighting against it for your brother's sake. He's out of the picture now, so let's fuck shit up." Laith threw an arm across his shoulder and pulled him close, up against his side, nose buried into his hair. The next part was a whisper. "I'm gonna fuck you so hard you'll forget your own name."

All air left his lungs. He couldn't even see straight, intoxicated by tobacco and amber, hand gripping the back of Laith's jacket as if it were his only lifeline. "Promise?" That was the only thing that came to him. It put a big grin on Laith's face.

Chapter 13

The Queen Bees

Tonight, I can feel your blood pressure rise
Let me crawl up into your mind

- Melanie Martinez, *Detention*

Walking down the hallway to Laith's place, the first thing he noticed was that Laith's gossipy neighbors weren't there anymore. He remembered they were perform-ers, so it made sense they'd be working on a Sunday night, when the crowd was at its largest. He took Laith's arm as a thought occurred in his hazy mind. "Your friends are performing," he blurted out.

"Yes, they are."

"Can we—can we go see them?"

They held the stare.

A smile slowly tugged at the corners of Laith's mouth, incredulous and candid. "You wanna watch them?"

"Yeah. That'd be cool."

Laith's smile fully formed. "Alright, let's do it."

As it turned out, each woman did something different; one was a come-dian and the other was a showgirl. Their acts were entirely separate and didn't even happen in the same place. For some reason, Theodore had thought other-wise. He was already not very bright on a good day, which practically turned his intoxicated brain into useless mush at the moment. Why would they work to-gether? They were neighbors, not business partners.

He wasn't doing well.

Ms. Intervention was the comedy queen; she had a permanent stand-up act five nights out of the week at one of the clubs in the Queen Bees. He remembered catching a glimpse of the name on one of the signs the first time he'd come around, but Hwan and the others hadn't ventured any further than the Unicorn Rave.

Just as Laith had described, The Queen Bees was incredibly chic and massive; a big area with multiple rooms, which Laith called clubs, that starred different queens with different talents. The one where Ms. Intervention performed was dimly lit with red velvet on the walls and smoke lingering in the air. Booths lined the back wall and small, round tables littered the center; some had tall chairs to go with them, some didn't. The stage was small and low, just like the ones in the movies, with a neon sign behind the microphone stand that glowed with the club's name.

By the time he and Laith arrived, the place was already packed, without a single seat available, so they had to watch from the sidelines, standing near the back. The only problem with that was how close they were to the bar, which could get pretty loud at times and completely drown out what the comedian was saying.

On stage stood a tall, black woman in a beautiful yellow dress that hugged her midsection and opened wide all the way down her legs. Her hair was done up in a beehive with shiny ornaments that Theodore could see all the way across the room. Her makeup was also exaggerated, eyeshadow all the way up to her eyebrows, halfway up her forehead.

Laith moved in his peripherals, leaning close. "I didn't know we were coming tonight," he whispered. "If we'd told her, she would've gotten us seats up front."

"I mean, it's not so bad back here."

The crowd laughed.

"When is she coming on?" Theodore asked.

"Who?"

"Ms. Intervention. When is it her turn?"

Laith pointed at the stage with a hand, palm-up. "That's her."

Theodore scowled. Staring at her, he took notice of the shape of her jaw and the proportions of her body, eerily similar to Laith's neighbor's. It was difficult to recognize her with the hair and makeup on, but that was definitely her; her voice and the way she talked gave her away. Damn, she looked incredible.

"She's a drag queen, Theo. Both of them are."

"Oh."

Well, that explained it.

"I thought drag queens were men," he commented.

"Some of them are."

Huh. Alright, then.

Part of the first act was difficult to follow, since he'd caught it halfway through, but as soon as the topic changed, he had no trouble keeping up. The jokes landed time and time again, a consistent stream of clever puns and hilarious punchlines that put the crowd into hysterics. She was really good. Some of her edgier jokes shot Theodore's eyebrows up, shocked at her honesty, at how open she was about her sex life and the gay men she knew. It felt subversive to be here, listening to such dirty language in the middle of a crowd that loved every second of it. His parents would've killed him if they knew. No, they would've called him a degenerate first, *then* killed him. Yeah. The irony wasn't lost on him, though, that his parents didn't condone this kind of stuff while directly making money off it. Hypocrites.

This was one of the best decisions he'd ever made.

Her exit was followed by roaring applause and loud whistling. Waving, she climbed the two steps down the stage and disappeared behind one of the curtains at its side.

With a hand wrapped around Theodore's arm, Laith started across the room, hugging the wall to successfully avoid the crowd.

"Where are we going?"

"We're paying her a visit."

The door that led backstage had a bouncer guarding it, but he made no attempt to keep Laith from walking in. In fact, after passing the two of them a glance, he even stepped aside to let them through. Laith definitely experienced the DP in a much different way than most people did, or more accurately, in a different way than the people who didn't work here. Being branded probably also helped grant him access to pretty much anywhere.

Ms. Intervention was very surprised to see them. She had her own room in the back, full of glittery clothes and feathery boas, with a big mirror and a wide desk, just like an actress. She'd been freshening up when they came in, and as soon as her eyes fell on Laith, her jaw dropped. Theodore saw it through the mirror. Before they could even say anything, she turned to look at them. "You rascal! I had no idea you'd be coming tonight. Why didn't you tell me?"

"I didn't know I was coming either. It was Theo's idea."

"Oh?" She grinned. "That's very sweet of you. I hope you liked it."

"You're very funny. I'm gonna think about that jockstrap story every day of my life now."

"The magic of comedy allows me to pass my burdens onto the audience and charge them for it."

He grinned. "I..." Oh god, should he say this? In his inebriated state, second guesses only lasted about a second. "I had no idea you did this. If Laith hadn't told me, I would've never known."

"That I'm a queen?"

"Yeah."

She stared at him. "Boy, how old are you? You have to be an infant not to look at me and know exactly what I do for a living. I have glitter on my face twenty-four hours a day."

"I'd just never met a drag queen before." His shoulders raised sheepishly. "I'm pretty new to this stuff."

Ms. Intervention glanced up at Laith. A moment later, her lips rounded into an O shape, eyebrows twisting with pity. When Theodore looked at him, he didn't see anything out of the ordinary, just Laith meeting his eyes. The smile that quickly formed there was very distrustful, though.

"You're not alone, honey." Her voice seized his attention again. "My parents didn't understand me either. It took me thirty years to come out to them and another six to tell them what I do, but the fact they didn't understand me didn't mean no one else would. I just had to find the ones who did."

His lips parted, mute, heart racing. What had Laith just told her?

"It can be very scary," she continued, "but it's also liberating. For me, it felt like breaking out of my cage. Of course, that was only the case because I no longer lived with them or needed them financially. By then, I already had my own place and a group of people who loved and supported me, so when the rejection came, I had a home to go back to and friends to embrace me. It's different for everyone."

He drew in a shaky breath. "How did it feel?" His voice was small, a quasi-whisper. "The rejection."

"Like a stab in the heart. No matter how much I'd prepared myself for it, it still hurt like hell, but wounds heal. They don't bleed forever."

A slow nod moved his head, eyes burning.

It was time to go.

"We actually—we have another show to watch, so we should probably get going now."

She gave him a small, loving smile. "I hope it's the best one you've ever seen." Her voice was perfectly serious, yet soft and caring all at the same time.

mmermlmlm

Apparently, D'angela performed at the Vapid Beasts, just down the hall. The music that blasted inside bled through the door, muffled like heartbeats, growing louder as they approached. Different from most other entrances, this one had a bouncer outside who patted them down before letting them in. The first thing that came to mind was what had happened to Qasim, the shootout and subsequent bloodbath. He still wasn't sure if Laith knew about it.

"There sure is a lot of security here," he commented, trying to sound inconspicuous, as if he were truly wondering why that was.

"Yeah, it's because of the Hollywood boys." Laith leaned in close to talk to him, speaking over the music. "Burman is very adamant about their safety. I'll show you where they hang out; it's this fenced off area with security out front. Here." A hand took his arm to pull him through the crowd.

That wasn't the reply he'd been expecting, but it wasn't untrue either. This felt like the second time he'd tried to get Laith to mention his brother to no success. It was possible that he really just didn't know about the circumstances of his death. If that was the case, should Theodore be the one to tell him? The mere thought twisted his stomach into knots, heart jumping into his throat. No, absolutely not. This had nothing to do with him.

The Vapid Beasts was huge, but still nowhere close to the Unicorn Rave. The stage took up a good portion of the room, with the middle part of it jutting out to form a T-shaped runway into the crowd where performers could come back and forth during the show. Smaller podiums also peppered the ballroom where half-naked men and women danced. The crowd centered near the stage, thinned out away from it, then gathered again at the opposite end where the bar was. The only tables available were in booths near the wall, back-to-back with each other, extending from one end of the room to the other. The last two booths, or more accurately, the two closest to the stage were fenced off like Laith had said, with a piece of velvet rope like the ones celebrities used and security guards in front of it.

It was only when they approached the ropes that Theodore noticed just how much of the crowd was actually only here for the Hollywood boys, disinterested in the show upstage. Well, not *fully* disinterested, but they did act like the performance was a secondary reason for coming here. They paid the Hollywood boys a lot more attention.

Laith brought him to the front of the line, where one of the security guards held out a hand to preemptively stop them from even thinking about going in. The guy gave Laith a much harsher look than Theodore, pointed, almost personal. Confirming they knew each other, Laith waved him off, saying he wouldn't try anything tonight. Tonight? As in, he'd tried something before? Laith indicated Theodore with a hand, as if showing the security guard he had company, therefore, he'd behave. The guy still gave him a warning, but other than that, let them hang out near the velvet rope. Laith nodded at the booths.

It was very easy to tell which of those people were the Hollywood boys and which were their patrons. As expected, they all wore designer clothes and were very, very attractive, with fresh haircuts and manicured nails, clearly in their twenties. Their patrons were all older, even if not by much, two decades at most, in expensive clothes and gaudy hairstyles that only extremely rich people thought looked nice.

Surprisingly, the Hollywood boys weren't all white; from a distance, Theodore could see all kinds of people, one of every type in the world. The only thing they had in common was that they were all clearly rich and handsome, but that was pretty much it. Some of them looked entertained by their partners, some looked a lot more interested in the drag performance, and some just looked bored, wrapped up in some annoying conversation with no way out of it. They glanced at the crowd every now and then, as if scoping it out, but never spent too long staring.

A couple of them took notice of Theodore, then immediately saw Laith next to him and looked away. Were they afraid of Laith too? That couldn't possibly be the case. Given his conversation with the security guard, it was more likely that the Hollywood boys wanted nothing to do with him, not because of his reputation, but because he'd annoyed them too much. They seemed like the type of people who'd block a friend just because they'd asked too many questions that they didn't feel like answering.

One of them, a light-skinned Asian with his hair parted on the side, elbowed the guy next to him and whispered into his ear. The recipient, a Native American with long straight hair and a sharp jaw, in response to his friend's comment, turned to glance at Theodore, pointedly holding the stare. His attention was unwavering. Theodore couldn't hear what the discussion was about, but he could accurately guess, as the two glanced him up and down. Done with the topic, they glanced away. Nothing came of it.

Despite how curious that was, Theodore had no idea what to make of it. He remembered how ecstatic Laith had been when he was once again in speaking terms with them, but Theodore didn't exactly sympathize. Their notice of him made him feel absolutely nothing. The way they acted reminded him of his parents' guests who looked at him as if he were vermin. He didn't know them and had no way of verifying that they thought that way, of course. The only accurate criticism he could construct was that their clothes, for as expensive as they were, didn't always look good. Shopping at Gucci didn't excuse those gaudy patterns that obviously clashed with one another. Those were supposed to be accent pieces, not entire outfits. If his mother were here, she would've wrinkled her nose in disgust. All he needed to look like them was a big necklace, some tall boots and a fur coat. That wasn't a compliment.

"So which one are you in love with?" He raised his voice so Laith could hear it over the music, safely out of earshot from the Hollywood boys.

"Uh." Laith scowled, eyes roaming the two booths. "No one in particular, really. It's more like stardom, I guess, wishing they'd give me the time of day and shit, you know. Feeling like I matter."

"You don't need them to feel that way."

"I know. It's just one of those things you can't really control." Laith's shoulders bounced. "I get the same feeling from what I do, though, so it's not like I need them to feel good about myself."

"Right." His mind whirred, puzzle pieces falling into place. "Your work for Burman, collecting her money. You're powerful."

He thought of the subway ride earlier, how the crowd had only stared until Laith had come close, the Great White Shark and the one who belonged to him. Marquis had said that the entire underground system knew Laith, especially the ones who wished they didn't. He was famous, in a way. Not to mention his influential connections; the Crow, who thought him intimidating enough to try and scare his son off, and Burman, the residing chairman, the mob boss. Had Hwan been serious about that? Theodore had brushed it off as a manner of speaking then, but he wasn't so sure now.

"That's not all there is to it, though, right?" he asked. "People are afraid of you. They get out of your way when you walk by and keep their eyes down to stay out of trouble." He met Laith's eyes, dark under a scowl. "Do you hurt them or just break their things?"

Laith's scowl deepened. "I didn't lie to you the first time. My job is to bring back what Burman is owed."

"And if you can't?"

Laith cocked his head aside, eyes glancing off, red under the neon lights. "Well, I'm not the one in debt. They know what happens next."

"You haven't answered my question."

His voice drew Laith's gaze back down.

"Do you hurt people?" he asked.

"No. That's what the dogs are for."

Fireworks erupted from the stage, pulling excited noises from the crowd. A loud voice announced the beginning of the drag show, consequentially ending their conversation—Laith's attention was fully seized. Colorful lights shone over his face, up at the stage, lips curled into a big smile—how could someone so beautiful be a criminal? Theodore stared at him for a minute, at the shape of his eyebrows and the angle of his nose, so delicate. He couldn't even picture Laith swinging a bat into the glass of a display case. When the crowd cheered again, Theodore turned to watch the show.

There was so much information up on stage that it took him a while to really absorb it all, to understand that D'angela had come out with another two queens to lip sync and dance rather than actually sing any of those extremely popular songs. They had an intricate choreography to follow and words to match their lips to as best as they could. Part of what gave him trouble was how good they were are it, which had led him to question if they weren't actually singing. What gave it away was Christina Aguilera's very distinct voice, the way she flawlessly held those high keys.

It was only after figuring all of that out that he managed to pay attention to each queen individually and try to find D'angela among them. She looked so different that he could only tell her apart from the others by height and body type, not face. The eyebrows and hair really threw him off; they were both bright pink with glitter on them, matching her outfit, a leotard with stars. She wore knee-high boots and elbow-long gloves, hair up in a ponytail with bangs. She honestly looked like a superstar. It made sense that the Hollywood boys would want to hang out here.

The performance was jaw-dropping; those queens high-kicked and summersaulted all across the stage, but what truly blew his mind were the death drops. The first one shot his eyebrows all the way to his hairline, pulling a gasp straight from his lungs. How weren't they hurt? The ones that followed were less impressive only because they weren't new anymore, but he still couldn't look away. Every time it happened, it still startled him.

Unfortunately, the tight security in the Vapid Beasts didn't allow anyone to go backstage after the show. Only the Hollywood boys had clearance to do so, and given Laith's reputation here, Theodore found it hard to believe they'd let him get close. A random guy off the crowd had better chances.

"I thought you and the Hollywood boys were in speaking terms again," Theodore commented. "What happened?"

That put a strange look on Laith's face. "When did I tell you that?"

Two years ago.

"A little while ago," he lied. "They don't seem to want anything to do with you, though."

"Yeah, well." Laith briefly glanced at the subjects of their conversation without holding the stare with any of them. "I may have done something stupid between then and now."

"Did you hit on one of them?"

"No, of course not; I'm not that far gone yet. I just thought, you know, since I work for Burman and her office is right next to theirs, maybe, like—we could meet. It didn't seem so crazy when I thought about it. Now I know it's insane."

"It doesn't sound insane to me. Aren't you guys technically coworkers?"

"That's what I thought at the time. I don't blame you for falling for it too; it's easy to think of them as employees when they bring in so much cash, but they just rent this place. They don't work for Burman at all."

Huh.

"I'm assuming you went to their office," Theodore commented, urging Laith to continue.

"Yeah. I should've known they never go there, 'cause they're always here, but that didn't cross my mind at the time. When I knocked, it was Burman's cousin who answered—their founder. Think of him as a CEO. I don't know what his real name is; everyone just calls him Punjab. It's a place in India. As far as I know, he wasn't even born there, but..." Laith shrugged. "It was a very awkward conversation. Before I'd even said anything, he already thought I wanted to do business with him. I tried to explain that I didn't, that I don't even have the money for that, but what he got from it was that I felt entitled to see the Hollywood boys 'cause I'm Burman's guy. The longer we talked, the worse it got; he didn't understand anything I was trying to say. He's so rich and so used to rich people coming to him for business proposals that he just couldn't possibly fathom why I would be there otherwise. It was like money had carved this massive chasm between us without a middle ground. It was bizarre."

"Isn't Burman richer than him?"

"Yeah. We've never failed to understand each other like that, though; Punjab's just weird. I don't know what he told the Hollywood boys, but ever since that conversation, they've been looking at me like I'll kidnap one of them at the drop of a hat. I don't know. They're probably traumatized."

Yeah, they probably were, but not for that reason.

"So now you're blacklisted."

"Pretty much."

A server cut through the crowd with a silver tray full of colorful drinks. The bouncer let them through the velvet rope to give the Hollywood boys their orders.

"It doesn't matter," Laith finally concluded, staring at them. "You're better than all of them combined."

"Oh, yeah?"

Green eyes found him through the flashing lights, pink and blue. A smirk slowly cut through Laith's face. "Yeah. I'll spell it out for you later, show you what I mean. You'll never forget it."

mmermlmln

Lying in a bed of flames, he asked Laith to hit him. It came out of nowhere, an urge that blossomed from a small slap on the side of his thigh, done mostly out of excitement, the sound of a firm grasp as Laith settled between his legs. He'd said it without thinking, an arm strewn over his eyes, chest housing a vicious feeling—*hit me harder*. Always good, Laith complied, slapping him once, nice and sharp. The sting traveled right between his legs, knees shooting both feet up, lip seized between his teeth. *Again, again*, he'd urged, drowning in an addictive need to feel his skin burn. His orders were carried out with the utmost pleasure.

Laith's surprise manifested in his speech, words pressed against Theodore's jaw, lips dragging across his skin. He teased him for it, whispering confessions into his ear, how he'd never thought Theodore would be into something so dirty, so rough—a boy like him. His nails dug into Laith's back, thighs stinging with each slap, open-palmed and precise. It was different, a degrading form of excitement, just one layer away from utter shame, driven home by Laith's judgment. He liked it, how lowly Laith spoke of him, how corrupt it made him feel.

He wondered what his dad would think about this, the fact he liked getting spanked after all, cock pulsing every time Laith's hand came down. The knowledge he was quite literally getting off on something that had ruined Ryan's life was almost enough to push him over the edge.

mmermlmlm

When he woke up, he found himself carefully wrapped in Laith's arms, blanket soft and warm over his shoulders. This was the first time in a long time that he'd actually fallen asleep at night. He breathed in tobacco and amber, reveling in the peace that surrounded him—every morning should start like this. His thighs ached, the result of last night's indulgences, but he really didn't mind it; jogging around campus every day used to give him the same feeling. At this point, it'd been missed. He didn't remember the end of last night, how they'd gotten back to Laith's place or how he'd fallen asleep in his arms, but he was sure Laith's sobriety had guided him through it all.

A quick peek over Laith's shoulder allowed him to glance at the alarm clock—10:15 a.m. Oh my god, ten fifteen?! His heart raced, blood growing cold—he'd already missed two classes and was on his way to miss another one. Could he make it before eleven? Sure, but that wouldn't guarantee his presence. Realistically, he'd already been marked as absent. Shit.

Leaving the comfort of Laith's presence, especially at a moment as serene as this, was the definition of a crime. Every move broke his heart, elbow propping him up, hand touching Laith on the face. The way he lay, half over Laith, pushed Laith to roll onto his back. A breath drew into his lungs, chest expanding with it, under the weight of Theodore's body. Still, he barely stirred. Fingers tightened the grip on his jaw, Theodore's face an inch from his own.

"Hey," he whispered, "I have to go."

Laith finally stirred, eyes cracking open just a slit. No words came from him, no retaliation or protest, so Theodore leaned down for a kiss. It was quick yet sweet, a heartbroken farewell.

As soon as they parted, three words shot up his throat so suddenly that he almost said them, a reflexive response, the natural progression of this moment—*I love you*—but they weren't there yet. Holy shit, they were nowhere close to something so loaded, so heavy. It scared him just how easily he'd almost said it, grenade hanging off the tip of his tongue. He stared at Laith with big eyes, speechless. Terrified out of his mind, he left the bed.

"When does your last class end?" Laith's voice was quiet, husky with sleep.

"At three," he spoke while picking up his clothes from the floor, head banging all of a sudden, shooting a horrible pain across his skull. Oh right, the hangover; he'd almost forgotten about that. "Why?"

"I'll be working at that time. I leave around eight, sometimes nine."

With his underwear back on, he glanced at Laith. "Okay." He wasn't sure where this was going.

"If you wanna hang out, I mean." A hand came up to rub one of Laith's eyes. He was still half-asleep. "I, uh—I'd like to see you tonight, I guess is what I'm trying to say."

Oh. His heart fluttered—really? A smile tugged at the corners of his lips, small, the ghost of disbelief. "Okay, yeah, that'd be nice. I'll come by around the time you're done, then."

Laith nodded.

Theodore had had no idea he'd have something to look forward to after class tonight.

Chapter 14

Four is a crowd

There is peace even in the storm.

- 1876 letter from Vincent van Gogh to his brother

*Classes didn't get any more interesting over the span of a weekend, but there was some-*thing distinctly different about this one, something he just couldn't put his finger on. Somehow, for the first time ever, he was able to pay attention to the lecture. The subject was still just as boring as ever, yet he managed to follow the profes-sor's train of thought anyway, without his mind wandering off like it'd done last week. That might be because it was the first time he'd come to class not high and relatively well-rested, even if hungover—no one was perfect. Either way, this class gave him hope that maybe they weren't *all* bad.

As soon as the professor wrapped it up, he walked up to them and asked after the textbook. Clearly annoyed, they told him that the bibliography used for their classes was listed on the website. They'd said that a million times last week, apparently—where was he? A quick glance down at some documents on their desk showed Theodore's acceptable attendance record, with only a couple of absences. His face burned, feet stepping away from the professor. With a brief thank you on his lips, he turned to leave.

It took him a bit of fiddling with the website to figure out where the bibliographies were kept. Luckily, every subject had a main textbook that the professor followed, so he made a point to visit the library during lunch. A quick stop at one of the sandwich places satiated his hunger before he rushed off to the library with no time to even glance around looking for the girls; he only had one hour to do this and his building was really far. They'd surely understand.

Walking fast made him feel pretty good, like he had somewhere to be on a timely manner, like he was important enough for appointments of that nature. No one had to know what business he had at the library, only that he couldn't dilly-dally on the way.

The library was way too big to navigate by himself and still find everything he needed, so he ended up asking one of the people behind the counter for help. The one who volunteered was a very old lady about half his height.

As she walked him through the aisles, she explained the reasoning behind the placement of each book. They were all separated by major and each of those sections were alphabetized by the author's last name. They all had numbers attributed to them as well, but Theodore didn't really understand that part and decided against asking; he probably wouldn't be here very often. The numbering system had something to do with the title of each book—that was all he could gather.

They went through the business section taking what he needed with a brief stop at the economics section and another at the finance one. He had no idea how those two sections were different, but he supposed he'd get to learn that as classes progressed. All in all, he checked out six massive textbooks, only to then remember he hadn't even brought his backpack. God. How had he gone from a straight-A student to this?

The afternoon period was much easier to follow along with the textbook over his desk. Who would've thought? The subject itself was still the most uninteresting one he'd ever had the displeasure to study, but the text kept him focused. The professor followed it pretty much to a T, and when they happened to make an interesting remark, he took note of it with a pen and a piece of paper he'd borrowed from the guy sitting next to him. He hadn't even bought any notebooks, still using the same pens and other office supplies from high school, which he'd left at home. Jesus Christ. If his parents could see him right now, they'd probably disown him.

His last period was the worst. Usually, by the time it came around, he was so tired from staying up all night that he could barely even function. This was the first time he even caught the name of the subject—marketing. Who gave a single shit about marketing? That was the worst one yet, regardless of sleeping schedule. He was tired, but nowhere near how tired he'd been all of last week; he had those two or so hours from last night to account for it. Still, he couldn't say he'd managed to absorb much about marketing, even with the textbook right in front of his face.

When he got home, carrying his books and notes in both arms like a freak, the girls hadn't arrived yet. That was usually how it went; he imagined they stayed on campus after class to make friends and hang out. Honestly, he had no idea. He set the textbooks on his desk and checked the time—3:30 p.m. Laith was at work. On a regular day, this was when he'd fall face-first on the mattress and sleep, but since he had plans at eight, he could only sleep for three and a half hours. He'd have to set an alarm for that. With his clothes hanging over the back of his office chair, he slipped under the covers.

The alarm went off what felt like two seconds after he'd set it. His eyes opened as if they'd never closed, not rested but not tired either. It was weird.

The first thing he noticed were the muffled sounds that traveled down the hallway, light shining through the slit under his door—the girls must be having dinner. He hadn't caught them awake in a very long time.

Getting up, he noticed how badly his body ached, worse in his thighs, arms sore from carrying heavy books all day. It felt like he had to physically push himself out of bed rather than spring joyfully from it. Hell. His phone had no notifications on the screen, so he placed it back on the nightstand and got up to take a shower. He really needed one.

The partial lighting in the hallway kept his presence inconspicuous, making it possible to slip into the bathroom unnoticed. Daisy sat nearest the hallway, the most likely person to catch sight of him, but she seemed too entertained by the girls' conversation to peel her eyes from the kitchen. Good.

Locked in the bathroom, he could strip down and turn a bit to glance at his thighs, where Laith had spanked him. His skin was a bit red, but other than that, he couldn't really find any bruising. His shoulders drooped with disappointment. The way it'd hurt had made him believe it'd been much worse, that he'd find his ass black and blue—how come? Incidentally, how bad would it need to be for a proper bruise? He kind of wanted one now.

It was a new feeling for sure, something he'd never experienced before, to want to be struck so hard that a bruise would be the aftermath, a trophy he could admire all day. My god, what was wrong with him? The hickey on his collarbone was still there, fainter than before, but still present enough to be seen. He liked it, the physical confirmation that Laith had touched him, that he'd been there. A bruise on his ass would be the same thing. Hickeys were extremely common; people did that all the time, he wasn't weird. There was nothing wrong with that.

Every time he walked somewhere and his legs ached, he thought of last night, how far they'd been spread, knees practically touching his chest. If they were going to do this regularly, he should really start stretching or something. Oh my god, was that why Hannah and Jessie had picked up yoga these last few months? That realization burned his eyebrows straight off his face.

Back in his room, he put on his patterned jacket, the one Laith associated with the Hollywood boys. That had nothing to do with what Theodore had seen last night; the Hollywood boys didn't actually know how to dress and only wore expensive clothes to show them off, so no, he didn't care to be compared to them. He just put this jacket on because Laith liked it.

He left the room at 7:45 p.m., while the girls were having dinner. Since the dining room was directly by the door, it'd be impossible to sneak out.

They caught sight of him right away, and with half-eaten tacos in their mouths, desperately invited him to have some. It was taco night, apparently. For as much as he loved that, he hadn't accounted for dinner; having some would make him way later than he wanted to be. There was a bit of a back and forth when he expressed that, with them trying to get him to sit down for a minute while he reasoned his way out the door and tried to say goodbye. The only argument that actually got him to pause came from Jessie, that Justin had texted her today. Theodore hadn't expected that. The way Emily had called Justin up to her apartment had given him the impression that something would happen between them after everybody had left. He supposed he was wrong.

"What did he say?"

Jessie folded her soft taco shell in half. "A lot of things. We've been texting all day." She brought the taco up to her face, just short of biting into it. "I might see him tomorrow." She took a bite.

"Are you flirting?"

She nodded, chewing quietly. Oh my god.

"Are you actually seeing him tomorrow?" Hannah asked. "On a school night?"

Jessie shrugged, mumbling the word *maybe* with a hand over her mouth. She swallowed before adding to that. "He said he could see me after work. He has a truck." That last part was spoken with a half-smirk. "Maybe we won't even need to go anywhere."

"Tell him to park around the corner, at least." Theodore made a face, hand pulling the front door open. "The doorman doesn't need to see *that*."

He left to the sound of laughter.

mmermmlmmlm

It was around 8:30 p.m. when he got to Laith's apartment. To his delight, the two queens were in their doorways again, chatting each other up, shooting judgmental looks up and down the hallway. When they caught sight of him, big grins stretched on their faces, hands waving at him with whistles to accompany their high spirits.

"C'mon, Diesel jacket!"

"Look at you. What is this Hollywood moment you're serving us?" A hand motioned to him, up and down, as D'angela talked. "It's posh, it's chic, it's rich boy on the street!"

"Give us a twirl, mama. Let's see it all."

He did as he was told, turning around while the women whistled. He'd never received a reaction like this before, so positive about anything he'd done. It was pretty wild. As soon as his eyes met theirs again, he found himself grinning wide, not even aware of when it'd sneaked onto his face. They made him feel as if he were on top of the world just for being here.

"That's a ten from me."

"Literally gagged."

He passed Laith's door a quick glance, feet approaching the queens.

"Your man isn't in yet," Ms. Intervention informed him, "but you can stick around until he comes back. It should be soon."

"Oh, I'm not—" Suddenly, words failed him. Yes, he *was* wondering that. He gave her a smile. "I've been meaning to talk to you guys, anyway. Ms. Intervention already knows this, but I went to your shows last night. Did you see me, D'angela?"

"Of course I did! You two were standing by the VIP area."

"They surprised us both."

"It was a last-minute decision," he explained. "I had no idea you two would be performing last night. I mean, I should've known, but I guess I wasn't thinking about it."

"Why didn't you come backstage to see me too?" D'angela pouted, arms crossed over her chest. Did she not know about Laith's little situation? Well, if she didn't, then he wouldn't be the one to tell it.

"Uh, I don't know. Maybe next time."

"You better!"

"I had no idea you guys dressed up and stuff. I thought only men did that."

"Anyone can do drag," Ms. Intervention clarified. "For example, I'm a proud transwoman and Brian is a gay man."

Wait, Brian? Theodore turned to D'angela only to see her playfully shove her friend on the arm. "Don't call me that! It breaks the illusion."

"Right, of course. I meant to say Brian is a biological woman."

"That's better." D'angela grinned.

Theodore was extremely confused. "So you're a guy and you're a girl?" He pointed at each one of them while speaking to illustrate his point.

"Correct."

"I don't mind if you call me a woman," D'angela explained. "I'm used to it. That's my stage persona after all, but yes, I am a man in a wig. Not right now, though!" She touched the baldness at the top of her head. "I don't dress up on Mondays."

"We work Wednesday to Sunday."

"Should I call you guys by your real names or your stage names?" He had absolutely no idea how this worked.

"It's up to you, sweetheart." Ms. Intervention's slender shoulders bounced. "Only very close friends call me Lucy."

"Oh, then I should probably stick to Ms. Intervention."

"Theo." She reached forward and cupped his face in a hand. "I'm your drag mother. You can call me Lucy."

He smiled.

"Do not call me Brian." D'angela flipped a strand of invisible hair off her shoulder. "Like I said, it breaks the illusion."

Theodore laughed. "Okay, queen. I'll keep your secret."

"Thank you very much."

It was clear to him that this was the perfect opportunity to ask them what he'd been meaning to know and gather intel on the man who only told certain things to certain people. He glanced at Laith's door again, heart skipping a beat. "Do you guys, like—do you guys hang out with Laith a lot?"

Ms. Intervention hummed. "I'd say pretty often. It comes with the territory, living so close to each other."

"Mondays and Tuesdays, mostly," D'angela added. "Last week was especially bad."

"What happened last week?" His eyes grew so wide he could feel them on his face.

"We don't have the full story, but he was really upset about something. He came to my room on Tuesday, sat on the floor near the bed and drank an entire bottle of Jack all by himself. He wasn't making any sense."

"For context, he was already drunk before leaving for work," D'angela explained. "He was drunk every day last week, actually. Drunk and high. We know he likes to indulge and that's fine, but it's not usually like that."

"He talked about Emily a lot. I don't know who she is and I have no idea what any of it meant, but he had her on his mind."

"Do you remember what kind of stuff he said?" Theodore's voice was small, pulse running cold.

"Something about making her angry."

"He kept asking us if we thought he was a bad person. I remember he covered his eyes with a hand and mumbled that he was good, or that he tried to be. It was really depressing."

"Yes, that's true; he was stuck on this dichotomy between good and bad. He really wanted us to know that he was good."

Theodore's blood cooled into ice.

Both queens glanced up from him, eyes fixed over his shoulder. Their subsequent smiles and waves let him know that someone came down the hallway, which he guessed could only be one person. With a deep breath in his lungs, he turned to see Laith approach, carrying the aluminum bat over a shoulder, leather gloves on his hands. He seemed delightfully surprised, with a small smile on his face. The bat came down as he stopped walking, completing the circle between Theodore and D'angela. If any resident needed to navigate this hallway, they'd have a difficult time; Theodore could hear their voices, disembodied arguments as shadows went up and down the stairs. People here were very opinionated.

"Hey, uh. I forgot to tell you something."

Laith's comment lifted Theodore's eyebrows.

"Earlier, I mean. I said I leave around eight, which is true, but I forgot to mention I usually hit the gym afterwards. I'll skip today, since you're already here, but yeah. I thought you'd like to know, for future, uh—" Green eyes glanced very briefly at the queens that watched them, posture stiffening. "Dates."

A smile tugged onto the corners of Theodore's lips. This was a date? In his peripherals, he saw the big grins on the girls' faces, heads turning to give each other looks. Despite that, no one teased Laith for it. They must know how difficult it was for him to say stuff like this.

"You don't have to skip tonight. I'll come with you," Theodore offered.

Dark eyebrows pinched together. "Are you sure?"

"Yeah. What's better than watching hot guys work out?"

"Amen, sister."

Ms. Intervention's comment prompted him to turn toward her. "Do you wanna come with? We could all hang out."

"Oh, I wouldn't want to ruin your date."

"It's not a date if it's four of us," D'angela reasoned. "I'd like to go. I haven't been to the gym in ages."

"Well..."

"I think you'll have fun." Laith shrugged. "Let me get my stuff." With that, he turned to unlock his door and walk in. Theodore decided to wait in the hallway, watching as both women also turned to their own apartments.

"Oh, I don't even know what to wear!"

"I have to beat this face, hold on."

mmmmmmmm

When Ms. Intervention wasn't performing, she wore a nice curly wig and very natural-looking makeup, while D'angela wore boy clothes. They both looked nice in their own way. Theodore understood what they'd meant now, that one of them was a woman and the other was a guy. Their drag personas just happened to both be women.

Since Laith was the only one with a membership at the gym, everyone else had to pay to get in. It wasn't too much, though. Both Laith and D'angela hit the locker room to get dressed, and since Theodore had no intention to actually work out, he stayed behind. To his surprise, Ms. Intervention felt the same way about it—they were only here for the hot guys. Not to mention he'd *just* showered and had no change of clothes; if these got sweaty and gross, he'd have to deal with them for the rest of the night. No, thanks.

Her excuse was that she'd never promised to exercise in the first place; her presence was a gift. She already exerted herself enough night after night, five days a week—a hand flipped some of her curls back, body swaying at the witticism of her comment, very similar to what D'angela had done earlier. This was probably just something drag queens did. Either way, the joke wasn't lost on

Theodore; he elbowed her with a big grin on his face.

The gym was much bigger than he'd expected it to be. The main floor was basically a big room with an aisle in the middle and all kinds of equipment on both sides, categorized by function; if their focus was the arms, the legs, the back and so on. Since half the group wasn't even here to exercise and D'angela had never actually been to this gym, they all just followed Laith around, hopping from machine to machine as his routine required. He spent about ten minutes in each one, so they were always moving around, scoping out the area.

Every time Theodore saw someone worthy of his attention, he made sure to inform Ms. Intervention about them, which kept the two relatively close to one another. If she sat on one of those stationary bicycles, he'd hang around, pretending to coach her; if he walked on a treadmill, she'd lean on one of the handlebars and pretend to coach him instead. That way, they didn't actually do any exercise, but still wouldn't get kicked out for not participating, if that was even a thing. Honestly, he didn't know.

He watched Laith a lot. In a tight tank top and short shorts, his body was in full view; biceps flexing, stomach tensing, thighs big and firm. It was a mesmerizing performance. Theodore tried not to stare *too* much, or Laith would notice, so his eyes would wander, his body would lean close to Ms. Intervention for a comment or two, and then he'd immediately glance back at what mattered. Laith's skin gleamed with sweat, tank top low on his cleavage, hair falling over one eye. The longer they spent here, the quicker Theodore's heart raced, growing more interested. By the time Laith's routine was done, Theodore could barely even look at him; the way his clothes clung to his body, tattoos stretching with the movement of his muscles. It was far too much.

While Theodore and Ms. Intervention waited for the other two to shower, she commented on how openly he'd ogled Laith up and down. She said it in a friendly way, with no intention to embarrass him, but his still face burned, eyes blown wide—he didn't know he was so obvious. Oh, but he was. Her laughter was affectionate, hand touching him on the back. He was mortified. Oh god, had Laith noticed it? Abso-fucking-lutely; there was no way he hadn't. If it was any consolation, though, Laith had stolen glances at him too, except he was much better at it. Knowing that only helped fuel the fire that swallowed Theodore's face.

On the way back to their apartments, Laith threw an arm across Theodore's shoulders and pulled him under his wing. It was nice, the casual nature of it, how thoughtlessly Laith did it now. Theodore remembered when he'd first found out about Marquis and Hwan and the jealousy in his veins, how he would've killed for anything even remotely similar to what they had. Now, this kind of affection seemed to come very naturally to Laith, to want to keep him close, pressed to his side. His heart still soared every time it happened.

The group talked about the most egregious topics he'd ever heard, things he never thought he'd hear anyone say. It went in line with what Ms. Intervention had brought up at her show; the sex positions, the intricacies of the act itself, the good and the bad. Theodore couldn't, for his life, add anything to the conversation, but ate up everything that was discussed. That way, he found out D'angela was—surprisingly—a top, that her type was soft and squishy, and that she was a big fan of rimming. That word alone closed a hand around his throat and strangled him. She loved doing it; she talked about it a lot.

As for Ms. Intervention, she preferred big and hairy, bonus points if he had a belly, double bonus points if he had children. She liked when they threw her down on the bed, turned her around, held her in a million different positions and pretty much just went to town. Theodore would never say it, but the whole time she expressed those feelings, all he could think was how similar they were in that regard. He understood D'angela's passion for being in charge and taking control, but the surprise of letting someone else take the reins was also exciting. He could honestly get down with both. What did that make him? It seemed he could never choose a side on absolutely anything. Was that what being bisexual really meant?

Laith was extremely predictable. Nothing he said was really surprising or even new information; Theodore already knew it all. He liked pretty much everything and was willing to try whatever his partner was interested in, an eclectic in every regard. He'd been with all kinds of men and had a wide range of preferences, but if he had to choose—and here, his eyes very briefly glanced at Theodore, pressed tightly against his side—he'd say his type was well-dressed and spoiled, like a model straight out of a Vogue magazine, covered in Versace. The two women whistled while Theodore simply squinted. For as much as Laith had made a point to be talking about him, that description very well encompassed every member of the Hollywood boys too. Again, perfectly predictable.

"What's your type, kitten?"

He parted his lips to answer, but suddenly, every word he ever knew escaped him. His mind drew a complete blank. He thought of his friends' dads swimming in the pool and how he'd fantasized about them; he thought of the guy from the threesome video and how he'd fantasized about him too, and lastly, he thought of Laith, the first person he'd ever been interested in. What did they all have in common? It bore noticing that, as soon as Ms. Intervention posed the question, nothing came to mind, not an image, not a single person. "I guess... bigger and older than me."

The two queens nodded.

"That's everybody's type until you realize that wanting someone older would mean visiting a nursing home," Ms. Intervention commented.

That pulled laughter from D'angela's throat. "Bitch, you're forty! Don't be dramatic."

Both women laughed.

"Does that go for girls too?"

Laith's question focused blue eyes up on his face, wide. "Huh?"

"Is bigger and older your type for women too?"

Theodore had heard him the first time; the confusion had come from surprise. His heart beat awkwardly in his chest, as if shifted a little too far to the side—they hadn't talked about this in months. In fact, the last time they'd discussed Theodore's attraction to women had been right before they'd first fooled around, when he'd told Laith about Jessie. Sure, Laith brought that up a lot and made fun of it, but it was different, a joke about something that had happened in the past, something that didn't affect Theodore anymore. He was completely disconnected from it. This question, however, touched on a part of his sexuality that felt strange to discuss with a bunch of people who were only attracted to men. Ironically, he'd feel a lot more comfortable talking about it with his father, of all people, even if his father didn't really get it either.

"Um."

He thought of Jessie and the time they'd gone shopping, when she'd caught him staring at her chest; he thought of Sherry and the curves of her hips, wider than any part of his own body, but what did those two even have in common? They were complete opposites. Well, when it came to skin color, that was true, but placing them side-to-side in his mind, he realized their body type was very similar.

"I guess tall and..." Oh god, how could he say this without sounding gross? "And, uh—tall with wide hips." He had absolutely no idea how to respectfully bring up the other thing, so he just cut it out. No one in this circle would

163

even relate to it, anyway.

Laith cocked his head aside, frowning. "I guess Jessie's tall."

"Of course she is."

"Yeah, but who really comes to mind is Sherry."

The breath that Theodore pulled into his lungs cooled at the base of his throat, stuck there for a moment, heart skipping a beat. Before Laith could see the shock on his face, he turned to the two queens who watched them curiously. "Do you prefer taller guys or shorter guys?" he asked. It was the first question that came to mind. Anything to end his previous conversation with Laith.

"Taller," they both answered.

"Or as tall as I am," Ms. Intervention clarified. "It's pretty difficult to find someone too much taller."

"Well, it's easy for me," D'angela remarked. "Tall and big is every-where."

"But aren't you a top?" Theodore asked.

"So what? I like to top men who are twice my size. I feel like a climber on top of Mount Everest. There's truly nothing like it."

Laith laughed. "You're fucking insane. How is that comparable?"

D'angela glanced him up and down. "I can tell you've never experi-enced it, but being on top of a massive man who could easily crush you to death is extremely liberating. I bet Theo feels like a bullfighter on top of you."

That comment reached an arm down Theodore's throat and pulled his soul right out. He was gone.

"Wouldn't he feel the same way riding the bull?"

Thankfully, Laith's question didn't affect him, because he wasn't here anymore. This conversation didn't touch him at all.

"Maybe, but the experience is different."

"He's not heavy enough to crush Theo," Ms. Intervention rebutted.

"No, but he could crush him with his arms. It doesn't matter *how* you can be crushed, as long as you know you wouldn't stand a chance against the man you're topping. That's the fun part."

"Well..." That word left him in a daze. His mind's autonomy pulled a memory from the fog, when he'd topped Laith that one time, how Laith had barely moved under his weight, unbothered in the slightest. Even now, he still wished he *had* bothered him. That he'd climbed Mount Everest and fought the bull. "It's a power trip," he commented.

"Right."

"How does it feel when you—" That question slipped out before he could process the rest of it, mind tackling the inner workings of his brain without consciousness, buried under layers and layers of thought. How would it feel like to *have* bothered Laith? To have done something to him, something good, the same way he did to Theodore. The exhilaration he usually got from sucking Laith off was more than enough to get high on; he couldn't even imagine what making Laith cum under different circumstances would feel like, what it'd do to him. If he were good at it, he'd probably never go back. Memories of Laith's hands coming down on his body and the sting on his thighs immediately caused him to reconsider that, though. Maybe they could take turns.

He stared at D'angela. "Do you ever hit them?" It was either going to be that or something *much* more embarrassing. His face tingled anyway, but thankfully, no one mentioned it.

Shaved eyebrows pinched together, manicured hand falling limp at the wrist. "Oh yeah, all the time. You'd be surprised with how much these bottoms love to be spanked, tied up and gagged. Girl, I've done all of it. Ask your boyfriend."

There was so much wrong with that last sentence that he wasn't even sure how to tackle it. If she knew they weren't together, why would she say that? *Did* she know? What had Laith told her? Also, and perhaps more importantly, why would Laith know about all the things she'd done in bed? Speechless, Theodore simply held the stare.

"To be fair, I haven't been to the dungeon in years," Laith commented, "and for as much as you brag about it, you don't really show up either."

The dungeon? Theodore's eyes widened.

D'angela shook her limp hand, waiving the air. "I was a lot more active when I was younger, okay? I just don't have the time anymore. Plus, it's really difficult to find people my age anywhere these days. I consistently come across twenty-year-olds and it makes me depressed. It's a whole thing."

Theodore glanced at Ms. Intervention. "Are they really talking about a sex dungeon?" he whispered.

"I don't know. I don't think so? I've never been, but a lot of people really enjoy these kinds of spaces."

He turned back to D'angela. "Are you talking about a sex dungeon?"

"No, not this one. I've never been to those. I liked the ones you went to for scenes. I was big into rope; it was my craft. I used to be really good too. People always came to me for my art; we'd play for hours. It was the most fun I'd ever had."

"What happened?"

"Nothing; I just don't really go anymore. I've become pretty anti-social these days. Now I just practice on my friends. Lucy and Shark have both seen my skills with the rope."

Theodore glanced between the three of them—a little grossed out, to be honest. "You guys sleep together?" That couldn't be right.

"No!" The limp hand slapped him on the arm. "Rope isn't sexual. I mean, it *can* be, but to me, it's an art form, just like drag. The rope I tie around Lucy's arms sometimes has nothing sexual about it."

"It's really beautiful, actually," Ms. Intervention added. "It's not really my thing, but I can still appreciate art in all its forms."

"Wait, so." He was really confused. "Do you tie people up for sex or not? You said you gag and spank them and stuff."

"Yes, but that's something else. That's what I like to do in bed."

That didn't make any goddamn sense.

"How's that any different than the stuff in the dungeon? I thought sex dungeons were the only kind of dungeon. You *don't* have sex in there?"

"Not in all of them—not in *most* of them. They're primarily a place for fun, not sex. For me, it was a place where I could show off my art and maybe meet a handsome guy who was interested in me. Handcuffing a man to the bedpost and tying intricate patterns on a stranger are two completely different things. The first one is hot, the second one is art."

"But that's a kink."

"Yes, but kinks aren't inherently sexual."

"How? Aren't kinks literally just what you think is hot?"

"No. A kink can be a preference, something you're interested in or your idea of fun. It really depends. Of course, a kink that's sexual to you can be non-sexual to others and vice versa. For example, some people find bondage really sexy, but I don't feel anything sexual towards it. Some people think of impact play as a form of athleticism, while I think it's sexy. It's different for everyone."

"Why would you get spanked if you didn't get off on it?"

"There are a million different answers to this. Do you know what a scene is?"

He shook his head.

She breathed in deeply, chest puffing out. At this point, the group was already back in the apartment building, climbing up the stairs. Laith led the way with Theodore right behind, followed by D'angela and Ms. Intervention.

"Okay, a scene is a space that we create with the person we're going to play with. We discuss what we want to accomplish, how we want to feel, how long it's gonna last, what will be the beginning, middle and end and anything else we find important. Usually, one of us is a dom and the other is a sub, but that's not a requirement. This scene can be sexual if we want it to be, or not, if we just want to play. For example, a sexual scene between me and one of my exes included tying him up, spanking him and making him feel dominated. That was what he got off on—the feeling of powerlessness. A scene that we liked to do that *wasn't* sexual included him servicing me, like fetching me glasses of water, changing the TV channel, standing on his hands and knees like a footstool, letting me tie him up and so on. That made him feel useful, but it wasn't a sexual thing; he just liked feeling that way. That's the difference."

Wow, that was fascinating. Did he have any kinks that weren't sexual? Probably. He'd never really stopped to consider the feelings he enjoyed and what he liked to do in relation to others, so he couldn't really put a finger on it. It'd be interesting to figure that out, though. He knew he liked feeling powerful, that when Laith did what he ordered turned him on, but just like the spanking from last night, it was a sexual thing. He still had a lot to learn about himself, sexually or not.

Chapter 15

And—scene!

You think you are possessing me —
But I've got my teeth in you.

- Angela Carter, *Unicorn*

After bidding the two queens goodbye, he followed Laith into his apartment. His mind still stirred, thoughts coming and going—did he like feeling useful? If Laith asked him to make dinner, for example, would he like doing that? No, probably not. He preferred the opposite, telling Laith to do things for him, being heard and obeyed. If he really thought about it, that didn't have to be sexual; he liked feeling in control, regardless of the situation. Was it only with Laith, though? He wasn't sure. He'd never really felt such strong emotions for anybody else, which was why identifying them in relation to Laith was so easy. He should try to pay more attention when hanging out with other people.

"Can we..." His heart jumped into his throat, a lump right in the middle, hands closed into nervous fists. Laith glanced at him while slipping his jacket off and hanging it behind the door. Theodore breathed in. "Can we do a scene?"

Dark eyebrows bounced with surprise, lips curling with the hint of a smile, somewhere between suspicious and confused. His lack of an answer prompted Theodore to elaborate.

"You mentioned you used to go to the dungeon and the way D'angela talked made it seem like you know something about this. I just think it could be fun. Anyway, I uh—I have something in mind."

Laith kicked his boots off while Theodore talked, tucked into the corner with his other shoes. Not once did he glance away, eyes trained on Theodore's face even when he fidgeted and broke the stare multiple times. "What's that?"

"Well, remember when you hit me yesterday?"

"Right..."

"I'm thinking maybe you could do it harder? I really thought—I thought it'd leave a mark, but it didn't and... I'm kind of disappointed by that."

Delight touched Laith's face so lightly that Theodore almost missed it. The hint was miniscule, but it was there, in the way his eyebrows raised and his lips parted. "You want bruises."

The mere word set Theodore's face on fire, pulse racing fast. "If that's okay." He practically swallowed that sentence as he spoke it, too embarrassed to hear his own voice at the moment.

"You know, I didn't wanna hurt you too much, in case you didn't like it. I wasn't really sure how far you wanted me to go; that was only your first time. Some people say *hit me*, but they don't really mean it. What they mean to say is *slap me around a bit*."

"I want you to turn me purple."

Laith smirked. "Okay, let's go over the scene then. I can't promise you I'll give you any bruises, 'cause it'll depend on how much you can take, but what I *can* promise is that it'll be fun. What were you thinking besides that?"

"Um." That was pretty much as far as he'd gotten. It was all that really mattered, anyway. "I liked what we did yesterday, so maybe we could do something similar, just harder."

"Alright." Laith walked over to the bed, gesturing vaguely toward it. "So, a classic scene would be if I sat down here and put you over my lap. It could be a chair or whatever; the bed is just closer."

Theodore's throat closed, pulse loud in his ears. His father used to hit Ryan that way. Carolyn would help hold him down as he screamed, face red with anger, eyes full of tears. No, maybe not that. They should try something else. "What if..." He could barely speak, breathless and shaky. His feet took a step closer to the bed, hands closed tight. "What if I lay on the bed and you sat next to me? I think—it'll probably be easier that way."

"We could do that. Do you have any toys in mind?"

"Toys?" Heat crawled up his neck.

"If you wanna use one, I mean. I don't mind using my hand, but I'm pretty sure I still have a paddle somewhere." Laith walked over to the wardrobe and pulled a couple of doors open for a glance. He moved some stuff out of the way, hanging jackets and swinging belts. My god, how did he live like this?

Theodore watched with his heart in his mouth, breath stuck in his throat. The mere thought of a paddle hitting him was enough to bring color to his face. How much would it hurt? He supposed it depended on how hard Laith would do it. He could definitely incapacitate Theodore if he wanted to, break skin and bone, but Theodore didn't think he would. The possibility was still exciting, though, in a scary way. Knowing it could happen, that Laith could seriously hurt him quickened his pulse. He could barely wait.

"Here." On one of the shelves in the wardrobe was a plastic box without a lid, which Laith pulled like a drawer for the paddle. It was very simple, a slab of wood like the ones in history books, that teachers used to spank their students with. At least, that was what it reminded him of. Was that it, or did they use rulers instead? He wasn't sure. Laith spun the paddle before offering it to him. "If you're interested. I have some other stuff too, but let's just take this one step at a time."

The paddle was heavier than he thought. He held it in both hands, appraising the weight, grabbing the width of the widest part. This could hurt. He slapped it into his own hand just to feel the impact, not nearly hard enough to sting. Part of him was too self-conscious to do it right in front of Laith.

"You wanna test it?" Laith asked, pushing the box back in its place.

Their eyes met.

"I'll let you hit me."

His eyebrows raised, blood pumping with excitement. Really?

Before he could even think of an answer, Laith pulled his shirt off with practiced ease. One hand threw it on the floor while the other slapped his own stomach, just over his navel. The muscles there tensed. "Use the wide part."

Of course. Theodore held it tightly, and with his heart beating out of his chest, hit Laith where he'd indicated. It was a weak hit, so he could see how it'd land and how much it'd hurt. It didn't even turn the skin red.

"You can do it harder. It's okay."

His eyes glanced up at Laith, then back down at his stomach. Okay, then—a proper hit. This time, the paddle made a sound upon impact, muscles reacting to the hit. Instinctively, he met Laith's face, not to find reassurance or comfort there, but to look for a sign that he'd actually hurt him. He wanted to see Laith bothered, but only found a big grin instead. That was just as well, he guessed. Moving the paddle away, he noticed it'd left the skin red.

"It's not so bad," Laith reassured him. "It just looks scary."

He turned the paddle around, inspecting it. Part of him wanted to hit Laith again, hard enough to get a reaction out of him, a hitched breath and a scowl. Instead, he gave the paddle back. "Make sure it leaves me purple."

Laith's grin turned into a smirk. "We'll see. Do you have an idea of what the rest of the scene should look like?"

Absolutely not, but he could use last night for inspiration. "If we start off with you hitting me, then the middle is probably fucking and the end is getting to cum. That'd be my guess."

"That works for me." Laith tossed the paddle into the air, spinning it. "Let me know when you've had enough."

Oh? He didn't think he'd have a say in that. If he was the one in charge, then what would happen if he didn't say a single thing? Would Laith keep hitting him indefinitely? Would Laith actually hurt him? Too excited to wait another second, he shrugged his jacket off and tossed it over the bed.

"Can we start, then?" he asked, already kicking his shoes off.

Laith watched him with a grin on his face, eyes sharp. "Sure. Is there a pet name you want me to use?"

Was there? He couldn't really think of anything at the moment, hurrying to take his pants off. He kept the underwear on, just because he wasn't sure if he was supposed to take them off or not, and climbed onto the bed. "I don't know." He lay on his stomach, elbows propped up and legs stretched. "Call me anything you want."

A muted sound prompted him to glance over his shoulder and see the paddle join him on the bed. Hands grabbed him by the waist and pulled him across the mattress, body sliding over the sheets until his legs were completely off the edge, bent at the hip and knees. The same way he'd get spanked over someone's lap, he'd now get spanked over the bed. That was fine. He faced forward again, hands gripping one another, pulse quick with anticipation.

Laith touched his ass, grabbed it, and landed a quick hard slap that made his breath hitch with surprise. It didn't hurt, because his underwear was still on, but he was sure things would escalate soon.

A couple of slaps later, he was already rock hard; his thighs spread apart all on their own, bottom lip seized between his teeth. He wanted the boxers off.

A hand slipped under his shirt and touched the low of his back, warm on the skin, pressing down. This change in pacing held a breath in his throat, waiting for it. His heart beat so fast that he could hear it against his own ribs.

Something brushed his boxers, rubbing on them a bit before the paddle came down, muted over the fabric, but hard enough to pull a gasp out of him. It didn't hurt in the slightest. The force there was similar to how Laith had slapped him the night before, but he knew it wouldn't be enough to leave a single mark.

Laith hit him again, harder this time, lurching him against the mattress—*that* one hurt. His toes curled, hands squeezing—holy shit. All he could think of was how it would've felt on his skin, the sting, the color it'd turn him. That one would've hurt bad. The paddle came down again, a few more times, just as hard. It never got harder than that. The force alone was scary enough, the way it pushed his thighs against the bed, even if it didn't hurt nearly as much as he'd wanted it to. His knees bent with the impact, little twitches every time the paddle came down, head hanging down, face burning in private.

As soon as the hand on his back pulled away, he breathed in deeply. The paddle fell onto the bed again, but other than that, he couldn't tell what Laith was doing, hidden behind him. He decided not to look; the excitement of not knowing was delicious. Two hands ran up his thighs and over his ass, pressing down, almost like a massage. "Let's see what it looks like."

Oh, so they could talk? The silence had given him the impression that that wasn't allowed, but Laith had probably just been very focused—focused on *him*. That little detail, so small but so important, would never go over his head.

Focused entirely on him.

Fingers slipped under the waistband of his boxers and pulled them down, not all the way, just enough to show off his ass. That small action shot straight between his legs, cock pulsing, trapped in his boxers. A hand touched his cheek very softly, feeling the tender skin there. He hadn't noticed how tender he really was, even though that should've been expected. In his mind, the boxers had protected him from everything.

"It's similar to the way I left you last night, but to my understanding, that's not what you want."

"No, it isn't."

Would Laith punish him for speaking? No, of course not; that wasn't part of the deal, but now he kind of wanted it to happen. Maybe they could have a list of rules for him to break, each one with its own set of punishments; some known, some not, varying in severity. Man, they should've talked about that beforehand. Next time, then.

"Let's take it a little bit further."

Yes. God, yes. His eyes shut immediately, head moving down, already preparing himself. Yes.

Laith pushed on the low of his back again and his cock throbbed in anticipation, hands squeezed together. The paddle touched his ass for a very brief moment, pulled back and came down. The surprise alone was enough to get a reaction out of him, stomach tensing, legs twitching. It wasn't sharp like a slap, but it stung all the same, even if the force used here was less than how Laith had been hitting him before. The boxers had made a big difference.

The paddle came down again, a little bit harder, and the sound it made against his skin sent shivers up his spine, toes curling. Every hit hurt a little more than the last, all stacked on top of each other, in the same spot. Laith only did it a handful of times, but still, as soon as he stopped, Theodore found himself breathing in deeply, muscles relaxing over the bed. Damn, D'angela wasn't kidding; this really *was* a workout.

Laith pulled his boxers all the way off, cock pressed against the side of the mattress, knees bending to help him out. Two hands grabbed his thighs and pushed them further apart, fingers digging into the softness there, spreading him. At this point, he could barely hold himself up anymore and decided to fold his arms under his face, lying flat over them.

"I'm not done yet," he informed Laith, voice muffled a bit. "I can take a lot more than that."

"I know. Be patient."

When the paddle came down this time, his eyes shot open, ice pumped into his bloodstream—that was *very* close to his balls. That was *dangerously* close to his balls. At least, it'd felt like it, since the boxers weren't covering them anymore.

Every time the paddle came down now, part of him was terrified he'd get his balls crushed; his breath came in sharp and his entire body started. He could barely even focus on the pain, paranoid, muscles tense, mind alert. The longer it went on, however, the sooner he realized Laith wouldn't actually hit him there; it was just a mind game. Some hits landed closer than others, but those were spread out, clearly to catch him by surprise. That helped him relax a bit, skin tingling, calling to his attention.

Laith widened the impact area from his ass to the back of his thighs, alternating between them, keeping him on his toes. Under that kind of diligence, it really didn't take long for Theodore to find himself out of breath, skin burning, cock dripping down the sheets. A couple of fingers pushed inside him just to tease, thrusting in every time the paddle met his skin. It was torture, but god, he'd choose it every day of the week.

Laith pushed in deeper, hitting his ass, making it sting. It was really starting to hurt now; every hit sent a deeper ache into his muscles, body trembling with how tensely it held itself.

Honestly, at this point, he just wanted Laith to fuck him. He was exhausted. Still, he didn't say anything; he wanted to see how much he could take and if Laith would keep hitting him forever. He gritted his teeth and squeezed his arms, toes curling, knees bending. He'd been pretty good at keeping quiet this whole time, breathing loudly instead; a gasp here, a sharp inhale there, but now, it was getting difficult. His eyebrows furrowed in pain, lips pressed hard together, muffling any whimpers that he failed to contain. His nails dug into the meat of his arms, throat closed around a lump. Fuck.

Just as his eyes began to water, Laith stopped. Breath immediately filled his lungs, body relaxing. A sound almost escaped him, but he swallowed it down before it could. His brain drowned, unable to formulate a single thought, lost in relief. He could've moaned right now.

"Are you sure you're not done?" Laith asked, breathless as well.

He was utterly unable to answer that. He couldn't even move, really; he was so fucking tired that catching his breath was an ordeal in itself, extinguishing the last of his energy. He felt like the victim of a roadside accident.

A hand touched him on the hip as the mattress dipped on the opposite side. Laith lay on top of him, but not with his entire weight; he must be leaning on an arm, keeping himself just low enough to meet his stomach with Theodore's back. His hips pressed against Theodore's, and even through the fabric of his boxers, it was possible to feel him pushing against Theodore's ass. He bit his lip.

"I think you're done," Laith whispered, low in his ear. It sent shivers down his spine. A trail of light kisses peppered his neck and jaw, nice and sweet as Laith ground against him, tender skin on soft cotton. The hand on Theodore's hip slid over one ass cheek, moving to pull Laith's boxers down.

As soon as Laith met his skin, his cock throbbed, and if he wasn't sandwiched against the mattress, he would've pushed back against him. Fingers pressed the head against the entrance, rubbing a bit. The way Laith shifted above him, angling his hips, lay weight over Theodore's back, Laith's breath warm on his neck. This time, when Laith thrust in, he couldn't stop the sound that came up his throat.

mmermlmlm

Something D'angela had failed to mention was that, apparently, after these types of scenes, aftercare happened. That was what Laith called it. He rubbed some ointment on Theodore's skin and assessed his emotional state, asking for his thoughts on what they'd just done. Lying there, a familiar feeling reached him, that they'd been through this before. The déjà vu was so strong that he didn't register the question Laith had just posed to him. His memories were hazy, because he'd been blackout drunk, but he was sure Laith had massaged him just last night; they felt far too real to be just his imagination.

"If this is aftercare, then was last night a scene too?"

"Not really. It was more like a spur of the moment thing, but it's better to be safe when it comes to these kinds of things. I didn't want you to feel uncomfortable and, like, regret it the next day, you know?" The mattress dipped and moved as Laith left it, hidden out of view. "You should get up and see how it looks."

His body felt like jelly, but he managed to slide across the mattress and sit on the edge anyway. An arm kept him propped up, feet touching the floor—he didn't want to do it. Laith pulled one of the wardrobe doors open for him, the one with a full-body mirror inside, so he could look at himself. It'd be easier than going to the bathroom for it.

He gingerly shifted his weight to both feet and turned around, still leaning a hand on the bed for support. His heart soared at the sight, blood cold—the bruises looked exactly how he thought they'd be this morning, deep purple spots all the way down his thighs, as if Laith had kicked the shit out of him. Would they last? "How long will it look like that for?"

"A few days. It depends on the person, but I don't think it'll stick around longer than a week."

Damn, really? All that for just a few days' worth of color? Hopefully, his body wouldn't get to it too fast.

Laith cleared his throat. "So, what did you think? Overall."

"I was thinking about something, actually." He sat back down. A deep ache immediately shot up his back, so he shifted some weight to his feet, which still rested on the floor. The hand on the mattress kept him off it a bit. "Next time, we could have like, a list of things that I'm not allowed to do, so every time

I break a rule, I get a certain punishment. Like, if I kiss you when I'm not supposed to, you'll hit me ten times or something."

"We probably shouldn't hit you for a few days."

He rolled his eyes. "Alright, then I'll hit *you* instead. How's that?"

"That's fine," Laith spoke with a grin, moving to take a seat next to him. "We could come up with some non-corporeal punishments, if you want. Like, you'll have to stay quiet for ten minutes or recite the alphabet backwards."

"No, look. What I want is to break the rules and then get beat up. Obviously, I'll be doing it on purpose."

"Then we'll have to give it a few days."

Theodore pursed his lips, sighing in frustration. "Fine. We'll come up with something else, then." He kicked Laith's leg. It was playful, with naked feet that wouldn't be able to hurt even if he'd wanted them to. "Next time, can you talk to me like you did last night? I couldn't think of a nickname, because I wasn't really thinking of anything, but I liked the way you talked to me, the stuff you said."

Laith watched him curiously, with eyes so thoughtful that they almost squinted. "Are you a masochist, Theo?"

He always mistook one for the other, but given the context, he was pretty sure that was the one that enjoyed getting hurt. "I don't know. I guess. I mean—" His shoulders bounced. "—you know, I'd just as gladly beat you up instead. I think they're both hot."

They held the stare. By all means, the care with which Laith studied him should be unnerving, but the attention that he received—the attention from *Laith* that he received—dwarfed every emotion that didn't fill his lungs with affection and his chest with warmth. He couldn't name it, the feeling that made it so easy to exist, that would love to live under Laith's gaze for the rest of eternity. If someone were to pull him apart at the seams, then it might as well be Laith. After all, weren't love and attention pretty much the same?

"We'll take turns, then. I'll let you hit me next time."

He smiled. "Does that make me a sadomasochist?"

"I think so."

"Aren't you one too?"

Laith shrugged, frowning briefly. "I don't really have much of a preference. I get off on getting *you* off."

"A man of the people."

"A real guy's guy."

His grin matched Laith's, laugher bubbling at the base of his throat.

"You're full of surprises, you know. You're nothing like I thought you were," Laith mused.

"What do you mean?"

"You're a wolf in sheep's clothing. You look like a goody-two-shoes, but you're really—"

"A freak?"

"No." Laith laughed. "You're much more similar to me than I thought."

"I know. We've been over this." Oh right, Laith had practically made no memories that night. "On Justin's porch, we decided that I'm you and you're me," he explained. "That you made me up in your head."

"We talked about that?" Dark eyebrows furrowed. "I told you that!?"

"Yeah." He shaped that word around a grin. "Why are you so surprised?"

Green eyes watched him wide. "That's..." Laith's throat moved with a dry swallow. "I mean, that's not really something I can explain without getting checked into a psych ward. It's... well, the kind of thought you have that you know is true because you feel it rather than make any sense of it. Obviously, you're a piece of me, but how do you explain that?"

"You don't need to explain it. I know that because you came from me too. You're more me than I'll ever be. I look at you, and you know, I see myself."

They held the stare. Laith's shoulders raised into a shrug that never fell, and before Theodore could even understand what that was, Laith got up from the bed. He crossed his arms and hugged them, turning to face Theodore again. "You're freaking me out. Don't say shit like that."

Theodore grinned. "I know what you're thinking, that this is what it feels like to talk to yourself. I know because I've felt that way ever since we met."

"Why didn't you tell me?"

"If I had, would you still have slept with me?"

Laith stared at him.

"When you said people can only fall in love with the versions of other people that they have in their heads, is this what you meant?" Theodore asked. It was a genuine question. Perhaps the one he'd wanted to know the answer to the most.

"No, this is the opposite."

"Because it's true?"

Laith's shoulders relaxed, arms falling back to his sides. His lack of an answer evidenced the end of this topic.

"Can we have dinner?" Theodore tried instead, head tilting aside. "I'm starving."

That night, he ended up falling asleep in Laith's arms again. He hadn't meant to; the exertion from earlier had just worn him out. That coupled with the fact he'd barely slept a wink the night before had only served to knock the lights out of him as soon as the movie began and the warmth of Laith's body enveloped him in a hug. It wasn't completely restful, though. At one point, Laith woke him up to show him something on his phone, a meme that Theodore couldn't comprehend but that Laith said was him, apparently. Then, he woke up again, but very briefly, to find Laith slipping an arm around him. In that moment, it didn't occur to him to wonder when the hug from before had ended, considering he was being pulled into a new one. His consciousness left him just as fast.

He woke up on Laith's side of the bed, eyes opening to stare straight at the alarm clock—9 a.m. Goddammit, he'd miss that same class again. At least he didn't have an 8 a.m. or anything earlier than this.

Without really thinking, he turned around to hug Laith one last time, a parting gesture that would hopefully burn an imprint of Laith's body against his own, something to think about throughout the day. As soon as he nuzzled into Laith's neck, he breathed in the faint scent of smoke, but not any smoke—pot. Did Laith get high last night? Had he gone somewhere? With his heart racing, Theodore propped himself up on an elbow and grabbed Laith's face with a hand, eyebrows drawn hard together. "Hey. Hey." He moved Laith's face a bit, pinching his jaw between his thumb and forefinger.

Laith breathed in deep, stirring beneath him.

"Did you go out last night?"

Green eyes cracked open just a slit, fixed on him. Laith quietly nodded. He brought an arm up and slipped it under his own head, sort of stretching under Theodore's partial weight.

"Why didn't you wake me up?"

"You were really tired."

A fist closed around his heart and squeezed it. There was no way around it; he'd have to change that. The problem wasn't only that he hadn't slept much yesterday, but that he hadn't found any time in his schedule to actually lie down and sleep. He'd exchanged his usual bedtime for a longer night with Laith, which had only resulted in him falling asleep while they hung out, leaving Laith by himself. That wouldn't do. He'd have to see Laith a bit later than right after class, maybe after Laith had come back from the gym. If he got home around 3:30 and fell asleep immediately after, he could get up around 10 p.m. or 11 p.m. and stay up all night. That should work.

Chapter 16

I don't understand, don't get upset
I'm not with you
We're swimming around
It's all I do when I'm with you

- Daft Punk, *Instant Crush (feat. Julian Casablancas)*

He had to drop by the apartment for his backpack, but since Laith only lived a couple of subway rides from his place, he was able to make it to second period just fine. Even though first period was utterly doomed, he still sat in for the last fifteen minutes of it. He might as well. That was when the professor usually brought up homework and recommended a few book titles, in case students were particularly interested in the subject or thought about specializing in it later on. He didn't think he'd read any of those books, but still took note of them, just in case. Who knew? He might want to become an expert in statistics later in life. He was pretty good with numbers, after all.

During lunch break, he decided to buy some new notebooks to write on, so he could stop using his old high school ones. Most of them were almost done with, anyway. A quick online search informed him of a graphic design store that sold office supplies just across the street from Gate C. Worried about the time constraint, since the store was pretty much all the way across campus, he didn't even stop to think about who worked there. He *knew* Ryan lived and worked nearby, but since they'd never run into each other, that fact lived in the very back of his mind, out of the realm of possibility. Ryan didn't go here anymore; why should they ever meet?

As soon as he walked into the store, his heart froze and shattered. The door closed behind him with a merry little jingle.

The look Ryan gave him was completely dead. The only emotion in his face was exhaustion, as if he'd been pulling twelve-hour shifts for three weeks straight. It bore wondering if that was how Theodore made him feel, if he was really so emotionally taxing. It hurt to consider that. Ryan's hair lay flat over his forehead, as if he hadn't brushed it this morning when he usually pulled all the stops, styling it up every day. As Theodore approached, he noticed the bags under Ryan's eyes, practically sunken in. His brother had no fight left in him.

"How can I help you?" Ryan asked, flat and joyless.

If this were any other day, Theodore would be getting ready to roast his uniform, how silly he looked in a polo shirt when he absolutely despised them. Today, it just wouldn't feel right. He approached the counter and cleared his throat. They were the only two people in the store. "Um, I'm looking for a couple of notebooks, maybe a binder. A place to keep my notes."

"We have these down here." Ryan pointed down the counter, where a glass panel turned the bottom into a display case with notebooks and pens inside. "As for binders, we have the ones behind me."

All the cover designs on those notebooks clearly pandered to certain types of people, all of which weren't Theodore. Some of them were pink with beloved cartoon characters in adorable poses, while others were cars and sports teams. The only normal ones were plain colors. The binders were the exact same too, so he ended up pointing at one of the plain black notebooks and a plain black binder. He could decorate them himself, if he wanted to. Ryan placed both items on the counter, plus a stack of lined paper, and rang him up. He handed Ryan his credit card.

Everything about this interaction was weird, but especially how impersonal Ryan was being with him, acting as if they didn't know each other. He took the card without a word, punched numbers into the machine, and passed it back to Theodore. The entire time, neither one of them said a word. As soon as the purchase went through, Theodore took the card back while Ryan slipped his things into a plastic bag. He took it with a tight knot in his throat.

"When are you leaving town?" he asked, lingering by the cash register.

"I don't know." Ryan kept his eyes down, hands moving behind the register. Theodore couldn't see what for. "I might stay for a while."

I thought you felt suffocated near me. Isn't that why you wanted to skip town in the first place?

He swallowed around a lump, nodding. Part of him crushed his chest while the other closed his hands into fists. What could he even do? Every time the two of them interacted, it felt like he was trying to build a castle on the dry corner of the beach, sand running through his fingers. No matter how hard he tried, he never got anywhere with his brother. Actually, he'd only managed to push Ryan away. "I'd like it if you stayed," he confessed. His voice was small, cheeks burning.

Ryan gave him the most emotionless look he'd ever received. "Thanks for shopping with us. Have a nice day."

That felt like a plastic bag wrapping around his head. The message was loud and clear, even if he didn't like to hear it. He'd known it forever. Without a word, he turned and left the store.

In the cafeteria, he managed to find the girls and take a seat at their table. The interaction with Ryan had left him pretty numb, without the smallest impulse to eat, but he knew he should at least try to have something, since he'd left without breakfast. The girls all spoke while he nibbled on a sandwich, eyes down at the void in his mind, body aching and sore. He felt like shit. It wasn't even a physical thing; he'd been fine a minute ago, dragging his ass across the subway system. The damp blanket Ryan had thrown over him had not only sunk his heart, but made the regular, everyday tiredness feel like total fatigue. Suddenly, he was fifty pounds heavier and just wanted to go to bed.

Tuning on-again, off-again into the girls' conversation, he caught part of a discussion about Jessie's plans for tonight. Apparently, she'd worked out a time with Justin and would actually go down to see him. From what Theodore could tell, she had every intention to fuck him in that truck. The girls all seemed very excited and proceeded to give her suggestions on what to wear; cute jackets, tights and hoodies for the cool weather they'd been having. That level of interest seemed a little out of place, since Theodore was pretty sure Jessie—and everyone else here—had sex all the time. What made this hookup different? It was true that Jessie and Hannah never made plans for this stuff, just hooked up with strangers at random parties. Still, that was all he could find; she didn't mention being in a relationship or dating Justin at all. The promise of an interesting night must be enough to look forward to. *That* he could understand.

At one point, the conversation turned to him and how his night had gone. Not wanting to be too graphic, he instead told them about the drag queens, the hot guys at the gym and how kinky those girls were. To his surprise, he didn't end up needing to explain anything about that; everyone here was already familiar with the concept. It made him feel a little dumb for being the only one confused by some of it, but all in all, it saved him time.

The girls' curiosity came from the fact that Laith was friends with actual drag queens. It was mind-blowing to them that drag queens were an accessible friend group rather than their own exclusive club. Theodore was sure they had their exclusive club anyway, but also hung out with their hot neighbor from time to time. That seemed to be the hook that had pulled them in—how hot Laith was. It explained why they weren't friends with anyone else in their building.

No one explicitly asked him how it'd been with Laith last night, so he decided not to say a thing about it. That wasn't the kind of information anyone here needed to know.

The ache in his thighs never left him, present at every breathing moment. If he didn't move in his seat too much, he could forget about it and focus on the lecture for a while, but as soon as he got up, he was reminded of what had happened the night before. It was awkward, to say the least. He couldn't think of an instance where he'd spent so long thinking about Laith's hands on his body, thighs spread apart. Every few minutes, he came back to it, struggling to stay focused. Part of him loathed how easily his cock stirred, at half-mast pretty much the entire time, legs bouncing under his desk, pen tapping on lined paper. His legs really didn't help; all they did was evidence the soreness in his muscles, how spent he was, how thoroughly Laith had worn him out.

The other part of him, for as horrible as this was, kind of liked the secrecy, the idea that no one around him knew what he was thinking about. It was a terrible dichotomy that hit him in waves of shame and excitement, made worse with his prolonged exposure to the public. The moment his last period was over with, he shoved all his things into his backpack and left the classroom.

He really thought he'd get home, hop into bed and fall asleep with no issue, like he usually did, but the problem was that he wasn't tired. Not physically. He'd slept through the night before just fine; the reasons why he didn't feel good had nothing to do with the amount of energy left in his body. As it turned out, there was plenty left.

He tossed and turned in the partial dark, unable to drown out his thoughts, thighs trembling with exertion. The silence opened a floodgate straight into his brain, and addicted to what Laith had done to him, he couldn't help reliving it, the sting of the paddle and the fingers that had pushed in. His cock throbbed with the mere thought.

A hand came down to grab himself over his boxers, holding his cock with no grander plan in mind. He could barely think; the only things that occurred to him were images and feelings, memories of what had happened earlier; Laith on top of him, pushing inside, holding their hips together. The ache in his muscles, how his thighs had hurt every time Laith had thrust against him. The weight of Laith's body, heavy enough to suffocate him if he'd wanted to.

He thrust into his own hand, absently, barely even there. It was an instinct more than anything else. As soon as he did it, he imagined his hand belonged to Laith, that he was pushing into Laith's palm instead. If he was here, what would he do? Would he grab Theodore where it hurt, would he make it worse? He'd said he wouldn't hit him for a few days, but that didn't rule out other ways to hurt him.

With his eyes closed, he pictured Laith walking into his room, watching him touch himself. There was a smirk on his face, subtle but present, that gave shape to the delight and the scorn that brewed with Theodore's utter incompetence at getting himself off. The real Laith didn't know, but *this* Laith knew that he didn't like doing it alone, that he felt weird about it, awkward. Laith was way better at it, anyway. Everything was better with him.

He slipped that hand into his boxers and stroked, picturing Laith kneeling between his thighs just how he'd done on Sunday morning. That felt so long ago now, the way Laith had folded him up and fucked him into this mattress. Then, later, the hand in his hair and Laith's cock all the way down his throat. Then, even later, the awakening of something deep inside as Laith had spanked his ass. My god, had they done anything but fuck these last couple of days? Jesus.

He pictured Laith jerking him off, leaning over him with a hand on the mattress. That made things much easier for him; it set his blood on fire and rose heat into his face, eyes screwed shut. He bit his lip, wrist working fast, lungs nonfunctional. Laith spoke to him in the same vicious way he'd done on Sunday night, calling him names, shedding light into his degeneracy, how surprised he was that an innocent guy like Theodore got off on such depraved, dirty shit. So he wanted Laith to hurt him, hit him, beat him up? How fucked up, how obscene. He pictured Laith grabbing his face and holding him down, mouth muffled under his hand, head pushed into the mattress. He panted.

As he got close, scrambled thoughts flashed through his mind, every climax they'd ever had together, shots of cum hitting him in the face, Hwan and Marquis fucking on top of him. His brain quickly switched Marquis for Laith and pushed his legs far apart so imaginary Laith could fit between them. Imaginary Hwan grabbed Laith's hips and thrusted into him, lurching him against Theodore, practically fucking Theodore through him. He pictured Laith's face, bottom lip seized between his teeth, eyebrows furrowed hard.

What would Laith think about that? He'd hate it, of course; there wasn't a single part of him that felt even remotely affectionately toward Hwan. He'd never let Hwan touch him like that. What would he think, then, if he knew Theodore was getting off to it? He'd call him sick. Both of them would call him sick for even thinking it up. Ironically, that would be the one thing they'd agree on. Would it bring them closer together?

In his mind, Laith leaned up so Hwan could land a kiss square on his mouth. No, it'd never happen; they'd first curse him out than do anything like that. Hwan's lips shaped around the word *freak* as Laith called him a degenerate. That was more than enough to push him over the edge with a strangled noise and an ache where his thighs met his hips. He breathed laboriously, eyebrows drawn into a scowl, cum dripping down his fist.

It was much easier to fall asleep after that.

mmmmmm

He hadn't set an alarm this time. That only occurred to him when he checked his phone for the time and saw the number twelve staring back at him. Still too groggy to make sense of that, he caught sight of the text notifications and unlocked the screen to check them. A few were from Justin while one was from Emily. Since Justin was still texting him, with new messages coming in, he tapped on that first.

Okay first of all I'm sorry.

Like I AM sorry but I'm not sorry, you know? I'm not sorry cause I really like her and she's amazing but I am sorry cause she's your friend and there are rules about this kinda stuff. I mean, just look at what happened between Ryan and Laith.

I get that their sitch is different cause you're his brother and that's way worse but maaaan... I don't want you to be mad at me!

I really like you!!!!!

Listen listen. She's a queen okay? And I tried to treat her like one I promise. I had every intention to put the seats down and turn on the heater and stuff. I even drove round back for privacy. I brought blankets for the windows!!!!

Theodore blinked a few times, staring blankly at the texts that just kept coming.

Look, I'm not a snitch but she's the one who didn't want to cover the windows up or put the seats down or anything, alright? I know she wouldn't misrepresent me but I just need you to know that. I came prepared. I was ready to take her somewhere nice too cause hey, not every girl is down for something like that, but she said she wasn't above it, so.
Bro I came with cash in hand jic the motel didn't take credit.
I have to say she surprised me tho. Like I wasn't expecting that at all.
She's like a tornado. She messed me up and left me crazy and all I could do was watch and let it happen cause there's no stopping someone like that. I didn't want to anyway but you know what I mean.
Oh god is that tmi? I don't want to scare you off.

His fingers moved over the keys.

Justin.

He blinked very slowly.

It's twelve in the morning. Didn't you just sleep with her?
Yeah. I was driving back home but I couldn't stop thinking about you so I pulled over to text you and get some coffee. I don't want you to be mad at me.
I'm not mad at you. Why would I be mad at you? Jessie and I have nothing between us.
I just don't want you to feel like I'm using you to get to the girls or something. You're my friend and I care about you a lot and I don't want you to feel like I don't!
Dude, I know that. It's fine.
I'm glad you like her and that it all worked out for you guys. I mean, you've

been needing that, right? You couldn't even remember your last nut.

Yeah yeah sure. That's really neither here nor there but yeah ok.

I can't believe your very first thought after busting one was me. You must like me a little bit. :)

I do!!!!! I like you a lot!!!!!!!!

His heart swelled. If only Laith were that direct.

Promise we're good? I don't want things to be weird between us.

Hey, you can fill Jessie up all you want and we'll still be friends, I promise.

You really didn't have to say it like that but yeah that's good to know. I feel much better now. I'm buzzed up and ready to hit the road!

I love you bro.

His pulse skipped. No, Justin didn't mean it like that; this was a guy thing, not a gay thing.

Love you too dude.

He'd never said that to anyone outside his family. It was weird to think that the first person to hear it was Justin when he'd almost said it just yesterday. His blood ran cold with the memories, how close he'd been, practically choking on those words. My god, what would Laith have thought? Would his eyes have shot open, would his mouth have curled with disgust? Under different circumstances, in a different lifetime, would he have said it back?

He decided to no longer think about that. Instead, he opened Emily's text.

I don't know if Ryan told you or if you even care, but he's not skipping town. For a while, at least. It might not be the case forever. Anyway, I promised him we'd hang out on Friday. Do you remember the schedule I mentioned? If you wanna party this weekend, Justin and I can see you on Saturday.

Did Justin know about that? Before answering Emily, he hopped back to Justin's chat window.

What's this thing about seeing Ryan this Friday?

He's not doing well... I'm sure you remember what happened. We're hanging out on Friday to help him feel better.

Saturdays are reserved for Laith tho so we'll probably see each other then. I mean you two are pretty much a combo deal now.

How interesting. Was he an afterthought because of his proximity to Laith—an unavoidable guest who'd show up anyway; Laith's plus one whether the others liked it or not—or did Emily actually mean to invite him? He wondered if Laith knew about it too and if he'd agreed with the others about Theodore crashing the party. Saturdays were reserved for *Laith* after all, not him. It would still have been nice to be invited, though, but he wasn't one of them. Obviously, invitations were for friends only.

Leaving both chats on read, he got out of bed.

mmemmlommlem

Laith's apartment building was always noisy. His neighbors never gave it a rest, arguing with each other on every floor, in every hallway, while others came and went, talked by the stairs and gathered in the corners. That was probably why the queens liked this place so much; the liveliness gave them something to gossip about. Theodore wouldn't be surprised to find out they knew everyone's darkest secrets without knowing any of their names.

This time, part of the commotion could be attributed to the queens themselves. Their laughter echoed down the hallway, growing louder as he covered ground. He couldn't make out their conversation, though, too quiet to eavesdrop on, discussed between bursts of roaring laughter.

He'd recognize Laith's voice anywhere.

His gradual approach evidenced the group's exact location, in Ms. Intervention's apartment, where the door had been left wide open. That seemed to always be the case. Instead of inviting himself in, which would be beyond inappropriate, Theodore only poked his head in.

This apartment had the same layout as Laith's, with a bathroom on the right and a small kitchen in the back. However, the way Ms. Intervention had decorated it gave it a completely different look. In the foyer, she'd pushed a console table against the leftmost wall under a round sun-like mirror. Underneath it were a couple of decorative vases, big enough to kill somebody with. He
188

was sure that was the reason why she'd got them. The floor was covered in a light blue carpet, brighter in certain spots where a neon sign shone. All the overhead lights had been turned off, leaving only this sign on, hanging on the same wall where Laith, in his apartment, had mounted a TV. Theodore couldn't read it from the doorway. Under it was a rectangular loveseat where the queens both sat and a corner table with empty beer cans on top. The bed had taken the same place as Laith's, directly in front of the sign. He sat on the edge of the mattress, the only one with a decent view of the doorway, bathed in pink and violet.

As soon as Theodore poked his head in, Laith spotted him. "Theo! Hey, come in," he said while beckoning him with a hand, head nodding to the rest of the room. "We're talking about old Hollywood stars that might possibly have been gay."

"How topical."

The queens both laughed. Their skins shone violet under the sign, hair neon pink; the room was bright where they sat and dark near the edges. They both sparkled; D'angela had stars on her eyelids and Ms. Intervention had sequins on her dress, mesmerizing to watch.

Theodore walked in tentatively, staring at the glow over Laith's jacket, shirt catching the light in geometrical patterns. That got his attention, since Laith never wore anything that wasn't plain black. The carpet muffled his footsteps as the three continued their conversation, speaking of old-sounding names that he didn't recognize. Approaching the bed, he was able to read the sign on the wall— *I'm your expensive taste*—with hearts floating up and a burning flame next to it. Close to Laith, he noticed that his shirt was covered in small triangles.

"Get him a beer, will you?" Ms. Intervention spoke with her eyes set on Laith, hand waving the air. Her rings shone and her bracelets rattled.

"Yes, queen." Laith hopped off the bed.

"Oh, get me another one," D'angela called.

Laith walked the three or so steps toward the kitchen.

"Go on, take a seat." Ms. Intervention referred to Theodore next. Her back leaned comfortably against the couch, legs crossed at the knees, covered in sequins all the way down. Aside from the corner table, which was littered with empty beer cans, Theodore also noticed a trashcan almost full to the brim with more of them, placed next to D'angela. She sat on one of her legs, in booty shorts and a loose t-shirt. Were they... drunk?

Theodore didn't have time to sit down before Laith was back with a can

189

for each of them. As the queens thanked him, he reclaimed his seat and opened a new one himself, foam threatening to come out. The sight shocked Theodore, hands cold around the can. Hadn't Laith stopped drinking? Wasn't he on prescription? Theodore couldn't move.

The three talked and joked, but he couldn't focus on anything they said. His ears were stuffed with cotton, the home of a sharp ringing that shook his skull and drowned out every sound as he watched Laith down his beer like it was water. Under the ringing was a scream.

He slowly placed his can on the bed and excused himself. Out in the hallway, he grabbed his phone and opened Emily's chat window.

I thought Laith had stopped drinking. Isn't he on prescription?

Before she even had time to read that, he followed it up with something very important.

Please don't call me. I'm within earshot.
Hey.
Yeah, he has a prescription for Xanax, but he was only on it last weekend.

Xanax? What the fuck did Xanax do?

Don't people stay on those for a while? Months?
I don't think you know how he works. He's had these pills forever, but he hasn't been on them.
Except for last weekend.

But I thought—he erased that message and started over. *You mean they're the same ones since the hospital.*
No, I mean it's the same prescription.
That's what I'm saying. Like he hasn't gone to Fred for a new one.
He hasn't seen Fred in a while.
If you thought he'd gone back to therapy, I don't blame you. When he brought up the pills, I thought the same thing too, but no. That's his old prescription.
So he's not on it all the time.

190

No, only when he wants to be.

What the fuck did that mean? Did he take it recreationally?

*I thought he was better. That he stopped seeing Fred because he was better.
If that's true, why would he be on his old prescription again?*
Maybe you should talk to him about it.
Why would he only take it for a couple of days and then stop?
Don't ask me.
Is he still on it?
Jesus Christ, Theo.

"Theo?" Laith's voice startled him to such an astronomical degree that his phone jumped from his hands and his breathing ceased. Luckily, his phone didn't fly too high up and landed safely in his hands. He hoped that, since he had his back turned, Laith hadn't seen any of that.

Before turning around, he forced a smile. "Yeah?"

"Do you wanna hang out? It's chill if you don't. I'm sure they'll understand."

"No, I do, I just—" He cocked his head aside at a perfect loss for words. His smile quickly turned sheepish, hands clutching his phone to his own chest. "Maybe we could have dinner first?"

"Yeah, sure." Laith walked back to Ms. Intervention's door and popped his head in. "Hey, we're grabbing something to eat. You want anything?"

"Where are you going?" D'angela asked.

Laith turned back to Theodore and repeated the question, as if he hadn't heard her from two feet away.

"Um, I don't know. A burger joint."

Laith turned back to D'angela and repeated the answer. He must be absolutely plastered.

"Get me some fries," D'angela ordered.

"And a diet Coke," Ms. Intervention added.

"Alright."

With a quest to his name, Laith followed Theodore down the hallway.

mmermemem

191

It was only under the overhead lights of the burger joint that he realized Laith's shirt *was* black, after all. The triangular pattern was made of a shiny kind of material, also black, that only appeared if light shone over it. Fancy.

They put their orders in at the counter—a burger, a medium Coke, two medium fries, a large Diet Coke and a large Irish Coke. Theodore had no idea it was possible to order something with alcohol mixed into it. This wasn't a bar.

"There's no law enforcement down here," Laith explained, pulling what looked like poker chips out of a pocket. "Any business can sell alcohol, no license needed. That's why no one cards you at the DP."

"So a middle schooler could order an Irish Coke."

"I'd like to see them try," the cashier cut in.

That comment pulled laugher from Laith's throat. "I mean, yeah, they could. It's up to the business owner to decide if they're actually gonna serve this kid."

"I"ve never seen that happen," the cashier added. "Teenagers usually get a pass, though."

"True. Thanks, Kasey." Laith turned to cross the establishment for one of the booths near the wall. On the way, Theodore kept his eye on the cashier to make sure they wouldn't listen to this next part, or they'd think he was stupid. As soon as the guy turned around, he spoke.

"Why did you pay with poker chips?"

"That's our currency. We get paid in chips. Credit cards and dollar bills are a surface thing. You pay with bills and people know you're not from here."

Huh. For a second there, he almost thought Laith had a gambling problem too. They slid into opposing seats, across from each other. Laith leaned back, shirt gleaming under the light, a slither between the breasts of his jacket.

"So, I had a pretty good day," Laith started. "Didn't see the dogs or anything; that's always a plus. Out of all the visits I made, only one couldn't pay up, which is rare. When I got back, the girls decided to come to the gym with me again—you're putting ideas into their heads. Even Ms. Intervention hit the treadmill a bit. They missed you, especially at the gym, but I told them you'd probably come around later. I wasn't wrong."

Laith was clearly drunk. His speech wasn't slurred and his walk wasn't yet affected, but the way he talked, speaking of himself when he never did, gave it away entirely. He grinned wide, happy and talkative, eyes bright.

Theodore's unimpressed silence prompted him to continue.

"I saw your dad, by the way. He's very pleased with how well you've been doing, following his orders and staying out of trouble. Obviously, I told him you're behaving. That you don't go out at all. He gave me two hundred bucks. What can I buy you with that?"

Theodore ignored the question. "You should come up with something else or he'll start to doubt it. Next time, tell him I tried to sneak out, but you caught me just in time. Tell him you made me stay in; that way he'll think you're useful."

Laith cocked his head, eyes up with his thoughts. "Okay. Do you think I should do it just once or more often? Like, maybe once every few days."

"Um, probably when there are actual parties going on. You could say I tried to go to Streisand's on Friday or some other place on the weekend. You know, when we actually go out and do stuff."

"That makes sense."

"With time, stop mentioning it, so he thinks I'm improving because of you. Make it crystal clear that you're important and actually doing stuff."

"I don't know if I can brag to your dad. That's like—that's lying."

"You brag all the time about everything. You'll be fine."

Laith laughed. "Okay, but not to your dad! That's different. When I go in and he's there, I'm not really lying. I tell him you were good that day—or that weekend—and I say it confidently 'cause it's true. You're a good guy; you do stuff from the heart. I just don't know if I can say you're that way because of me. It wouldn't be true at all."

"Just fucking lie."

"No, I'll find a way around it. I'll think of something, like maybe I'm a good influence 'cause I'm a cautionary tale or you see me as one. Maybe you're doing well 'cause you want him to know that and I'm the messenger. Maybe—"

"Tell him if it wasn't for you standing in front of my building late at night, I would've gone to Streisand's. That you're the only reason I didn't go."

"Yeah, but that's not really true, is it?"

They held the stare.

"I'm hanging out with you, right? If I wasn't, where do you think I'd be right now?"

"Uh, at home, I guess."

"Wrong. I'd be getting high with Justin or grabbing a drink with Hwan, but I'm perfectly sober here with you."

Laith thoughtfully touched the bracelet on his left wrist. "I offered you a drink two minutes ago."

"It doesn't matter; I didn't have it."

The cashier walked over with their orders, placing a tray in front of Theodore and a to-go bag in front of Laith, which probably had D'angela's fries in it. He also placed a cup-holder with the two large Cokes in it and left. This was a small business; the sitting area wasn't nearly big enough to warrant any servers. Plus, it seemed that most people ate at the counter anyway.

Laith unwrapped a straw, stuck it into one of the large Cokes and sampled it. The face he made implied it was the wrong one, so he put it back, pulled out the straw and stuck it into the other cup. Most people would've made that face while drinking the Irish Coke, but not him. He drank in massive gulps, the way he always did when alcohol was involved, eager to get as drunk as possible, as quickly as possible. That brought to mind the beer he'd started before Theodore had left. By the time he'd come to the hallway, had he already finished it? Theodore watched him with a lump in his throat, heart jumping into the roof of his mouth.

A moment later, Laith brought the cup back down. "How was your day? Did you make it in time for class? I have a feeling you've been missing some of them 'cause you haven't been setting any alarms."

"I made it just fine."

"Really? Your internal clock must be incredible. It's easy to lose track of time, especially down here; that's why we have so many signs that tell the time. Have you noticed that? Some signs outside have deals written on them, scrolling left to right, followed by the time. Inside, stores and restaurants usually have a clock on the back wall. Look." Laith pointed at a big neon clock above the cash register, digital numbers bright pink.

In response, Theodore simply nodded.

"The chairs in my tattoo parlor all face the clock. It's right above the window, so you can people watch and know exactly how long you've been there. Do you think that's a type of torture?"

"You're being poked with needles the entire time. I feel like you know the answer to that."

"The needles aren't so bad; what really matters is where they're hitting you. If it's over a bone or somewhere sensitive, then yeah, it's torture, but most places are fine. The arms and legs are good starters, 'cause they don't hurt."

Theodore nodded again, keeping his silence.

While Laith picked up his cup again, Theodore glanced down at the sandwich in front of him, neatly wrapped over the tray. He wasn't really hungry. Realistically, he knew that he was, but the anxiety that bounced his legs under the table killed any other feeling, disinterested in doing absolutely anything that didn't involve Laith's on-and-off medication mixed with alcohol. Couldn't that kill a person? He pulled his phone out for a quick search.

First, he found out Xanax was a kind of anxiety medication. Then, he found out taking it with alcohol wouldn't kill anyone straight away, only make the side-effects of the medication, as well as the alcohol, worse. It seemed that, for it to actually kill, both would have to be ingested in great quantities. With how heavily Laith drank, it wasn't hard to believe he'd end up back at the hospital if he popped a few pills during the night.

"What kind of stuff are you learning in business school?"

He put his phone down. God, if there was one subject he didn't want to talk about, it was this one. He should probably bring something up then, a different topic that would invalidate Laith's question and change the course of this conversation forever, but what? Oh. "I saw Ryan today." There, that was a good one. "He says he's not skipping town just yet. Did you know that?"

"I figured. He blocked me, so."

Huh.

"I thought it was the other way around."

"It was, until I unblocked him and found out I still couldn't text him. It doesn't matter; I'll find new people to hang out with. I'll make some new friends. I really don't care." Laith's shoulders bounced in an attempt to illustrate his point, but they weren't committed enough for that. Despite the carelessness of his words, nothing in his body actually corroborated that feeling; his eyes were downcast and his eyebrows furrowed. His lips almost even pouted.

"Except you do care," Theodore interjected. "You care a lot. You wish you were still together."

"Sure, but what can I even do? I've made my choice. Don't take this the wrong way—I don't regret it—but I wish I didn't have to choose at all. It just sucks, you know? He was my friend."

"He was a terrible fucking friend."

"He saved my life."

Theodore crossed his arms and leaned back in his seat. So Emily wasn't the only one who put Ryan up on a pedestal for that, huh. There was nothing he even wanted to say in response.

"We were pretty close," Laith continued. "Guess I just miss him, is all."

"Don't worry; I'll start bullying you, so you can feel like he never left."

Laith scoffed out a laugh, lips stretched into a smile. Without a come-back, he brought his cup for another sip.

"He's seeing Justin and Emily on Friday, you know. They're partying without you."

Dark hair swayed with a nod, hand setting the cup back on the table. "Yeah, I'll have to find something else to do. They'll be at the DP, so we should probably not go there. There are a bunch of other clubs around, though; it's not like we're out of options. They're all the same."

"Assuming I'm coming with you."

Laith stared at him. "Do you have plans?"

No, he just wanted to see the look on his face, his big puppy eyes, deso-late and round, lips parted with surprise. What a sight.

He grinned. "Of course not, but don't take my presence for granted. In-vite me, at least."

"Oh." A smile tugged at the corner of Laith's lips. "Do you wanna party with me this Friday? We'll make some friends and have some fun. We'll forget we even knew Ryan at all."

"I've been meaning to do that for years."

Laith grinned, eyes dropping to his cup. He pulled the lid off and brought the cup up, not for a sip, but to eat a mouthful of ice. It crunched loudly.

"I didn't know you were an ice-eater," Theodore commented.

"Not really, but this is the good kind." His speech was muffled by the ice, hand tilting the cup so Theodore could see inside. It was the pellet type. "Small and crunchy."

They held the stare for a moment. Disinclined to really talk about any-thing, Theodore decided to just watch Laith munch on the ice, green eyes drop-ping to the tray in front of him. A hand motioned to it. "I thought you were hungry."

That comment drew his eyes to his perfectly untouched burger, still wrapped in the restaurant's logo. No, he wasn't hungry; he was too worried to be hungry. The only reason he'd asked to come here was because he'd wanted to leave Ms. Intervention's apartment, not because he was hungry. They could've gone anywhere. He'd just needed Laith to be away from alcohol for a moment, but leaving the building hadn't really changed that after all.

The Xanax that coursed Laith's veins was the only thing he could think about; it swallowed his mind the same way Laith drank from his cup. He glanced up to find Laith eating some more ice.

"I thought you were on prescription." There, fuck it; he could no longer keep it in. They had to have this conversation.

Laith crunched loudly, eyebrows furrowed. "That was last weekend."

He hated how he could hear Emily's voice through those words, even if she'd only texted them.

"Yeah, people don't usually get on prescription pills for just a weekend. Sorry for being under the impression you'd be on them for a while."

"No, it's an old prescription. I don't need it anymore; I only take it when things get bad."

"Please, finish eating the ice."

The crunching slowly stopped. "I'm not on Xanax all the time," Laith continued, speaking properly now. "I haven't been on it for about a year. That's something my doctor put me on after the hospital. Xanax and some other things; it doesn't really matter. I'm not on anything right now."

"What do you mean, you only take it when things get bad? Is that how prescription even works?"

"Yeah. Sometimes, when you're in a bad place, you need them just to get through the day, but as you get better, prescriptions change."

"So you only take stuff when you feel like it."

"No, when things get bad. It's..." A hand gesticulated vaguely. Laith's voice dropped for the next part, growing sheepish. "It's a relapse thing."

"Are you recovering from alcohol too?"

Laith squinted. "I don't have an alcohol problem."

"Are you sure? Because you live in a fucking dumpster. When I first got to your place, there were empty bottles fucking everywhere. It made me so worried I had to clean it up."

Laith's face burst into flames, green eyes wide. "I promise it's not always like that; you just caught me at a really bad time. I told you last week was rough, but I'm fine now. I've been fine for a long time. I don't drink to cope anymore."

Both queens immediately came to mind, the brief conversation he'd had with them on Monday, how worried they'd been over Laith that week. Then, he remembered what Hwan had said at Atlantic, that a lot of people had seen Laith walk around drunk enough to cause a scene. "A lot of people seem to think you have a problem."

"I promise I don't. I can function just fine without drinking, like it's not destroying my life. These last few days, I didn't have a single drop and I was just fine. This is the first time I've drank since Friday. The girls wanted to have a few beers, so I joined them. That's all."

Without anything to say to that, Theodore stared at him. He could feel the worry in the crease between his eyebrows, jaw tense.

"You know, all things considered, I think I've been doing pretty well," Laith continued. "I know it doesn't look like it and I should probably clean up the apartment a bit, but I'm surprised by how fast I bounced back. That's never happened before, like it's always been a huge struggle for me. I know it's because of you, though. As soon as I fell into the lake, you fished me back out. Crawling out by yourself takes much longer. It's messier too; you're covered in mud and keep slipping back in." Laith touched his metal bracelet again, nails scraping over the links. His voice grew softer for the next part. "I'm glad you've been visiting me these last couple of days, you know. It helps a lot."

Theodore swallowed a lump. "So you really have been doing better."

Laith nodded.

"Can your psychiatrist sign off on that?"

They held the stare.

"Do you want me to see him?" Laith asked.

"If that's okay. One session would do; I just really need his opinion on this. It's not that I don't believe you, I just—I need something else to help me stop worrying about it."

Green eyes dropped to the space between them, lost in the light green surface of the table. Laith stared at it for a minute, head slowly beginning to nod. "Yeah, I could do that for you. You do so much for me already."

Like what? he decided not to ask.

"Thank you."

His hands moved to unwrap the burger.

198

Chapter 17

Usually I put something on TV
So we never think about you and me
But today I see our reflections clearly

- Glass Animals, *Heat Waves*

The walk back to Laith's apartment was a nebula of thoughts snowballing down a moun-
tain with Laith's voice in the background. He couldn't find it in himself to believe Laith when Justin had told him before just how secretive he was about that
topic, how adamantly he kept it out of discussion. On the one hand, the fact that
Laith had managed to open up a bit could mean that they'd finally grown close
enough for that. On the other, well, he was piss drunk. He'd been *trying* to dismiss Theodore's arguments this whole time and hadn't he said that each one of
his friends only knew parts of the story? That no one had the full picture? If
Emily was the one who knew the most about his mental health, then it'd make
no sense for Theodore to get clued into it this late into the game. Not to mention
that Laith had—apparently, allegedly—spent the entirety of last week wrecking
himself only to bounce back a day later, which yeah, Theodore didn't buy at all.
Sure, it *could* be true, but to him, it just seemed unlikely. Every rat knew about it,
every rat talked about it and even the queens, who were the calmest people he
knew, had been worried. Did they still feel that way? If anyone had borne witness
to the development that Laith claimed had taken place, then it'd be those two.

Up in the hallway, he swiped both the bag and the drink from Laith's
hands. "It's alright," he reassured him, walking off ahead, "I'll make the delivery.
You can go on and unlock the door. I'll be just a minute."

Shock and confusion took turns pulling on Laith's eyebrows, but ultimately, no interjection came. Laith simply watched as Theodore flashed him a smile before slipping into Ms. Intervention's apartment.

The door was still wide open, and inside, he found both women in the exact same places where he'd left them, laughing at each other's stupid jokes. They waved as he approached, practically breathless.

"Hey, here's your drink and here are your fries," he started. His voice was low, so it wouldn't travel outside the room. "Can you guys tell me something? I don't have much time."

"Ooh, a secret? What is it?" D'angela spoke with a fry pinched between two fingers while her friend drank from the straw.

"The way Laith's been acting these last few days..." He shot a brief glance over his shoulder and saw Laith with his back turned, unlocking his own door. "Is that how he usually is?"

"Oh god, no!" Ms. Intervention waved dismissively. "That's all a front, girl. He's putting on a show for you."

"He's *really* trying to impress. It's actually really hard *not* mentioning it."

Ice gnawed at the corners of his heart, eyebrows furrowing with concern. "What—what's he like? What's he usually like, then?"

"Not this."

"This Prince Charming act will not last forever. He's putting a lot of effort into it, which means he won't be able to keep it up for long."

"I'll be honest—I've never seen him so dedicated. It's impressive. If only half the ladyboys in these tunnels were taking notes!"

D'angela nodded her agreement.

"What Prince Charming act?" Theodore asked. "I'm talking about his mental health."

"Oh."

The girls exchanged looks.

"Well, it usually isn't like this either," Ms. Intervention added. "What happened last week was out of the ordinary."

"It scared the hell outta me."

"So if this is all fake, then he's not really better, is he?" His voice was a shaky whisper, hands cold.

"Sweetheart, you misunderstand me. I didn't mean to say he's lying to you; it's more like he's trying to look good for you. He seems to me to be doing better."

"He's really not the kind of person who can cover up a relapse. If he were lying about being better, I promise you would've known."

A quick glance over his shoulder showed Laith's apartment door cracked open. He must've already gone inside. "You really think he's better, then?"

D'angela shrugged.

"Do you see him spending twenty-five minutes trying to unlock his own damn door?" Ms. Intervention clicked her tongue. "That's already an improvement from last week."

"This is a transitionary period, to be fair," D'angela explained. "He's bouncing back from a pretty rough time. If you're worried about him, maybe ask what you could do to help."

From what they had to say, it seemed they hadn't seen anything suspicious; no more binges before work or mumblings about being good. That alone brought air to Theodore's lungs. The possibility that Laith wasn't lying, but had actually not drunk since Friday felt a little more realistic now. He left with a brief thank you, feet walking on their own, mind stuck far away.

As far as he could tell, Laith had been put into a bad place—as he'd called it—on Justin's farm, when his friends found out the two of them had slept together. He knew they'd been arguing with him way before that, against him even existing near Theodore at all, but since the relapse had happened last week, Theodore could safely say he'd played a big part in it. He'd probably even been the cause of it; after all, he'd been the one to tell the group of their night together. If it'd been up to Laith, he was pretty sure they'd remain a secret forever. Had Laith's friends pushed him to the breaking point? Perhaps Theodore had lit the match, but they might all have caused the fire.

The moment he walked into Laith's apartment, he noticed some changes. First, that the pile of pants tossed over one of the chairs was gone, and second, that the pile of shoes by the door was no longer there. The door closed behind him with a soft click. A brief stretch of the neck gave him a glance into the bathroom, where the pile of dirty laundry was no longer on the floor.

"Hey." Laith's voice drew his attention forward. He stood by the wardrobe with an arm reaching out of sight, probably to close it. Without his jacket on, it was possible to see that the shiny triangular pattern spread across his whole shirt, short sleeves tight around his biceps. Theodore approached slowly. "I put some stuff away. I know it's not much, and I've essentially just moved the problem out of sight, but hopefully, it'll make you feel better. I'd never actually used the shoe racks in here—"

The hand out of sight pushed on the wardrobe to indicate it. Theodore's approach allowed him to catch sight of it, and as soon as his eyes dropped to Laith's arm, his entire body froze. Right there, semi-hidden under the metal bracelet, was a series of fresh wounds, thin and deep just like the scars beneath them. Theodore couldn't move. Scabs alternated and crossed over each other, not in spaced out lines, but in a mess of blind emotion—the result of violence. He could almost picture it, the way Laith had done it, his state of mind at the time. Laith's voice was a muffled noise in the expanse of the room, silent in deaf ears. So that had been the extent of his relapse. Theodore's eyes filled up with tears, heart punched into a pulp, aching under bloody knuckles.

It was all his fault.

"I'll find a place for everything later." Laith moved away from the wardrobe, but Theodore's gaze remained locked in place, staring into the abyssal nothingness in his mind. A single tear dripped down his cheek.

How could he have been so blind? Self-centered to the point of hurting the one person who he cared for most in the world. Above everything, he'd wanted Laith to be happy, but thinking back, that must've gotten lost in translation. He had definitely not been thinking of Laith's happiness when he'd told the group they'd had sex in the master bedroom.

A very gentle hand touched his face and forced his eyes to meet Laith's, wobbly behind a wall of tears. He didn't even feel the next one that fell. "What's going on?" The softness of Laith's voice ripped his chest open. His throat swallowed around a hard lump, hands coming up to push Laith away. He didn't deserve his affection right now.

"I'm having a bad day," Theodore mumbled, eyes barely blinking. Tears streamed down regardless.

Oh my god, was that why Laith had so consistently been wearing his brother's jacket? He was a man of tank tops and spiked vests, yet he'd covered his arms every day this past week. Theodore took a step back, disoriented. Nothing he looked at actually registered in his brain.

"You know, I should—" *probably go home,* he didn't finish, because Laith had just told him his visits had been helping. If he left, he'd only make things worse. No, he had to be strong right now. A shaky breath filled his lungs halfway, shoulders squared as best as he could. He blinked the tears away, hands rubbing hastily at his eyes. He was okay. He was fine. He *had* to be fine. He had to be strong for Laith right now. Sniffling, he swallowed his emotions down.

"I should—" He glanced up at Laith's face, finally able to take notice of the genuine concern that furrowed his brow. The way he stood, with his chest puffed out, indicated just how weirded out he was by all of this. Theodore didn't blame him. "—probably tell you what's going on," he finished.

"Please." The apprehension in Laith's voice was a perfect match with the look on his face.

Theodore swallowed—the lump was still there. "Okay, I'm not gonna lie; I was worried you were mixing pills and alcohol. I know you were very clear about that last weekend, that you weren't doing it, but seeing you drink with the queens just made me think of it. I'm sorry."

Laith's posture relaxed a bit, scowl softening. "You're not wrong to think I'd do that. I used to, but it's not a good trip. Not worth it."

His breathing slowly came back to normal, nose clearing up. One deep breath filled his lungs to the brim. After a second, he monitored his exhale.

"Hey." Laith touched him on the shoulder. "Why don't we lie down for a while? I'll put on one of those movies you like, with the couples that always get together in the end."

A smile threatened to pull at his lips. "I thought you said they were un-realistic."

Laith grinned. "And they are."

~~~~~~~~~~~~

They didn't really cuddle like this. The only time Laith got close to him—outside of sex, of course—was to either sleep next to him or walk around with an arm across his shoulders. Even though he wanted much more than that, the strides they'd made weren't lost on him, so when Laith motioned for him to get close, his heart practically jumped out of his mouth. Without a word, he scooted over and let Laith wrap an arm around him. It was very similar to how they'd fallen asleep last Sunday, with his head pillowed on Laith's chest and his stomach pressed to Laith's side, except the body below him wasn't asleep.

Actually, Laith didn't seem even remotely close to being tired. He laughed at the silly scenes and made fun of the main characters, lying with an arm under his own head and the other one across Theodore's back. His right hand hung half an inch from Theodore's face, so close he could almost feel the warmth of Laith's skin and the softness of his touch. It was tantalizing. If he turned his head just a bit to the side...

He didn't. Honestly, he had to stop thinking about that; this obsession with intimacy wouldn't get him anywhere. He knew Laith wasn't into physical affection, that he barely even hugged his friends, so expecting him to suddenly play with Theodore's hair or take his hand only served to set himself up for failure. He had to stop. Squeezing his eyes, he turned his head so Laith's hand was out of view.

He couldn't focus on the movie. His mind was a minefield of deeply emotional trains of thought that he knew, ultimately, wouldn't do him any good. Remnants of the guilt from before still gnawed at his insides, blaming him for turning Laith against himself, for forcing him to pick up a blade after so many years of recovery. The knowledge that his hand dangled close enough to brush his hair squeezed his heart into a fist, throat tight around a lump. On the screen, lovers held hands and told their families of their newly formed relationship. Beneath him, everything he'd ever wanted; a reminder of how close he was to the goal. He just needed to calm down and let Laith take his time.

In silence, he traced the triangles on Laith's shirt. The shiny ones were interlocked with dull ones, plastic on cotton, all the way down to the hem. He couldn't help himself; no matter how he felt, his eyes always ended up wandering to Laith's crotch. The way he sat never gave Theodore anything, though; it was a matter of habit. One leg was bent at the knee, showing some skin through the slit there, the gashes that made Laith's pants his signature pair. His boots had been left by the bed.

Laith's laughter shook his rib cage—Theodore could feel it under his palm, the vibrations, how much deeper his voice sounded with an ear to his chest. The hand by his hair touched it, fingers slipping through the locks, closing around the shape of his skull. His eyes slipped shut right away.

"So *he* was the one who crashed into her car!" Laith laughed. "Did you see that? He owes her at least three more dinners."

"Maybe even four."

"Maybe even four!"

His lips curled into a smile despite himself. It was the glee that emanated from Laith, who claimed not to care about romances, yet seemed thoroughly entertained by them anyway. His hand brushed Theodore's hair, touching the curve of his ear before slinking off, back to the space next to his head. Had he only meant to catch Theodore's attention? Maybe that had been part of his excitement, a reaction to go with the surprise of that scene. Theodore breathed in deeply—could he really complain? A crumb was better than nothing.

"I need a haircut," he blurted out.

That was something he'd been meaning to do for a long time now, but hadn't managed to get around to it. It was another item on the list of things his mother used to take care of, along with doctor's appointments and shopping for school supplies. To think he'd have to start making his own appointments... it was fair to say he'd probably never see a doctor again.

"I could take you to my barber," Laith offered. "It's not too far from here."

"After the movie?"

"Sure."

mmermlmler

It was very clear to him that he'd been skirting closer and closer to danger, inching his way into the giant mouth in hopes it'd spare him. He knew it'd never done that before and had no reason to treat him any differently than the others, but something inside still held out hope that it'd let him make a home out of sharp teeth.

Emily had warned him about this. Laith's affection was dangerous; it felt too nice. The more Theodore got, the more he sincerely believed he was special—*that* was the dangerous part, thinking he mattered more than he actually did. In Laith's arms, it was easy to forget where he stood, and in his bed, it was easy to believe the lies he'd been telling himself. He knew Laith would never be his, but part of him still worked to make that happen. He was a fool trying to fit a square-shaped piece into a star-shaped box.

The barber shop was much more populated than he'd thought. Multiple hairdressers worked on a row of different clients staring at their own reflections. Laith managed to flag down his preferred professional and asked to put Theodore in line. The man was significantly older than them, in his forties, with a pair of round frames on his nose and an apron down his chest. Luckily, he was just finishing up, so the most they had to wait was a couple of minutes.

"What can I call you?" the barber asked. One of his arms was outstretched to indicate the chair nearby. "I'm assuming Prey is not what you want to be called."

"Call him Blue," Laith jumped in. "Baby Blue."

Theodore glanced at him, body sliding into the chair. Baby Blue, huh.

Wasn't Burman in charge of names like that? He didn't know they could pick and choose.

"Alright, Blue." The man turned the chair to stare at his client through the mirror. "Tell me what you want."

"I'll wait outside," Laith informed him. "It's pretty crowded in here."

Theodore nodded, watching the door jingle after Laith. As soon as he turned back around, his eyes fell on the barber that stared back at him. "Do what you think would look nice on me."

"A lot of things would look nice on you. What kind of style are you looking for?"

"Any. Just do whatever you want."

Two thin eyebrows raised from behind circular frames. "Alright, then. Scissors or clippers?"

He shrugged. Without any pointers, the man stared at his hair, contemplating it in silence. A moment later, he put the clippers down. "Let's start with the basics."

The guy cut off all the excess hair around his head, making the sides shorter and the top a little longer. When he asked Theodore what he thought about it, Theodore told him to keep going, so he took some length off the sides and about a quarter of an inch off the top. What about now? Theodore turned his head around to inspect it only to come to the upsetting realization that he still looked like himself. Perhaps he should've told the man to make him into somebody else.

Before he answered, the barber explained that this cut was what he called a chameleon, since it could be worn in a multitude of ways; brushed to the side, brushed forward or even styled up. The last one turned him into Ryan, so he decided to never do it. No, he'd keep it brushed to the side, the way Laith liked it.

Dissatisfied but too disillusioned to try anything else, he told the man that was fine. They were done here. He let the guy blow dry his hair, paid him in cash and left the shop. Part of him didn't like that his mother would approve of this haircut, while the other part was relieved that she would. In a perfect world, he would've left the shop as someone who Laith would've wanted to call his.

With his hands in his kangaroo pocket, he stood by the door and looked around—Laith wasn't here. This corner of Blaze was pretty calm; small groups of friends walked down the passageway speaking in indoor voices that didn't travel very far, which allowed for a good line of sight, only mildly obstructed. If he had Laith's number, he could text him.

Just as the thought emerged, Laith walked out of a diner across the way. Since the tunnels were unregulated, it was common to see people drinking pretty much anywhere, so Laith carrying a beer in the open was normal. He smiled when their eyes met, walking perfectly straight somehow. The buzz from earlier must've worn off during the movie.

"You look good." His voice was low, a sincere compliment. It sent Theodore's heart flying despite the nonchalant shrug he gave in reply.

"I bet my mom will say that too."

"I bet she will. When are you seeing her again?"

"I don't know. Whenever I want to, I guess. If anything, I'll see her on Thanksgiving."

Laith nodded, beer bottle coming up for a sip. The angle of his arch was wide enough to evidence that not much was left to drink.

This time, as his eyes began to wander down Laith's neck, he tore them away. The detachment had to start somewhere, even in the little things.

"How come you called me Blue?" he asked. Still not staring at Laith, he watched the casual flow of the population instead, the people who came and went. In his peripherals, Laith brought the bottle back down.

"Figured it's time you got a proper name, so people will stop calling you that Prey shit."

"I *do* have a name."

Laith clicked his tongue. "You know how much you've been talked about, right? It's traveled far. Would you want your name, in association with mine, to get to your dad?"

Hm. That was a good point.

"Blue could be anyone," Laith concluded.

"Sure, but I mean, it kinda sounds like…"

Laith stared at him, waiting for him to finish.

Like we're together. He shrugged. "Like I'm one of you, a Dead Pony. Like I work for Burman too."

"People know you don't. If you did, they would've seen you smashing stores or walking around with the dogs. They already associate you with me, anyway; they know you're not here because of her."

"They could get the wrong idea, you know. Giving me a name like that."

"They've got you wrong this whole time. At this point, we might as well play into it."

His heart skipped. Still, he refused to look at Laith, training his eyes on the neon signs that crawled left to right. It was 4:30. "How far do you wanna go?"

"What do you mean?"

He swallowed thick. This was the textbook definition of playing with fire. "How much are we playing into it? Like, what do we want them to believe?"

"I don't know. I don't think that really matters. I'm thinking we do what we do and let them think whatever they want."

"Yeah, but you know what they'll think. What they *already* think."

Laith shrugged—he saw shoulders bobbing from the corner of his eye. "So what, Theo? What difference does it make? It's not like they're too far off the mark anyway."

"Blue."

"Sorry—Blue."

"But they *are* off the mark. They're *way* off the mark. If you let them think we're together, that's gonna kill all your game in the dark rooms."

Laith laughed. "You underestimate the number of people who'd come to me *because* of that. It's the same reason married men are so coveted—the unattainable is magnetic."

It sure fucking was.

"So you're married now." He finally turned to glance at Laith, to see the beautiful grin that pushed into his cheeks.

"C'mon, you know what I mean. Plus, it's not like I'm seeing anyone else. I'm already missing out."

His chin lifted in a nod that never fell, heart quivering. Oh, he loved hearing that. He kind of already knew it, but god, he loved hearing it anyway. "That's on you, though. I'm not keeping you out of the DP at all."

"No, I know." Laith tipped his head side-to-side, which made it seem like he had more to say, but no elaboration ever came. Instead, he changed the subject. "Why don't we hang out at Salamander tonight? I think you'll like it. They have six different flavors of iced tea."

"Is that a bar or what?"

"It's a Mexican place. All their drinks are spicy, even the tea."

He nodded.

A wide arch flipped Laith's beer upside down, allowing him to finish it.

When he was done, a tongue swiped over his lips, hand tossing the empty bottle into a nearby trashcan. Theodore watched him absently, picking up pace as he started down the street.

"If people associate me with you, but don't consider me a Dead Pony, then... what am I?" He'd wondered that for a while now.

"Word is you're a Poison Dart. I blame Tae-hwan's friends for that."

"So your friends decide your allegiance."

"Not necessarily. It depends."

"On what?"

A hand came up to motion vaguely in the air. "You know, on a lot of things. If you have family down here, you belong to their faction. If you're from upstairs, then you're not *really* one of us; you're a visitor. If you're from upstairs but you know one of us, then your rat friend decides your allegiance for you. If you visit often and do a lot of business down here, then you *have* to pick a side. It's complicated. People think you're a Poison Dart because they saw you with Tae-hwan's friends first. If we keep hanging out, you'll end up switching sides, though. That's up to you."

His lips parted to ask about his address theory, but before the first word could come out, he noticed how stupid that'd sound. Allegiances were clearly far more intricate than living on another faction's turf. Actually, he was pretty sure people's addresses above ground had absolutely no relation to what happened beneath them. Then again, when he'd pointed at his apartment building, Hwan's Poison Dart friends had seemed to take that as his allegiance to their faction.

"I'm assuming addresses don't have much to do with it, then," he bluffed, trying not to sound stupid.

"Well, people tend to live near their faction. I'm not saying the opposite doesn't happen, but it's not very common. It seems inconvenient."

He'd gotten that backwards, then. People moved to certain areas because they were already in a faction, rather than becoming part of a faction due to where they lived. On second thought, yeah, he had to be Earth's biggest dumbass to believe the latter.

"So... wait. If Hwan's a rat, then how come his friends are all still Poison Darts? As far as I know, they don't live underground. Shouldn't he make them into Gorgons?"

"There's probably another rat there, or maybe they do business with Poison Darts. I don't know. I don't know them."

"They seem to know you."

"A lot of people give that impression."

Hm. Even though Laith had met them all at Streisand's, he hadn't really talked to any of them. He'd only spoken to Hwan—a fiasco—before the girls had come over, and even then, the two factions had stood opposite one another, with the Poison Darts on one side and the Alvorada on the other. They hadn't mingled at all.

Chapter 18

The breaking point

How come I see you and ache instead?
How come you only look pleased in bed?

- Glass Animals, *Pork Soda*

Something inside him just wasn't right. No matter how hard he tried to loosen up and enjoy himself, it was simply impossible to ignore the gaping chasm that ate him up inside. It grew with each passing moment, a reminder that he was wasting his very precious and finite time with Laith not really there. His body was present, but his mind was far away, on the inevitability of their demise, on how quickly he'd have to say goodbye. The fact that he didn't know how soon that would be only made it worse.

When would Laith finally get tired of him? Minutes slipped away like sand spilling through his fingers. Once again, his efforts were useless; he couldn't keep either Laith or Ryan around. What was so undesirable about him? Tangentially, how much longer would he be able to swim against the current? His arms were getting tired. The longer he forced it, the more it was starting to seem like giving up was his only option. The goal was unachievable.

"Hey." Laith's voice drew his eyes up, eyebrows raised. He found concern there, digging a crease into Laith's forehead. "What's going on with you? You've been out of it all night. Feels like you're not really here."

"I'm sorry. I—" His mouth moved, yet nothing came out—useless. To make matters worse, a knot tied around his throat, eyes growing damp. God, he wanted to kick himself into unconsciousness. "This just isn't a good day for me," he finally explained.

"Did something happen?"

"Um."

He could be truthful. That was the first thing that crossed his mind, telling the truth, screaming from the top of his lungs that, actually, he'd changed his mind and wanted off this ride now. It wasn't all fun and games anymore; a prize off the shelf could never satisfy him. He wanted far too much. Then again, if he said any of that, Laith would kill what Theodore so desperately fought to keep alive. What he so desperately *needed* to keep alive.

"I guess seeing Ryan messed me up more than I thought. Sorry."

A dark eyebrow arched with Laith's skepticism, but nothing came of it. Instead, he opened another beer. "Let me know if there's anything I could do to help."

"I will."

Both of them knew that he wouldn't.

The closeness was unbearable. Each kiss tore into his heart with a sharp blade and each touch burned his skin with branding iron. He hated how convincing Laith was, kissing him like he meant it, holding him like he loved him. It was agonizing. It hurt like nothing he'd felt before, an ache that closed his throat around a lump and shoved rocks in his mouth. Was this how Laith treated every one of his partners? The amount of care and attention he put into it could make anyone feel special. It was hard to believe he didn't have a group of lovesick ex-nothings following him around all day.

Theodore just couldn't take it. Cut up and burned, he told Laith to be rough, to fuck him like he hated him—*and mean it*, he almost added. *I want you to fucking hate me.* Somehow, that put a big smirk on Laith's face, playful and mean. Oh, he thought it was a kink, that Theodore was experimenting again, the way he'd done all week. That was fair. Any normal person would've jumped to that conclusion. Laith still complied, so he didn't have a reason to explain himself.

With his face buried into a pillow, it was much easier to forget who he was and just focus on the hands that grabbed and pulled. It didn't hurt. Actually, it was much nicer than he'd wanted it to be, with none of the suffering he'd hoped for. He wasn't really sure what he'd wanted exactly; all he knew was that he didn't really want to enjoy it. He'd been looking for a clean cut between him and Laith, a reason not to come back. Unfortunately, Laith could make even pain feel good. The fingers that pushed into the bruises on his thighs were a big argument to keep him coming back.

As soon as they were done, Laith was nice again—as if he'd ever really been bad in the first place—kissing down his neck, pulling him close. A whisper asked if he was okay, and ironically, the affection in Laith's voice was what hurt him the most. His heart writhed, snapping arteries like twigs. Yeah, he was fine. An arm pushed Laith off to make room for an escape—he couldn't be here anymore. Looking at Laith's face earlier was already difficult enough; he couldn't possibly do it during the afterglow. He wasn't that strong.

"Are you leaving?"

That question bashed him over the head. There was no heartbreak in Laith's voice, just curiosity, but the shame it invoked practically burned him alive. His lungs drew in shallow breaths, face warm. With his back turned, he slipped his boxers on.

"Yeah, I have class soon." A quick glance at the nightstand let him know that his lie had been a relatively good one. His first period was in two hours. "I need to get ready and get my things," he continued, stepping into his pants. "It takes a while to go home and then go to college. Plus, I need a shower and breakfast, so." As his brain scrambled for more excuses, he realized Laith didn't actually know what time his first class was. He could lie and say it'd be in an hour.

"You could leave your stuff here next time," Laith suggested. "Bring it with you, so when you leave, it's a straight shot from here to campus. What do you want for breakfast?"

His throat closed. What did he want for breakfast? He didn't have breakfast. The last time he'd had breakfast was at Justin's place. His vision threatened to blur, arms working his shirt into place. "Yeah, that's a good idea. I'll, uh—I'll bring my bag next time." He picked up his hoodie and began to put it on, eyes searching for his shoes. His movements were frantic and quick; if he did three things at once, he'd be out the door within the minute.

"There's a diner nearby." Laith's voice was closer than before. Theodore didn't have to look to know he'd gotten out of bed too, large in his peripherals, a presence that towered over him. "Do you like eggs and bacon? I think it's my favorite dish. Breakfast-wise, I mean. Eggs, bacon and orange juice."

Theodore quickly turned around, eyes wide. "I can't stay."

Those words left him without a thought. The suddenness of it put a look on Laith's face, curious.

"You mean for breakfast?"

"Yeah. I have to go home anyway, so I'll just grab a bite there." He found his shoes half-hidden under the bed, right behind Laith's feet. On an impulse, he approached and took Laith's arms to move him out of the way. Confused but still compliant, Laith stepped aside, letting him toe his shoes on.

"Okay..." A hand touched him on the arm very softly. His eyes dropped to it, body halting all movement. Both shoes were on. "Are we good?"

Frozen in place, he couldn't look up. The stare prompted Laith to pull his hand away.

"Was it something I did? 'Cause if it was, you can just tell me."

His heart shattered. "You didn't do anything." He spoke while facing the bed, unable to look Laith in the eye. If he did, he knew every nerve-ending in his body would scream in pain. He couldn't even picture the look on Laith's face without feeling like he'd swallowed a dagger—what a coward. His feet took a couple of steps backwards, eyes down on the floor. "I'll be back later."

A few quick steps rushed him over to the door, where his hand lay on the knob but didn't immediately turn it. He squeezed it instead, arm shaking— the moment he walked out, his time with Laith would be over. His jaw trembled, heart lodged in his throat. Oh god, he wasn't ready for it to end. He didn't *want* it to end. The prospect of leaving Laith erased the pain of being around him the same way a gunshot was a possible cure for a cut on the hand—or wrist. He squeezed his eyes, breathing in quickly. He couldn't leave him. He was helping; his friendship was helping and if he came back only to find Laith with even more scars, he'd never forgive himself.

He slowly turned around. Knowing the look he'd find on Laith's face didn't shield him from the emotional pang that came with it. Green eyes watched him under furrowed brows, upset and concerned—his fault. He wanted to shoot himself point blank in the face. With his heart bleeding in his mouth, he walked back over to Laith and took both of his elbows, staring him hard in the face. He had to do it; there was no way around it. His lips pursed, tears threatening to fall—he didn't let them. A big breath filled his shaky lungs.

"I love you."

The utter shock that widened Laith's eyes and drained all color from his face was all Theodore needed to see. Now he *really* had to leave. His hands gave Laith's arms one big squeeze before letting go, feet adding some space between them. There was nothing else to be said, and anyway, he didn't want to hear anything either. Without another word, he approached the door and pulled it open.

The outside embraced him like an iron maiden, door closed behind him—the last nail in the coffin. He'd finally done it.

mmermmermer

The part that hurt the most was the fact that he still had an hour and a half before his first class and all he could think was how he'd have to spend it without Laith. Opportunity wasted, tossed out the window; everything related to Laith hurt. He had a knife stuck in his chest and every time he moved, it shot an ache down his body. Well, now Laith knew. Would he still want to hang out? Laughter came up Theodore's throat, but what actually came out was a sob. People glanced at him, so he pulled the hood over his head and kept walking. It didn't matter; he was already dying inside.

Luckily, the girls were still asleep when he arrived, so he could crawl into bed and scream. His face was pushed deep into his pillow, further than a moment ago, when Laith had climbed on top of him. He screamed his throat raw, fisting the sheets, casually on fire. It burned every organ very painfully and very viciously, but in a detached sort of way, where the fire didn't really attribute itself any of the blame. Theodore didn't either; it was *his* fault, after all. He deserved to burn. In fact, the fire did him a favor.

When his scream died out, the tears came. He couldn't help it; they squeezed out painfully, as if two hands wrung his heart out like a wet rag. In the hands' defense, his heart *was* very heavy. What were wet rags good for anyway? They wrung violently, twisting his insides. It hurt so bad that Theodore would soon rather swallow a razor blade than see this through. Unfortunately for him— because fortune just seemed to have abandoned him altogether—this was inescapable. He was strapped to the passenger seat of a moving car.

He sobbed and hiccupped as if attending his own funeral, small and pathetic. If anyone saw him, they'd think he'd just lost a loved one, not that he'd confessed his rotten guts to a stranger—but god, Laith was so much more than that. Laith was so much more than that. Laith was—well, he was everything. He was Theodore's entire life. Without him, what would Theodore do? What would he strive for? He didn't have a single goal in life other than getting near Laith. Now that he'd climbed the mountain and seen the other side, was there anything left for him to do? Living beyond the mountain had never been an option. He knew the rules; he'd signed the contract of his own free will. Idiot.

A sudden movement shook his stomach, startling him. It scared him so much that his tears almost rushed back into his eyes. When the movement repeated, he realized it was his phone, buzzing in his kangaroo pocket. He sat up near the edge of the mattress and pulled his phone out, bright in the dark, the only light source in his room. Coming in, he hadn't even bothered to turn on a light. Emily's name was on the screen—why would she call him so early in the morning? A hand wiped his cheek while the other swiped right to accept the call. He sniffled quietly before bringing the phone to his ear.

"Hello?"

"Hey, Theo. Are you okay?"

He stared at the empty desk across from him. Had Laith told her something? "Uh, yeah, I'm fine. Why? Do you need anything?"

"Yes, actually; there's something I need to tell you. It's about Laith."

His heart skipped.

"If you're not busy, I'd like to discuss this over breakfast," she proposed. "How's eggs and toast?"

"At your place?"

"Yeah. Ryan's not up yet, if that's what you're worried about."

"Why can't we talk over the phone?"

"Oh, I'm old-fashioned. I want to see you."

He swallowed. God, he probably looked like shit. "Okay."

"Great; come as soon as you can. We wouldn't want Ryan to wake up in the middle of our talk."

Alright, message received.

"I'll be there in ten."

"See you then!"

He brought the phone down with a shaky breath. Was this actually about Laith? Something told him it was a trap, that Emily already knew what had happened between them and had only used the Laith tactic to lure him over. If she *did* know, then Laith was quick on the draw. How long had it been, twenty minutes, half an hour? He wiped both of his cheeks and got up.

Chapter 19

And I love you so much
I'm gonna let you kill me

- Florence + The Machine, *I'm Not Calling You a Liar*

She pulled the door open with a smile on her face. It came off as disingenuous to him, so he didn't trust it, squinting at her on the way in. Why was he *really* here? A deep, rich scent filled the air as he squeezed past, something that reminded him of the color purple, a dark shade. Lilacs, maybe—were they purple? He breathed in when she walked past him again, this time to go through the archway. It must be a new bottle of perfume if he was only now noticing it, the scent of lies and deceit. Who knew they'd smell so nice.

The kitchen area was too small for a table and chairs, so Emily and Ryan had put them in the living room corner, right next to the kitchen door. That way, the TV was left undisturbed if one of them was setting the table, walking back and forth. It made sense. She'd set down two plates with eggs and toast and two glasses with what seemed to be apple juice. Simple, but still nice and thoughtful. Theodore placed his backpack on the floor before taking a seat.

"Do you like cayenne pepper?" she asked. Her tone was way too friendly, instantly suspicious. Had she doused the eggs in pepper? Would he choke on them?

"Yeah, I love it." He'd never had it before.

"Good."

She sat directly in front of him, easy to watch. For the first time ever, her eyes didn't have the winged liner on them, but a different kind of makeup, softer on the lids, a smoky look in warm colors. On second thought, that was probably how she did her makeup on a day-to-day basis, saving the eyeliner for the weekend. She hadn't done her lips yet, probably because they were about to eat. Was this how her mornings usually went? It almost felt like he was intruding somehow, like he shouldn't be seeing this side of her, too intimate. Picking up his fork, he mirrored her, having some of the eggs. They were actually really good, not too spicy at all.

"I want you to tell me something," she started, looking him straight in the eye. "Why did Laith call me to ask if I could keep an eye on you today?"

He stared at her, suddenly unable to breathe. "What?"

"He seems to think you're going to do something stupid, you know, hurt yourself. He said you were acting weird all day, and that just before you left, you said the three forbidden words."

His eyes grew wide. Oh, shit. Well, there it was then, the trap he'd suspected all along. This wasn't about Laith at all. Stunned into silence, he blinked.

Serious now, Emily put her fork down. "What's going on with you, Theo? You're losing it."

"I know." Fuck it; there was nothing she didn't already know, so he might as well start being genuine. At this point, he had absolutely nothing to lose. "I'm an idiot," he confessed. "You told me to be careful, that it was too easy to fall for him and get hurt, but I didn't listen and now guess what—that's exactly what happened. I feel like a fucking dumbass. We hang out and all I wanna do is hold his fucking hand. He looks at me and it feels like I'm dying, like there's a scream ripping through my throat." His right hand motioned to his own neck for emphasis, fingers bending into a claw.

"He's perfect," he continued. "He's everything. It's not his fault; I'm just—I should've listened to you, but I guess I wanted it, in a way. I kept pushing my luck on purpose, because deep inside, I wanted to see it happen, the heartbreak, the falling out. I wanted it to burn."

"So you said what you shouldn't to set it all on fire."

"Yeah. Might as well, you know? I already feel like shit; it can't possibly get any worse, so fuck it. Let him hate me."

Emily leaned back in her seat, arms crossed. Her shoulders poked out of her sweater; it either had two thin straps holding it up or she wore a tank top underneath it, just as black. He couldn't tell, but it looked nice, a classy fit that matched the velvet choker around her neck. This one had a heart rather than spikes. She looked very fancy. Was this how she usually dressed?

218

"You sound like such a loser. Man, what happened? Where's the confident guy who stole our hearts? Who elbowed his way to the front of the line and pushed Ryan out of the picture? You're *such* a turn off right now. I'm not even hungry anymore."

His eyebrows furrowed, lips parted with indignation. What the fuck?

"Listen." She leaned forward and placeed her forearms on the table, folded over one another. Her nails were black, silver rings shining in the light. "You've gotta quit whining. Laith *doesn't* hate you and he never will. What you said scared the living shit out of him, but wasn't enough to make him want to stop seeing you. You're more than a random fuck, anyway; you're his *friend*, so you get chances that other people wouldn't. Think about that."

They held the stare. He wasn't sure where she was going with this or what her point was, so he kept his silence. Naturally, she continued.

"I have to tell you about the Serpent. I'm assuming you don't know about him yet."

He shook his head.

"Laith dated him a long time ago—five years now—and yes, I mean *dated*, as in they were in a committed relationship. You're probably not surprised, I mean, someone who doesn't date was clearly done in by a relationship, right? Yeah. Well, the Serpent was a motherfucker. He was so possessive of Laith we could barely see him, and when we did, the Serpent was always lurking around, breathing down his neck. He was a creep. A good-looking creep, but one nonetheless. He hurt Laith in ways you can't even imagine." She leaned forward as she spoke, adding pressure to her arms. "Obviously, I'm not going to tell you the details. If you really wanna know, you'll have to ask Laith himself. Just know that if you do, he might shut you out entirely. We've only ever talked about it once."

Her eyes dropped to the table between them, introspective. "He's a lot to handle. I don't think the Serpent knew that at first, but he figured it out soon enough; it's not very difficult to notice. They met at a really bad time, right when Qasim died. Laith went down for his jacket and didn't come back for a week. When he did, the Serpent was with him."

"They went to this one dungeon a lot. I don't know if you know this, but people in these places tend to know each other and talk. It's a community. At the time, the Serpent wasn't welcome there—like I said, he was a motherfucker. When he showed up with somebody new, people started talking and what Laith heard surprised him. Let's call it a series of red flags, reasons why the Serpent had been banned. He was a grown man, by the way—almost thirty—but still couldn't handle any sort of criticism."

Her lips pursed, eyebrows up on her forehead. "Let's just say Laith's questions put a lot of *strain* on their relationship; arguments that ended on bitter notes and were always his fault. He's sensitive, so the whole thing took a huge toll on him. As the relationship failed, he got worse, and when he gets like that— when it gets bad—it's impossible to know how much of it he's going to internalize. That's the thing about him—he'll always take it out on himself. The Serpent just used that as more evidence that Laith was the one at fault. He even blamed him for the breakup, despite being the one to do it. It was the worst case of gaslighting I'd ever seen. That was when I made Laith promise me he'd never get too close to anyone again."

Theodore could feel the scowl that had dug between his eyebrows, heart bleeding quietly. His hands squeezed each other so hard they hurt.

Their eyes met.

"I need you to stop being a huge fucking loser and get over yourself. So you opened up a little too much—so what? He already knew that. You've never managed to hide it very well in the first place. Okay, now it's out in the open. Do you really think Laith's gonna do anything about it? He's gonna continue seeing you regardless, so your self-destructive plan didn't work. Weh, weh." She mocked crying with two hands closed into fists twisting under her eyes, fourth grade bully style. He hadn't seen anyone do that in years. "Now what?" she continued. "You're going back there later, aren't you? What the fuck are you gonna do?"

His hands shook, jaw setting. "I don't know."

"You're going to be the charming and confident guy we know," she cut him off. "The guy who swept Laith off his feet the first time and gave me three weeks' worth of headaches. The guy who's so relentlessly cunning and smart that an entire group of people still couldn't stop him from snatching the prize from right under their noses. You'll be *that* guy—*you*, not this embarrassing caricature of you." She lifted a hand, face turning slightly aside. "Put those sad eyebrows away; they're making me sick."

His lips moved wordlessly, mute as the gears in his brain began to turn. He wasn't even sure what to say. "I don't think you're getting the point," he started, voice low. "I can't stand pretending I'm not in love with him, that I'm not dying to make him my boyfriend. Every time he looks at me, the question rushes up my throat and hangs off the tip of my tongue, one bad decision away from slipping out. I can't be near him without being *with* him."

"Then win him over."

He stared dumbly at her, so she elaborated.

"Make him so obsessed with you that he'll have no other option than to want to make you his. It'll be easy; you've done it once, so do it again. Whatever you did the first time, replicate it. Make him want to spend every single day with you, and when he does, I'll deliver the killing blow." She reached her hand to the center of the table and mimicked dropping an imaginary a-bomb on it, fingers stretching out to emphasize the impact.

"Why would you do that?"

His question drew her eyes up.

"You don't want Laith dating anyone," he explained. "Why would you let him break his promise?"

"That promise is a defense mechanism. If he's ready for a relationship, he'll break it. All I'm gonna do is plant the seed in his mind, that the possibility is there and he's practically already taken it. At the end of the day, the decision is his."

His leg bounced under the table. "I don't think I can do it," he blurted out. "It hurts too much. Being next to him hurts."

"Then let it hurt you. It wouldn't be worth it if it didn't." She waved at the plate in front of him. "Now eat your breakfast. I spent time making it."

The next few minutes were spent mostly in silence, as the two of them ate and Theodore mulled over the conversation they'd just had, replaying Emily's words in his mind. Her plan made sense, but he wasn't sure he'd be able to manufacture so much confidence, fake it till you make it style. It was one of those things that he either had it in him, or he didn't. Up until yesterday, he did. When he'd asked Laith out and paid for his beer, he did. When had he lost it? Probably when it'd dawned on him that, sooner or later, Laith would grow tired of him and move on to somebody else, but he supposed he'd gone about it the wrong way. If he made himself interesting, then Laith wouldn't have any reason to part from him. That was the sort of thought process Emily must've wanted from him, the winner mindset, ways to slide down the hill and make himself a home rather than plans to turn back and surrender. He'd been so sure Laith would be his; every stride they'd made in their relationship was because of *him*.

Where had that confidence gone?

Nowhere—he still got it. What had happened earlier had been a simple lapse of judgement, a moment of weakness; he was fine now. He could do this. Laith already cared for him; one strong push the right way would do the trick. Saying the forbidden words hadn't helped his case, he'd admit that much, but maybe he could turn it around and use it in his favor. It'd been genuine, after all; now Laith knew how serious he was about it. At the very least, he knew he was loved. How many people could confidently say that? Theodore had been the one pining over Laith for far too long; it was time to turn the tables. He'd make himself so enviable that Laith would simply not be able to pass him up. He'd turn himself into one of the Hollywood boys, a perfect recreation, starting with his hair. As Emily hastily did the dishes, he looked at his own reflection, standing in front of a circular mirror near the table. He pulled his hood down and ran his fingers through blonde locks.

"You got a haircut," Emily commented. Her voice came from a couple of feet behind him, on her way across the room. Instinctively, he followed.

"Do you like it? It's not very different from how it was before."

"It's very chic, like a classy version of the old one."

"Hollywood worthy?"

She pondered his question with a tilt of the head, leading him to the door at the end of the hallway, directly across the entrance to the apartment. Unsurprisingly, it was a bathroom. "If you're asking whether you look like one of the Hollywood boys or not, you already know the answer to that."

He didn't follow her inside the bathroom. Instead, he stood in the doorway, watching her retrieve a dark red lipstick from a drawer and put it on.

"A haircut isn't gonna change what your face looks like," she continued. Her eyes were trained on her own reflection, hand carefully coloring her top lip. When she was done, she pressed her lips together. "If you're trying to look like one of them, you just need some extravagant clothes. Coats with feathers on them and bright colors. Think peacock bright."

This was the first time he'd seen her without the Cheshire cat grin painted on. The way she'd just lined her lips gave her a heart for a mouth, full and round on the bottom, cute in a different way. A hand slapped the lights off before she squeezed past him, out into the hallway. He followed.

"If I just showed up with a feather coat on, don't you think that'd be a little too obvious?"

222

"Of course it would be. Everyone would talk about it."

She walked into her bedroom, a door on the same wall as Ryan's but on the opposite end of it. Her bed was a twin on the right side of the room, under a big window that allowed some brightness in with none of the sunshine. Next to it was a nightstand, followed by an L-shaped desk with two computer screens and a tablet pushed to the left corner of the room. Her wardrobe was on the same wall as the door, behind the two of them.

A pair of knee-high platform boots stood by the foot of the bed, which she promptly stepped into and zipped up. As soon as she bent over for that, Theodore's first instinct was to look away, but he quickly realized that no one was around to catch him staring. It was a victimless crime. In mischievous silence, he watched her sweater ride up to show the near-invisible outline of her underwear, difficult to see against the black of her skintight pants. His pulse skipped, blood rushing to all the wrong places.

She straightened up soon enough, hair flying up in the air. Her hands fixed some strands out of her face before she turned around, going for the bottom of her sweater next. He quickly moved out of the way to let her through, but this time, she didn't leave. Dark eyes squinted, scrutinizing him instead. It held a breath in his throat.

"What did you do?" she asked. Her tone was very suspicious.

His face must've blown his cover.

"Were you staring at my ass?"

"No," he lied. "I didn't mean to," he lied again.

Her lips parted with surprise, head cocking aside. "Theodore Elizabeth, I thought you were gay."

"That's not my middle name."

"Are you bi or am I just hot?"

"Yes."

She laughed. It didn't last long though, cut short by an alarm clock that went off in the other room—Ryan. They held the stare, and without another word, hurried out of the apartment. She slipped a jacket on before shutting the front door.

In the silence of the elevator, he felt his face burn. Goddammit, he shouldn't have looked. Actually, he should refrain from doing anything like that again until he learned how to properly cover it up. It'd take some practice, considering Jessie had caught him almost immediately that one time and Emily had

223

been able to tell just by looking at his face. Girls seemed to have an incredible eye for that stuff.

"I'm sorry." His voice was quiet, almost a whisper.

In his peripherals, Emily fixed her jacket in place and swung her backpack over a shoulder. "It's fine. Honestly, I'm more surprised to learn you're not gay."

"Why does everyone think that?"

"Oh, I don't know. Probably because you're head over heels for the gayest man I've ever met?"

"All that means is I'm not straight."

"I know. Going from straight to gay is a bad habit; it's like bisexuals don't exist."

"Aren't *you* bi?"

"Yeah. This habit I'm talking about is societal. We grow up being told that if someone's not straight, then they're gay, but that's not true at all."

The elevator dinged, and a second later, its doors slid open. Naturally, he towed behind her.

Since both of their first periods didn't start for another hour, they ended up hanging out on campus. The fact that this was the first time they'd ever hung out wasn't lost on him; he felt the weight of it banging into the back of his mind every time she spoke. Nothing serious was discussed, but a sense of awkwardness still lingered inside. He felt unbecoming next to her, the unpopular kid and the older girl who was far too cool to give him the time of day. He used to think that about Laith too, but his massive ego had soon gotten rid of that feeling. The biggest difference was that, every time Laith had caught him staring, he'd decided against mentioning it. Emily, on the other hand—god, he'd feel like shit about this all day long.

In class, he thought about asking her out to lunch. He knew her times were probably different than his, since she wasn't an undergrad anymore, but guessed that lunch should have remained the same. His guess was right; the reason why she couldn't hang out had nothing to do with it. Apparently, she was an intern for Laith's tattoo artist, who saw her every afternoon after class; she was only on campus in the morning. Laith was usually working when she went down, so they couldn't really meet. It was no big deal, though; Theodore ended up having lunch with the girls instead.

This time, the talk of the table wasn't Justin, but what the girls would be doing that weekend. Until further notice, the plan seemed to be Streisand's on Friday, some club downtown on Saturday and somebody's house on Sunday. Would Theodore be partying with them? Uh, maybe; he had to check with Laith. His answer pulled *awws* from the girls, both sincere as well as ironic—the latter could be attributed to Hannah and Daisy, the skeptics.

"So you're not dating," Hannah remarked. "You're married."

"It's not like that; I just want to know if he has different plans. Emily and Justin are seeing us on Saturday, but I don't know what we're doing on Friday."

"They are?" Jessie asked. "Where?"

"Probably at the DP—that's where they like to party."

"The DP..." she echoed, eyebrows pinched together. "That's where Justin works."

"Yep."

"He works at a club?" Hannah asked.

"Apparently." Jessie's shoulders bounced. "I'll ask him about it tonight. If you guys are going to the DP on Saturday, then we'll go too."

Oh, she didn't know about Justin's job. On second thought, it made sense, because that wasn't a conversation topic for a first date, but still—she'd have to know at one point. Tonight, from the looks of it. Did Justin lose a lot of people like this? Maybe. Then again, he also got to know a lot of them *because* of it, so ultimately, it was a tradeoff. Theodore wouldn't be the one to tell her.

The nonchalance with which she'd agreed to hit the Dead Ponies with the others clearly alluded to the fact that she didn't know it was underground. If she knew, she would've never agreed to it. Theodore decided not to be the one to tell her about that either. She was Justin's problem now.

"Well..." He cleared his throat. "I'm just guesstimating, to be fair; I don't actually know where we're going."

"If you have any suggestions for Friday, let us know," Daisy added.

"It has to be a good one, though!" Nadia jumped in. "Streisand's is throwing a zodiac sign party this week with quizzes about your sign and compatibility charts, so whatever you have to offer has to be better than that."

"We talked about the zodiac just last week," he defended, "before you guys showed up. How interesting can it be?"

"Oh." Nadia stared at him. "So you don't know anything about it..."

"Oh god, here we go." Daisy rolled her eyes as a big grin slowly cut through Nadia's face. A hand reached across the table to grab Theodore's wrist, dark eyes glinting with excitement.

"I have so much to tell you. What's Laith's sign?"

"Why don't you guys have that conversation on Friday?" Daisy suggested. Her voice was nicer than Theodore had ever heard it, eyes fixed on her girlfriend's face. "It'll be much more interesting with Laith there to participate."

"You're right. It's settled, then; Laith's coming to Streisand's with us."

"Well..." Theodore tipped his head. "I still have to talk to him about it. He doesn't really go to Streisand's anymore."

"But he will this week."

"Now he has to," Jessie argued.

Hannah was the only one who didn't have anything to say about that, sitting with her arms crossed.

He supposed there wasn't much of a way out of this one.

mmermermem

This time, he actually set an alarm. It woke him up at eleven to messages from Justin, Hwan and Emily, in that order. Since Justin's was the newest one, from only twenty minutes ago, he decided to check it first.

Soo you guys are hanging out at Streisand's on Friday huh? Very cool

Jessie told me about it but as you know I can't make it

I told her I could hang out on Saturday tho... it'd be cool if we could all meet up and stuff

I miss you :(

An absent smile tugged at his lips.

Hey, papa bear. I miss you too.

Promise I'll see you this weekend?

I don't think the girls would want to hit the tunnels so maybe the DP is out.

While Justin didn't reply, he tapped on Hwan's message. It'd been sent to the group chat with Marquis about an hour ago.

Seems like your relationship with Laith is getting serious. You've been to

226

his place every day this week. Does that mean we've lost a friend?

Does it?

I didn't realize being with him meant I was choosing sides. I don't want that.

I might not really be a Poison Dart, but at this point, I'm not sure what I'm supposed to be.

Justin got back to him just as he'd typed out that last text.

Baby boy we don't need to make plans to see each other! YOU'RE the one with a tight schedule (and tight everything else...)

If you ever wanna see me just say the word and I'll come running to you. You know that!

What if I DO wanna see you? Would that clash with your plans of seeing Jessie too?

Noo listen... I'll see you one at a time. There's enough of me to go around. Yall don't need to fight.

I'm at Sunset by the way... ;)

Hm. Seeing Justin was always a good idea, but he had to speak to Laith first. There was an entire can of worms to address, all of his own doing. He'd bought it, taken it to Laith's place, opened it, thrown the worms everywhere and left. Now, he had to clean up.

I'm always down for debauchery, especially if you're involved. How long are you gonna be underground for?

Probably until sunrise. Business starts to dwindle around four tho so if you don't wanna be surrounded by people that's probably when we should meet up.

Alright, daddy. I'll keep you posted.

Hwan had replied during this back and forth, so he went back to the group chat.

If you keep hanging out with him, you'll be a Pony pretty soon.

I wasn't suggesting you took sides though. What I mean is that you'll prob-

ably stop speaking to me as time goes on.

I won't blame you for that. Unfortunately, it's a side-effect of being his friend. You'll end up taking his word over mine, and before you know it, we're not friends anymore.

I won't do that. I respect you just as much as I respect him.
Actually, I think I respect you more, but don't tell him that.

When the next part came to mind, his heart skipped. He didn't mean it that way, but it'd still be pretty damning, depending on how Hwan—and his boyfriend, who could read all of this—decided to interpret it. His fingers hesitated for a moment, hovering over the screen.

Can I see you tonight?

There. He stared at the three dots that came up as Hwan typed, bouncing in a little bubble. The dichotomy between these texts and the ones he'd just sent Justin was massive. Somehow, he had a much easier time faux flirting with a straight guy than making the mildest of plans with someone he'd already slept with.

Are you sure about that? I wouldn't want to make your boyfriend angry. My dad's store doesn't deserve a visit from the dogs tomorrow.

He wouldn't do that, and anyway, we're not together. I can see you as much as I want to; he can't tell me what to do. How about 7 a.m.?

I usually go to bed at six, but I'll stay up for you.

Those words made his heart swell.

Would six be better for you? I don't want you to lose sleep over me.
Either one is fine.
I hope you know that, even if you don't tell him about this, he's gonna know.
Oh, I'll tell him.
See you soon. :)

He tapped on Emily's message next, the oldest of them all, sent a little after 5 p.m.

Sorry for blowing you off earlier. If it's any consolation, I just left work, so I'm free now.

Ah, shit.

I was asleep! Do you still wanna hang out?

At this point, his invitations were less about actually seeing his friends and more about how many he could cram into one packed schedule. Laith from 12 to 4, Justin from 4 to 6, Hwan from 6 to possibly 8 and Emily from 8 to 9. What was that, an entire night and morning reserved just for his friends? It seemed like a good deal to him, the opposite of lonely. If he could manage to do that more often, it'd be the perfect life. Was that why his parents liked having the neighbors over so much? They were all friends, so it made sense. Perhaps he was much more similar to them than originally thought. A faint echo of Ryan's accusations last weekend rung in the back of his mind, but he quickly waved those thoughts away. No need to think about that ever again.

Since Emily didn't immediately call him, he supposed he'd missed her; she was probably asleep at this hour. That wouldn't be much of a stretch, considering she studied all morning and worked all afternoon. Did she have any time for Ryan at all? Did they even have meals together? The possibility that they didn't filled his chest with wicked warmth.

Every time he undressed in front of a mirror now, he turned to check the color of his skin. The mere sight of his purple bruises was enough to put a smile on his face, heart beating deeply. He wasn't sure what that feeling was, that spread through his veins like hot sauce and flames, but he liked it. Seeing physical proof of his involvement with Laith reminded him that they were more than just friends, even if he didn't belong to Laith the way he wanted to. They weren't strangers or best friends either, but something unnamed, stuck in between. It'd be nice if Laith let him brand him too. It was his turn, after all.

Back in his room, Emily's voice drew his hand over to the colorful jacket he'd bought two weeks ago, telling him about the peacock style of the Hollywood boys. He was pretty sure they wouldn't actually wear this, much more

229

interested in Versace and Gucci anyway, but Laith liked it on him, so he put it on. It was the illusion that mattered; looking like one of them was enough. He brushed his hair to the side, the way Laith liked it, and left the room.

This next hour would fucking suck.

Finish the series with
An Obsession With Success:

Success: the final objective, the ultimate addiction. There's nothing quite like getting what he wants, even if he has to bend the rules for it. Eventually, his parents will know about his relationship, so why not go ahead and tell them himself? Have the upper hand, take the initiative. If he's the one doing it, he can manufacture the perfect outcome. If the presentation is fantastic, even the worst dishes can be served.

For that, however, he will need to come out.

Other titles by the author:

Unfollowing Stacy Lee
This is what happens to mean girls after high school.

Shady Lane is an anonymous profile that keeps tabs on the popular kids, spilling all the embarrassing things they're doing. Stacy Lee is the most popular girl in school. But when graduation rolls around, the author doesn't stop writing; they enroll in university with her. The posts keep getting more and more personal. They're getting closer.

Rich and dating the cutest boy on the football team, Stacy seems to have the perfect life. Only her very close friends know the truth: her boyfriend is seeing someone else and anxiety is eating her up inside. Surrounded by liars, is there anyone she can trust?

How to kill an angel

In charge of paradise's security, Nathaniel works hard to keep the angels safe. Danger comes from below, the pit of demons right beneath their feet, so when a human starts to cause trouble up above, it makes him question the system he'd deemed infallible. Who's Aiden, and more importantly, can he trust him? Why do his fingertips leave goosebumps in their wake and his kisses feel as warm as sunlight?

Intoxicated by vetiver leaves and cedar wood, in a world where their eyes meet through the dark and the warmth of Aiden's body feels like home, Nathaniel puts his integrity at risk. Humans aren't supposed to make him feel this way, and never have; the only one who'd ever come close was one of his own, gone with the years, an aching memory. How is Aiden so like him? The golden curls on his head, the depth of his eyes, the color of his skin...

Is Aiden going to ruin everything?

READ ALL THESE TITLES FOR FREE AT <u>SEADEMONS.NET</u>

About the author:

Olívia S. Zanini, also known as seademons, has been writing for the LGBT community since 2009. Passion and love are always at the very center of her works, but something else lurks beneath the surface too—something dark and twisted that just doesn't sit right. The protagonist isn't always the good guy and the love interest isn't always who they claim to be. Through the lens of unreliable narrators, it's up to the reader to see through the veil. No matter the amount of angst, hurt and pain these journeys might bring, one thing is always accounted for: couples will get together in the end. The LGBT community deserves happy endings too.

How to kill an angel is seademons' debut novel. *An obsession in glitter* is her latest series. *Unfollowing Stacy Lee* is her latest release. Stay tuned for more!

Follow her on Twitter <u>@seademons</u>, tumblr <u>@sea-demons</u>, Goodreads @ <u>Olívia S. Zanini</u> and Facebook <u>@seademonsauthor</u>.